DARKEST FEARS

By Tabatha Shipley

eBook 979-8-9880129-7-9
Paperback 979-8-9880129-6-2

Tabatha Shipley Books

Also by Tabatha Shipley

KINGDOM OF FRAUN NOVELS

Breaking Eselda

Redeeming Jordyn

Training Tutor

Empowering Sawchett

Tin's Tale and other stories of Fraun

Kingdom of Fraun (omnibus)

STAND ALONE NOVELS

30 Days Without Wings

Projection

A Spark of Magic

Noises from the Other Side

How to Schedule a Death

In Trust We Fall

CHAPTER 1

The worst part about driving home from the night shift at the mall, in Keith's opinion, is navigating through the woods this late at night. The town of Flagstaff has city ordinances in place to keep the lighting low so the observatory on the mountain has full visibility of the night sky. This is not something anyone is ever going to allow the council to change, because someone had discovered a planet at that observatory a long time ago. This makes the entire place important. It doesn't seem to matter that Pluto is no longer a planet. The darkness remains.

This means that when Keith has to maneuver the small SUV his parents let him take to college through the back road after nine PM, his headlights are pretty much all he has to guide him. There is the occasional streetlight, but they are few and far between usually only signaling a possible road ahead or a business parking lot.

Coming around a blind corner, his headlights reflecting off trees, he flips his high beams off. High beams are just one thing he hadn't learned to use until he moved to Flagstaff. Keith had grown up in a suburb of Phoenix, where headlights alone are practically unnecessary but high beams certainly are. There are so many people, streetlights, other cars, and businesses in his hometown that it just isn't necessary to take your own source of lighting with you. As Keith pulls the wheel straight at the end of the turn, noting there are no oncoming cars, he flips the high beams back on to illuminate the trees on either side. He knows people who have encountered deer and even elk on this road. Better safe than sorry.

Spotting nothing ahead, he lets his eyes check the notification bubbles on the CarPlay screen in the center console. No missed calls. No new messages. He lets out a groan of frustration. Craig, his roommate, is supposed to be dropping the rent check off today at the rental office. He is notoriously forgetful about things that resemble responsibility, so Keith has been calling off and on all day to try and remind him. He has yet to get through.

He hits the button on the steering wheel that will tell his phone to take commands. "Call Craig." He hears the annoyance in his own voice before the sound of ringing fills the car. Keith listens to it ring four cycles then hangs up before the answering machine can trigger. He has already left one more message than anyone should have to leave since the phone will tell Craig he called. At this point, it doesn't matter anyway. The rent check is either in the closed-for-the-day office or it isn't. He only keeps trying because it is starting to worry him that Craig isn't answering. This is unusual behavior. Unusual is never good. Unusual is especially not good considering the messy situation Craig's libido had gotten him into lately.

Keith steps harder on the gas pedal. His best course of action is to get home, yell at Craig for not answering his phone all day, and then have a beer or something and laugh about all of this.

The parking lot for the apartment complex is completely full. As he's done many times before, Keith curses the management for not designating parking spots. He manages to find an empty one, but it is nowhere near their unit. He locks the car, a habit from his city childhood that he is having trouble breaking, and starts walking quickly toward their unit. It is chilly outside. Not cold yet, but a promise that cold is on the way. There are no people in the lot tonight. No noise coming from any apartments. It's eerie, actually. Keith can't remember the last time their complex has been this quiet. This complex, despite being directly across from the local police station, is known for having college students who sometimes get out of control.

Keith makes it to his own building and picks his way down the steps. Craig and Keith have a unit on the very back of the complex. Directly across from their unit is a line of trees, a slightly busy street, and then that police station. As his door comes into view, Keith pauses.

It's hard to tell in the dark with only a small porch light to aid his eyes, but it looks like the door is ajar. His heartbeat picks up and his fingers start to tingle, a sign he is panicking. Keith tries to take a deep breath. He snaps his eyes closed, telling himself to calm down. He slips his cell phone out of his pocket and dials Craig's number. He thinks he can hear it ringing from somewhere inside the unit, although that has to be impossible. He hits the end button with his thumb and takes one step closer to the unit. He still can't be sure, but it looks darker around the edges of the door than it should.

He flips on his phone's flashlight, shining it in the direction of the door. Then he curses. The door is definitely open. He backs up and pulls up the non-emergency line for the police department from his contacts. He makes a mental note to never mention to his mother that she was right about him needing that particular phone number. The phone rings only once before it is answered. "Flagstaff police, what is the nature of your call?" the voice asks.

"I just got home and my front door is open. It looks like it may be a break-in. Also, my roommate isn't answering his phone. So I guess I'm worried." The words all tumble out of Keith in a rush.

"Give me your address and I'll send an officer to enter the residence with you." Keith rattles off the address and unit number. Then, not knowing if he is supposed to stay on the line or not, he waits. When he hears nothing further, he pulls the phone away to see he is back on the home screen. They hung up on him, ending his curiosity about if he was supposed to stay on the line. He locks the phone, turns off the flashlight, and slides it into his pocket. Then he waits.

The police take seventeen minutes to get to him. Seventeen minutes during which Keith got himself worked up about how stupid he was being. Seventeen minutes during which he almost just entered the apartment alone three times. Seventeen minutes during which he called Craig's phone, still no answer, six times. His feet are going numb and he has goosebumps all over his arms.

When the police officer finally pulls up right near the stairs, Keith has to fight off the urge to snap at him for taking too long. "Did you call about a break-in?" the cop asks, stepping out of the vehicle. He is not much older than Keith, although the uniform makes him look a little older. His brown hair is cut short and his name badge says Marino.

Keith nods. "Yes. I just got home from work and the front door is open."

"You live alone?"

"No, I have a roommate. But he's not answering his phone so I don't think he's home. Plus, he never leaves the door open." One of Marino's eyes narrows, showing his skepticism. "We're from Phoenix, man. We don't leave it open. I swear."

Marino shuts the car door and comes down the stairs. "How about you and I just go in together, we'll see what's going on." His voice has an edge, almost like he is teasing Keith. He stops when he is even with Keith, his eyes going immediately to the open front door. Then he looks at Keith again. "That sound like it would make this less scary for you, big man?"

Now Keith is sure he's being teased. He hates guys like this. Guys that think they have to talk down to other guys just to feel like the biggest man on the scene. He rolls his eyes, suddenly not nervous anymore but angry. "You know what, I shouldn't have called. This is stupid." He stomps to the front door and pushes it open.

The inside of the apartment is completely dark. Keith can hear the hum of the appliances but no other noise. No television, no radio, nothing. If Craig is home, he's sitting in the dark in total silence. Keith takes a step into the doorway and freezes. Something is wrong. Besides the door being open, which is obviously a problem, something else is wrong. He can't put his finger on what it is. Something just doesn't feel right.

He hears the officer's footsteps behind him. "Want to step out of the way, son?" Marino asks. Keith takes another step into the apartment and he hears Marino echo the movement. Behind him, there is a sharp intake of breath. "Do you smell that?" Marino asks.

Keith turns to look at the officer over his shoulder. He is frozen in the doorway, exactly how Keith imagines he must have looked a few seconds ago. He wants to point out that the cop must feel it too, that sense that something is wrong. Instead, he sniffs the air. Yes, he smells something. He isn't sure what it is. It's faint. "What is that?" he asks.

Marino puts his arm out and Keith sees he is holding a flashlight and a gun. When did he pull those? "I'm going to sweep the rest of the unit. Why don't you wait for me on the porch?" It doesn't sound like a suggestion, so Keith steps outside.

Standing there in the cold, he wonders what changed. Marino had been teasing him when he showed up, making it seem like it was foolish of Keith to call the police. But the second he stood in that doorway, his entire demeanor changed. Suddenly all business, he relinquished Keith to the patio. Why? What was that smell? Why was Marino taking so long? The apartment has two bedrooms, a bathroom, and a small kitchen. Maybe three closets. Surely it doesn't take that long to check out the entire thing.

Curiosity powers Keith's feet back toward the door frame. This time the smell is stronger, as if someone has brought whatever is causing that odor closer to the door. It smacks Keith in the face. Pungent, rotten, and foul. His stomach clenches, threatening to let go of the chicken sandwich he'd had for lunch. He pinches his nose and takes a step back from the door, trying to get away from the smell.

Officer Marino appears in the shadow of the hallway toward the bedrooms. He is moving faster than he had been before. The gun is no longer in his hand, but the flashlight still is. He crosses the room quickly and puts his hands on Keith's shoulders, walking him back away from the unit. Both men stand there in the chilly night air, taking deep breaths to get that smell out of their noses. Marino meets Keith's eyes. "Stay here. Right here on this spot. Don't move."

Marino takes a step back and pulls a cell phone from somewhere near his hip. Keith can tell he is trying to speak in a quiet voice as he gives the address of the unit and tells whoever is on the other end that he is going to need backup and a morgue van.

When he ends the call and turns to Keith, he looks sorry. "Do you think it's my roommate?" Keith asks, saving Marino from having to explain that the smell plus the word 'morgue' he overheard equals someone dead in the apartment.

"I've never met your roommate, son, and I'm not taking you in there to find out. In fact, once my backup gets here to secure the scene, I'm taking you to a police station where we can talk about this and get warm."

"Yeah, alright."

It almost feels like a normal conversation to be having. Just two guys chatting on the porch around 10 PM. No big deal. Except, Keith realizes with a pang, one of them is a police officer and the other one has a dead body in his apartment.

He feels his knees wobble and Marino grabs his upper arms before he can fall, guiding him gently to the ground. "Breathe," Marino commands. "In through the mouth, out through the nose. You need to calm down."

"There's a dead body in my apartment," Keith says. He looks at Marino's face for confirmation. He wants to be wrong. He wants to be corrected.

"Yes there is," Marino says. "But it's not you. You're still right here. Breathe."

It's good advice. Keith closes his eyes and tries to follow it.

Sarah Rodriguez leans back away from the table at the locally-owned Italian restaurant and lets out a sigh. "Honestly, I'm in love right now," she says.

Her date smiles. "With the entire town?" she asks.

"Yes. The lush greenery, the fresh smell, the bustling energy of the college campus, all the things to do within walking distance so I don't have to use my piece-of-crap car and the cooler weather? Where has this place been all my life?

I'm in love."

Mariana laughs. "Flagstaff is beautiful, I'll give you that. But I can't imagine it's the only town in the country to offer all of those same things you talked about. Plus, it doesn't prove your first point. You've probably been in love with other inanimate things incapable of loving you back before. I accused you of never being in love. You were trying to prove me wrong." She leans close across the table as if she were about to share a kiss with Sarah if only she would be met halfway. "I meant with a person."

Sarah smirks. "Oh." She lets her eyes trail up to the ceiling as if looking for the answer written there. In reality, she is stalling. The truth is easy to locate in her brain, but not always received well by other people. The truth is Sarah has never been in love with a person. You're supposed to love your parents, but Sarah's made that impossible. Her father was never in the picture, claiming Sarah should have been aborted "like he wanted" and refusing to see her. Her mother was not capable of keeping herself safe, let alone a baby. Sarah spent her childhood and teenage years bopping around foster homes and never really belonging to anyone. The times when she did get to see her mother it was for long enough to decide she was never going to let herself be like this person. She would never think she was in love with everyone who showed her attention. She would never make her life about what someone else wanted or needed. She was never getting addicted to drugs just to numb the pain of not feeling good enough for everyone she thought she loved. She was never going to struggle to hold down a job. These were promises she made to herself daily, but they weren't good first-date conversations.

Sarah returns her eyes to the cute Latina across the table from her and smiles. "Then you're right. I've never been in love."

Mariana sits back and snaps her fingers. "I knew it. You have this way of carrying yourself like you're putting distance between you and everyone else. I'm telling you, I just read people so well." She is enjoying this, which makes it easier for Sarah to laugh off what otherwise would have felt like an insult.

The waiter, who looks like he might be a student either of the girls would encounter at one of their own college classes, approaches the table, smiling awkwardly until his patron's laughter dies down. Sarah's laugh stumbles and threatens to start up again as she tries to reign in her amusement at his sour expression. "Is there anything else I can get you ladies?" he asks, eyes flitting down to the check he'd dropped off at least twenty minutes ago.

Sarah knows this is waiter-speak for 'Why the hell are you still here, I want to go home'. Guilt consumes her as she realizes they are the only patrons left in the otherwise silent restaurant. She doesn't need to look at her watch to know they are probably past closing time. This always happens to her when she has to squeeze an actual sit-at-a-table-dinner into her tight schedule. She quickly grabs the little black book with the check inside and drops her credit card on top without even opening it. "Sorry, no. We're all set."

"Great." He takes the card and stalks off.

Sarah turns her attention back to the beautiful Mariana with her mirror-straight and shiny black hair and huge brown eyes that are perfectly symmetrical beside that adorable button nose. She'd originally met Mariana at a study group for a summer session she was taking on communication. Mariana had not been part of the class but had been tagging along to the study group with a friend because she'd heard that the coffee shop where the group was held often gave away pastries to the group. According to her, she'd come back the following week even though there were no pastries because she liked Sarah's vibe.

It had taken them three months of occasional conversations on the phone to nail down a first date. This was not Sarah's fault. She had been upfront and honest right away. She wasn't looking for anything serious, but she had no problem enjoying the company of another person. In other words, she liked going on dates but hated dating. Mariana had, originally, claimed to be looking for something more. Two weeks ago, she'd decided casual was fine. Enough was enough. Now, here they were.

Sarah risks a glance at her watch when it won't seem rude. Then, when the waiter drops the black book back down, Sarah signs the receipt, adding a generous tip since it is almost eleven o'clock at night in a restaurant that said they closed at ten thirty and stands up from the table. "We need to get out of here so these poor folks can clean," Sarah says. "Plus, I have to be at work in ten minutes."

Mariana stands up to follow Sarah out of the restaurant, but her face twists in confusion. "Weren't you at work earlier today? Isn't that why we had to come out so late?"

"Second job," Sarah explains over her shoulder as she pushes the door open into the beautiful fall night air. Her small white Kia is parked right by the door. She stops beside it, leaning on the driver's door as if claiming ownership. "I work retail at the mall on weekends and in the afternoons. I work the front desk at the police station on campus at night."

"You're a cop? I thought you were in school."

Sarah laughs. "I am in school. The police station isn't open at night. They just need someone to man the front desk, answer calls, and sometimes take emergency statements from someone who rings the after-hours doorbell out front. I have sensitivity training, sign a disclosure, and that's about it."

"What if, like, someone needs to be arrested?" Mariana asks, her voice rising as if the thought of Sarah handling that was exciting, instead of incredibly dangerous.

Sarah emphatically shakes her head. "Not my job. There are police officers on call. There's a list of their contact information and a copy of the shift schedule at the desk. Honestly, it's an easy job. Most days I sit there and do my homework in peace."

"I'd fall asleep. You work there all night?"

"Eleven at night until six in the morning. Nice and quiet."

Mariana steps closer. "When do you sleep?" She is using a quieter voice, sensual somehow. Sarah could easily see herself melting into this version of Mariana. The one who sounds like soft sheets and cool-to-the-touch pillows.

Instead, she clears her throat. "Whenever I can. Hey, seriously, I had a good time but I have to get to work. Call me later."

"You know I will." Mariana is still using that sensual voice, Sarah notes. She is working this date angle, for sure.

Sarah reaches behind her and pulls the handle up, opening the car door with an audible click. The interior light clicks on. Mariana takes the cue and steps back, putting distance between them. "Are we doing this again sometime?" Mariana asks. "A date, I mean. I've been on this campus for three years and I can count the number of lesbians I've met in that time on one hand. We can't squander this opportunity."

"I'm not a lesbian," Sarah points out. She realizes the knee-jerk answer makes her sound a little harsher than she'd intended. She smiles to soften it a little, then explains. "I'm bisexual." She thought they'd talked about that on at least one of the phone calls. She usually makes that clear right up front. "Is that a problem?" she asks.

"No, I knew that. Sorry, I didn't mean to use the wrong term. Still, you knew what I meant. The prospects here for dating are seriously limited. Can we do this again?"

Sarah closes the gap between them and brushes her hand along Mariana's cheek. It makes her feel something when Mariana leans into it and lets her eyes slip closed. Sarah leans closer and touches their lips together, lightly, just a wisp of a promise. "We can and we should. Call me." Then she reaches behind her and pulls the door open fully in the space she had vacated to give the kiss.

When she drives away, Mariana is still standing there with stars in her eyes watching Sarah drive away. Sarah shakes her head. Is this girl falling too hard too fast? That could be a problem. She likes Mariana. She's funny, kind, and a little cocky. Really, she is the type of casual date Sarah usually likes. But if she can't accept casualness that is a problem. Sarah is absolutely not derailing her plans for anyone else. There will be no serious dating. There is no exclusivity. There is no time for any of that.

Sarah has a plan. She is getting her degree, getting a full-time job that pays her bills, and making a name for herself at that job. Then, and only then, will she allow herself to even start considering something else. She will absolutely not fall in love right now before she finishes college. She will not end up dropping out. She will not be supporting someone else's dream just because she "falls in love" with them. She will not turn into her mother. Absolutely not.

The Kia slips into the usual parking spot as if nothing is different tonight but Sarah can tell right away that something is off. The parking lot is more crowded than usual, meaning there are more than the three campus cruisers and Alicia's car. She opens her car door and uses the overhead light that pops on to make herself more work-ready and less date-ready. She pulls her red hair up into a ponytail, securing it with one of the rubber bands she perpetually wears around her wrist. Then, grabbing a makeup wipe from where she keeps them in the center console, she scrubs off the makeup. If she happens to have a quiet night at the desk and nods off for a second, she'd hate to have mascara run down her face. Lastly, she pops three small breath mints from the red tin on the dashboard to make sure there's no lingering scent of garlic from her Italian dinner.

She grabs her bag of things she might need to finish her homework from the trunk and hits the lock button on the key fob before making her way across the parking lot to the front entrance. She doesn't spend much time thinking about what might be going on inside.

It's the last time she'll get a chance to cross a parking lot without thinking about it for a long time.

CHAPTER 3

The front door of the campus police station is not open at this hour of the night. The official hours posted on the door show it closing at eight PM. Beside the posted hours is a sign that says "Front desk is monitored 24 hours a day, 7 days a week. Ring bell for service." Sarah pushes the button which is wirelessly connected to a base at the desk. She knows this will sound the chime to alert someone to her presence. She also knows there are closed-circuit security cameras out here watching her from three angles. They are recording even if no one is watching them. But the button alerts whoever is at the front desk to pay attention to the feed on those cameras. Sarah waves in the general direction of a camera and hears the buzzing of the front door unlocking.

Pulling it open, she enters into a flurry unlike anything she has seen in her year of working here. Despite it being eleven at night there are four uniformed officers in the lobby behind the desk. Alicia, the bubbly blonde-haired clerk who works the three to eleven shift, is standing behind the desk at the coffee machine pouring mugs full of steaming liquid. She turns and waves in Sarah's direction. "Put your stuff down, I'll be right there," she calls.

Sarah nods, crosses the lobby, and rounds the desk to the employee's side. She nods politely at the officers, only one of whom she recognizes at all. Behind the desk she can tell that Alicia has packed up for the night, her belongings secured and off to the side to make room for Sarah's. She deposits her bag and laptop underneath the desk. She watches as Alicia hands off the mugs one at a time to the uniformed officers who disappear back around the corner and into the heart of the station. Sarah drops into the rolling chair she'll occupy for the next seven hours. "What is going on?" she asks.

Alicia pulls a folding chair from the closet at the back of the lobby area and opens it on her way back to sit beside Sarah. "Oh my God, girl, you won't believe it. The rumor is that someone …" her voice drops to a whisper, "died".

"What? No way."

Alicia holds her hands up on either side of her torso. "That's the rumor. I don't know. They don't tell me anything." She shakes her head, sending blonde curls flying. "All I know is Marino was covering over at the main station tonight because they were short-staffed or something. Then, just after 10, he called someone in for backup. I heard parts of the conversation when the guys were leaving." She tips her head toward the hallway. "After that Marino showed up here with some guy. Looks like he might be your age, really shaken up. They have him in Interview One right now."

Sarah sits back in the chair, letting out a dramatic sigh. "You're letting your mind run away with you. People don't get murdered in Flagstaff, Alicia. More likely he got in a bar fight or a car accident. Something typical."

Alicia scoffs. "Typical comes with four uniforms in here just to complete an interview?"

In the year that Sarah has been working part-time at the police station she has always been on the middle of the night shift. It suits her lifestyle and homework patterns just fine. Most days she sees exactly zero uniformed officers. Occasionally she will have to call one for something or see someone who just can't let a case go still working when she arrives. But never, in her entire time here, has she seen two at once. Let alone four. "Ok, good point." Sarah shakes her head. "But we can't sit here spreading rumors. If we get caught doing that —" she lets her voice trail off because, in reality, neither of them really knows what would happen. Sarah just gets the impression it wouldn't be good. She needs this job.

"I know, I know." Alicia stands up and yawns. "It's been a long day and I'm ready to go home, eat something bad for me, and get some sleep." She collapses the folding chair again and returns it to the closet. "I do know that they already have a witness statement form in there so they shouldn't need another one. You may want to make sure there are enough phone record request forms printed, just in case. Besides this, it's honestly been a pretty quiet night." She reaches down to grab her purse from the ground. "When I tell you I didn't see a soul after Ted locked up when he left at eight, you'd have to believe me." She reaches around Sarah to retrieve a refillable water bottle from the back of the counter, bringing her face close to Sarah's ear. "You let me know if you hear anything juicy though. I want all the details." Alicia straightens up and winks at Sarah. "Are we clear on that?"

Sarah puts her hand to her temple and salutes. "Yes, ma'am."

Alicia is halfway to the door before she spins around and gasps. "I forgot to ask about your date. I'm such a bad friend, I'm sorry." She walks back to the front reception desk, leaning on it from the civilian side. "How was it? Did she dress cute?"

Sarah laughs. "She looked great. Jeans were just the good side of tight and a red shirt that looked really good with her skin tone. We had a good time."

"Red shirt to Italian food, smart girl. Hides sauce stains." Alicia nods as if judging Mariana as passing an assessment Sarah wasn't aware she'd signed her up for. "What did y'all talk about?"

"Nothing really. She told me a little about her last failed relationship. She told me how she's studying psychology at school because she can read people so well …"

"Oh no," Alicia says. "She tried to read you, didn't she?" Alicia lays her hands on her sternum and rolls her eyes. "I hate it when college students try to prove themselves in the right field and show off like it's some parlor trick. What did she say?"

Sarah smiles at the display. Alicia dropped out of college herself only a few years ago because she wasn't sure what she wanted to do with her life. Now, at twenty-three, she is the oldest of the desk employees. Whenever she has the chance, she likes to remind them all of this fact. "She said she could tell I'd never been in love." Sarah widens her eyes, waiting to see if Alicia will try to defend her or agree with this assessment.

"Well that's not exactly a good first date

conversation, is it?" Alicia says, going for the safe cop-out. She sets her water bottle down so she can prop her elbow on the desk and rests her chin in her palm. "Did you run out of there like there was a track meet somewhere you forgot to finish?"

Sarah shakes her head. "I told her she was right."

Alicia drops her hand with a dramatic slap on the counter. "Well look at you all mature and honest. Good for you. I like a girl who knows herself well enough to listen to feedback like that and not let it knock her down." She grabs her water bottle again. "Will there be a second date with this girl?"

Sarah pauses to think, letting her eyes trail up to the ceiling. "I think so, yeah. I like spending time with her."

Alicia points at her. "I like that. You gonna fall for this one?"

Sarah shakes her head emphatically. "You know I won't. I'm not looking for anything serious."

Alicia turns and heads back toward the exit. "Good. You remember that. You don't let this girl change you unless you're ready to change your mind. Keep those morals, Sarah."

"I always do," Sarah calls. "Good night."

"Good night, girl. Be safe." The door closes behind Alicia and in the sudden quiet, Sarah can hear it click. She takes a deep breath, letting it out with a sigh.

She pulls out the drawer at her feet and checks all the folders. Each one contains a blank form they often have to hand off to either civilians or officers. She checks all the folders, just scanning to make sure there are enough copies of everything. As Alicia suggested, she pays special attention to the cell phone request form. There are at least ten in the folder, more than enough for whatever is going on in Interview One. Satisfied that there are enough copies of everything, Sarah pushes the drawer closed.

Next, she pulls up her company email and checks for anything new. Unsurprisingly, she finds nothing. She leaves the tab open on the computer, just in case.

Then, as if this is any other normal night, she checks the feed from the cameras out front. When all is quiet out there, she pulls out her bag from under the desk and slips out a green folder. Opening the folder on the desk she extracts a sheet of questions she is supposed to be studying for her upcoming biology exam.

She reads the first question and mentally answers it. She grabs a pen from the holder on the desk and puts a checkmark next to the first question. That one was easy. She reads the second question. This one is a little harder, she has to close her eyes and try to recall the memory of the lesson. Then, even after she thinks she remembers, she pulls out her phone and Googles just to be sure. When the search engine pulls up a reliable page confirming her answer, she circles the number two on the sheet. This one requires more studying, but she knows it.

A door closes behind her, bringing Sarah's attention away from the study sheet. She glances over her shoulder, seeing Officer Marino has stepped out into the lobby behind her. He looks a little pale. Sarah takes the opportunity to check the monitors, finding nothing unusual about the parking lot, and then spins fully in her chair. "Need something?" she asks Marino. She's not used to having uniformed officers around during this shift. She isn't well practiced in small talk or helping with cases. On a normal shift, most of her job is sitting alone and keeping herself busy. She is uncomfortable in this new role where she has to interact, nervous about saying the wrong thing.

Marino nods. "I just needed to step out of that room for a second and think. Do you ever get that? Too much information all at once just causes you to feel sort of overloaded?" He shakes his head. "I just needed a change of scenery for a second."

"Makes sense," Sarah agrees pleasantly. Honestly, she's not sure it does make sense but it doesn't seem productive to tell him that. Why would a change of scenery help you think? Personally, Sarah is capable of shutting out distractions in any situation. It seems like that would be a good skill for a police officer to have. Of course, that isn't a respectful thing to say.

Instead, she chooses to point out the obvious. "You're not usually here for this shift. It must be late for you. Can I get you a coffee or a chair? We have folding chairs." She gestures toward the closet where Alicia pulled the chair from earlier.

"No. I'm alright. I just needed to breathe and think for a second. Then I'll have to head back in." Marino is younger than most of the officers she's met on the force. Sarah has met him only a few times. The last time she saw him during her shift he told her that the only reason he's ever been around this late at night is because he has trouble letting things go. Sarah wonders if that's the case tonight. If so, she wonders if it also explains why he's so pale right now or if that is the result of something else. She certainly hopes the rumor Alicia was tossing around was just that, a rumor. The last thing this little town needs is a murder.

Finally, Marino takes a deep breath and straightens his spine, throwing his shoulders back. "Alright, I'm going back in. Can I have a couple of phone record request forms?"

Sarah pulls the drawer open and takes three sheets of paper out of the appropriate folder. When she puts her attention back on Marino, he's looking more like his old self. Whatever inner pep talk he's giving is working.

He takes the three papers and disappears back into Interview One.

Sarah checks the monitors again, finding no

new activity. Then she resumes her studying with question three.

CHAPTER 4

Keith picks his head up off the small wooden table when he hears the door close. He has been in the interview room for over an hour. He feels like they've gone over every single question and every single detail at least three times. First, he had to answer a bunch of seemingly random questions for Officer Marino when they arrived at this building. Then, he had a few questions of his own which required a phone call to a different officer. That officer, who showed up in a suit with no name tag and didn't offer his name, answered as many of Keith's questions as he could.

Yes, the body had been positively identified as Craig Macdonald.

Yes, there was reason to suspect foul play.

As for the questions, was there forced entry, am I a suspect, and who did this … well they were all met with the exact same answer. "We are not at liberty to discuss an ongoing investigation."

Then the man in the suit walked Keith through a line of questioning that was almost exactly the same as Officer Marino's. If it weren't for his center seat in this entire fiasco, he might find it in him to be a little proud of the young cop who obviously got all the questions correct. As it is, he found himself annoyed that he had to run through it again.

After the well-dressed guy left Keith alone in the room again, he put his head down and tried to think of all the people he would have to call when this was over. Immediately he thought of Craig's parents, but obviously, they had already been called. At least, Keith assumed so. Who else would be able to positively identify Craig's body on short notice like that? In fact, he wondered, how long had he been here?

It was at that point he had pulled out his cell phone to check the time. The door to the room flew back open, harder than any other time, and slammed against the wall. A uniformed officer with a name tag reading Smith filled the doorway.

"Could we have a look at that cell phone?" he asked. "You mentioned earlier that you made a few calls to the victim. It could be relevant."

Keith had handed over his phone, knowing he had nothing to hide. Then the third round of questioning had started. Marino was back for this one, but he stood off to the back of the room, handling the cell phone, while they ran through it all again.

This time, when he was left alone in the room, Keith merely put his head down and tried to get his body to relax. He had been up early this morning for his eight AM class. He'd been in and out of classes until about one. Then he'd grabbed lunch on his way to work. He was driving home from work when this all happened. That meant, if his calculations and estimations were correct, he'd been awake for about seventeen hours. Really, he was exhausted.

Marino looks like he understands how tired Keith must be when he takes a seat on the opposite side of the small table. The first thing he does is place Keith's cell phone face down in the center. "Alright, we've taken a look at this. Thanks for letting us do that. We have a request for records form here which we'll use to get Craig's records. But you'll be able to give us a good head start with what we got from you. Thank you." Marino places a few sheets of paper face up on the table beside the phone. Keith can see that they have a heading indicating they're the forms

Marino mentioned. He returns his eyes to the officer's face.

"We're just going to run through a few last details together, make sure I have them right. Then we'll have you sign the statement. Does that sound acceptable?" Marino produces another stack of papers, this one stapled. Keith nods.

Marino sets the stack down in the center of the table. "Check this first page for me and make sure your contact information, name, and date of birth are all correct." Keith runs his eyes down the page listing all his vital information. Yes, there's the information Marino mentioned but he also sees height, weight, eye color, hair color, and demeanor listed. He shakes his head a little at noticing "distraught" is listed on that final line. What else should he be right now? Honestly, he feels a little like he is not handling this well. Like maybe he should be showing more emotion. How is someone supposed to act at a time like this? He has no idea so he defaults to thinking he's doing something wrong.

He meets Officer Marino's eyes again. "It's all correct."

"Great." Marino turns the page. "This next page here just refers to a few details from today. The date, the address of the incident, and the time you called the police department. It also lists the make and model of your vehicle and your license plate. I know this is all correct since I have that information from our dispatchers or officers on location. But would you like to check it yourself?"

Keith shakes his head. He doesn't want this to take longer than it already has.

"Perfect." Marino turns the page again. This page is full of small text boxes. Marino picks up the packet to be able to read all the text squeezed onto the page. "I'm going to read this and you just tell me if I have anything incorrect, alright?" Keith nods. "You work at the Dog Haus at the mall. You were there from two in the afternoon until about quarter after nine at night. During that time you called Craig without an answer twelve times." Marino looks away from the paper for a second. "Your boss already verified that your times are correct for work if that helps." Keith isn't sure how it would help, since he already knew it was right. So he doesn't acknowledge the comment. Marino continues, "At that point, you drove home in your vehicle and called the police when you found the front door ajar."

A flash of memory cuts through Keith's exhaustion. His heartbeat speeds up again just at the thought of that front door. What if he hadn't called the police at that second? What if he had gone into the apartment alone? What if he had been the one to find Craig's body?

"Keith, are you with me?" Marino is asking.

Keith nods. "Yes, sorry. That all is correct."

"Great." Marino flips a page. "You still have

no one you recall making threats to Craig? No one Craig would have had problems with?"

Keith sighs. "Alright, look," he says "I don't actually know anyone who made threats or anything but I know Craig was sleeping with a married woman. I told you that, right? Like, if her husband found out, something bad could've happened." Keith feels his eyes burn a little with the realization that something bad did happen. He stops himself from spewing more negative talk about the roommate he will never see again, swallowing his sadness to process after he gets out of this damn building.

Marino's eyes track down the page. "Right, we have that here under relationships. You know he was having sexual relations with at least three women, one of whom was married. But you weren't sure of any of their names, when the relationships started, or if they are still ongoing."

"Yeah, that's true. His cell phone will probably have more information," Keith says.

"As I said, we'll be putting in a request for that." Marino's eyes return to the paper. Suddenly Keith understands this is the last thing needed from him. Something about the way a tired Officer Marino keeps bringing them back to this packet makes it obvious. He can't believe he didn't see that sooner. If they can get through this packet, Keith can go home. He sits up in the chair, ready to focus on the task at hand. He makes no corrections to the last two pages and signs his name on the final page with a flourish.

Officer Marino stands up, leaving the packet opened to the last page where Keith's signature shows boldly on the plain white page, and offers his hand to the slightly younger man. "If you think of anything new or helpful, give me a call," he says.

Keith shakes the hand. "I'm free to go?" he asks.

"You are. We'll be in touch if we need you." Officer Marino reaches behind him to spin the knob and open the door. The hallway they walked in probably close to two hours ago looks exactly the same as it did before. There are no windows along this little corridor so no way for anything other than the fluorescent lighting to affect the appearance of the hallway. Keith wonders if it causes problems for the officers, the fact that they can't tell just by looking whether it's night or day.

He follows Marino back down the hallway and into the little reception area. Here there are windows, high up on the wall clearly showing the dark outside world. At the desk sits a girl about Keith's own age with bright red hair tied up in a knot on her head. She has what appears to be two ballpoint pens sticking out of the knot.

She turns and smiles at them both, her green eyes immediately friendly. "You two need anything?" she asks. Keith appreciates her including him in the question. For some reason it makes him feel more human than anything else she could have done.

"Sarah, can you get Mr. Armendariz the contact information of the grief counselor from our information sheet?" Marino asks. He turns and lays a hand on Keith's shoulder. Keith assumes the gesture is meant to show a kind of camaraderie, but he has trouble taking it that way. Perhaps it's because he remembers the attitude Marino showed up at his apartment with. That cocky, why-can't-you-just-go-check-out-your-own-apartment attitude. "Keith, you just tell the doctor that Officer Marino recommended you call him. He's a good guy, he'll help you work out anything you might have going on. I really suggest you give him a call."

"Thanks," Keith answers. Right this second, in the middle of the night, after finding out his roommate was likely murdered in their apartment, he would tell you he doesn't plan to call. Of course, that can always change after a little sleep and the sunrise.

The thought of sleep reminds him of something important. "I can't go back to my apartment, right?" It's a crime scene, he assumes.

"Right. You mentioned you had a place to stay. Is that still true or do you need me to call someone?"

"No," Keith pulls out his cell phone and shoots off a quick text message to his friend, Brad. *Call me. Sorry, I know what time it is. Important.*

Sarah, who has been writing something on

a bright yellow sticky note, turns around to face the duo again. "Alright, here's that number for Doctor Carmen."

Keith takes the sticky note and smiles at her. "Thank you."

His cell phone chooses that moment to ring, the sound of a quacking duck filling the room. Keith reddens in embarrassment at the insane ringtone he selected as a joke and hurries to unlock the phone. "Hey man," he says, noting Brad's number is the one showing on the screen. "There's been an emergency situation," he says. He turns away to whisper a short explanation, followed by a promise to explain more in the car. Then, when Brad agrees to come rescue him, he hangs up and turns around to find Marino has disappeared.

"You need water or anything?" Sarah asks.

"No, thanks. My buddy will be here in about five."

"Ok." She crosses to a little cabinet and pulls out a folding chair. "Have a seat."

Five minutes later, she wakes him up when she sees a car pull up out front.

The desk phone rings just as Sarah picks up her study guide. On the camera feed, she watches the car that picked up Keith turn out of the parking lot. She puts her study guide back down again with a sigh and takes the phone off the cradle. "Campus police, how can I help you?"

"I think my cell phone was stolen," the voice says. The caller sounds like they're about Sarah's age, female, and the slight slur to the voice hints at a possible inebriation.

"I'm sorry to hear that. Unfortunately, you'll have to come by the campus police station to fill out a lost or stolen item form. Do you want directions to the building?" Sarah follows the script she was given in her new hire packet, which she used to have to have in front of her for calls like this. She's proud of herself for having these answers off the top of her head now.

"No, you're on North Campus, right? Up near the pool and the gym?"

"That's us. The building is well-lit and the desk is manned twenty-four hours a day. You can come by whenever it is convenient for you."

"I'll be there in ten minutes," the caller says before ending the call. Sarah replaces the handset of the phone at the desk and wonders, briefly, if she'll see that girl before the night is over. Just in case, she takes a lost or stolen property form out of the correct folder and places it on the desk. Then she checks the cameras again, still clear, and picks up her study guide. She reads the next question and tries to remember the answer.

"... can head down to the Coroner's now if you need me." Marino's voice pops up behind Sarah. She sets her study guide down again and turns in her chair to see him walking toward her down the hallway, cell phone nestled between his shoulder and his ear. "That makes sense. Let me know if you need anything else. I'll get this form sent off right away." He takes the phone away from his ear, hits the end button, and sets it face down on Sarah's counter. "What a night," he says.

Sarah tries to smile. The thought of a coroner needed for a case in her town makes the smile shaky. She's pretty sure only half of her mouth cooperates. "Morning, actually," Sarah corrects, pointing to the wall clock that clearly shows it's after midnight. "Maybe you should get some sleep, Officer Marino. Is there anything I can do to help you get your paperwork done so you can call it a night?"

The officer sighs, runs a hand down his face, and moves his head to the right to stretch out his neck. "I just finished these phone record request forms. Can you send them to the email addresses at the top of the form for me? I think I'm going to head home and get a few hours of sleep before the Coroner's report comes in."

Sarah takes the forms and drops them on the scanner. When she hits the button, they slide through the machine, sending digital copies to the computer in front of her. This time, Sarah feels like she can acknowledge the big C word since it was said directly to her instead of overheard on a phone conversation with someone more important. "Coroner?" she asks, tilting her head as if the word confuses her. "Someone died?" She feels a little guilty for delivering this question as if she's a blonde movie extra hired for her body more than her acting skills.

Marino narrows his eyes. "Don't tell me you're trying to get more gossip for the front office rumor mill. You're better than that." He tips his head toward the desk behind her. "And you have a person walking up to the front."

Sarah spins in her chair to find a young brunette with long legs and a short skirt making her way up the sidewalk to the front door. By the looks of her, she's having a little trouble walking in a straight line. Sarah grabs the form she set out earlier and a pen, setting them on the top of the desk. She buzzes the door as soon as the girl approaches, which turns out to be a good thing since the girl didn't even attempt to stop at the phone provided to ask for permission to be buzzed into the building. As soon as the door opens, the girl is already using her loudest voice. "Someone stole my cell phone," she hollers into the quiet.

Behind her, Sarah hears Marino chuckle. She hopes he will take this opportunity to duck out of the room. "Come on up here and let's get this form I told you about all taken care of so the right people can help you find it," Sarah says. In reality, most cell phones are recovered by the person who lost it before they are even searched for by police. Even if they weren't, unless someone else finds it and turns it in, you're not getting your cell phone back. The police are not actively out there searching for lost items. The form serves one basic purpose: to give you something legitimate to hand to your insurance company to file for replacement. But Sarah will get to that.

She walks the girl through filling out the form. While the girl concentrates on printing, Sarah attaches the forms she scanned for Marino into an email and fills in the correct address. After double checking both attachments are included, she hits send.

"Are you all set with that?" she asks when the girl hands over the form.

"I think I did it right," she answers.

Sarah scans it, finds no blank spaces and answers that make sense. "It looks good to me," she says. Then she takes it to the copy machine and makes two copies. She brings one copy to the girl. "Alright, here's your copy. You'll want to provide this one to your insurance company if you have coverage for the phone."

"What?" The girl looks genuinely confused now. "You aren't just going to give it back to me after all that writing?"

"If someone turns in the phone or it is found, we'll obviously return it to you. An officer will contact you with the details tomorrow morning. But in the meantime, you can give this form to your insurance company if you have coverage for the device to secure a replacement."

"Just give me my phone." The girl slams her palm down on the counter.

Sarah squints in confusion. "I don't have your phone. You came here because you lost it. This is a police station." Usually, Sarah has no problem at all with talking to slightly inebriated people, but this girl is getting on her last nerve. "Is there someone I can call for you? Someone who can maybe walk you home to make sure you get there safely?"

"No. I don't have my phone."

"Right. I have a phone right here." Sarah points to the desk phone. "Is there someone I can call?"

The girl turns her entire head in a circle like she's following the hands of a clock moving in reverse. "Oh my God, you're not listening." She claps her hands together. "I don't have my phone." She claps her hands repeatedly to emphasize every word in the sentence.

Sarah closes her eyes and takes a deep breath to keep herself from snapping at the girl. "I'm aware of that." She sets the form down on the counter between them and picks up the phone. "Are there any phone numbers that you know off the top of your head without having to look them up in your phone?"

"My Moms, I guess."

"Great. What's that number?" When the girl starts with a long-distance area code, Sarah holds up her hand to stop her. "Your parents don't live in Arizona, do they?"

"No."

"Right, so they wouldn't be the best candidates for picking you up right now. Do you know any other phone numbers?"

"How am I supposed to know all of those

without my phone? No one remembers all the numbers for everyone in their dorm rooms."

Sarah smiles, tugging the answer free from that mess of a sentence. "Which dorm do you live in?" Sarah hangs up the phone just long enough to pull up the directory for the campus. Then she dials the front desk of the residence hall the girl lives in and gives the girl's name. After a small pause, she's connected to a roommate. She explains who she is and that the girl needs someone to come pick her up from campus police because she lost her cell phone. The roommate promises to wake up the neighbor who has a car and be there as soon as possible. Sarah hangs up and turns her attention back to the girl. "Your roommate will be here shortly. Do you want a cup of coffee?"

She lets the girl come around the counter and sit in a folding chair while she makes her a cup of coffee. "Why can't I just walk home?" the girl asks.

"It's pretty late and it's dark out there. I'd just feel better if you had someone with you," Sarah answers. The truth is, even on a normal day, Sarah wouldn't have felt comfortable with a girl this drunk walking home across campus. But today doesn't feel normal. In the back of her mind she can still hear Marino's voice asking about a coroner. Someone in Flagstaff, probably close to her age if she can judge by the fact that Keith looked about her age and must have known the victim, was killed. Someone who might not be much older than this girl didn't get to go home safely tonight. Doesn't that warrant a little extra caution? Sarah checks the cameras again, more carefully this time, looking for any cars or people that may be lurking on the edge of the frame. She finds nothing but feels her heartbeat quicken anyway.

"So, where were you when you lost your phone?" Sarah asks, trying to make conversation. She turns her head to see the girl has fallen asleep in the chair, her head tipped back and her mouth wide open. She chuckles to herself. Most of the time she sits here by herself all night long without interruption. Tonight two people have fallen asleep in that folding chair waiting for rides. That just enforces the idea that this is a weird night.

She picks up her study guide and gets through ten more questions before another car pulls up on the camera feed in front of her. She wakes up the sleeping girl, which proves more difficult than waking Keith, and points to the monitor. "Is this your ride?"

"Yeah, probably," the girl mumbles.

Feeling absolutely no confidence in that answer, Sarah helps the girl up and gets her through the front lobby to the door. She can't walk further than that with her or the door will lock her out, which would be a huge problem. Instead, she settles for watching the interaction between the passenger and the girl. Clearly, they know each other. The passenger gets out of the car, meets the girl halfway, and waves at Sarah. Then she helps her into the back seat and they drive away.

Back at the desk, Sarah manages to get through the rest of the study guide without further interruption. She only thinks about the coroner and what that might mean three times.

CHAPTER 6

The alarm on Sarah's phone goes off at 5:45. She wasn't asleep in the chair at work, but she also wasn't fully awake. She was staring off into space, not thinking about anything. She shakes herself fully conscious, turns off the alarm, and starts the process of packing up for the shift change. Everything she brought in with her needs to be put back in her bag. Her belongings need to come out from under the desk so that Greg has a place to put his things when he takes over. The folding chair goes back into the closet it came out of. A pot of fresh coffee gets brewed. Sarah clicks a button to log her email out of the server, making room for Greg to log in when he gets here. Then she grabs the set of keys from the top drawer of the desk and makes her way to the front door. The building officially opens at six. Sarah's policy has always been to unlock it whenever she's ready for the day to begin, even if that's a few minutes early. Today it's eight minutes early.

Sarah spots Greg walking up to the building from the parking lot and waves at him. He returns the gesture while picking up speed. It feels like it would be rude to shut the door when he's obviously trying to hustle her way so Sarah leans on it and waits. "Good morning," she calls when he's close enough to hear her.

"Morning." Greg lays his hand on the door behind her and pushes backward a little, making it clear he intends to hold it while she goes in first.

Sarah rolls her eyes. "Stop it. You don't have to try and be the guy who insists it's your job to hold a door I was already holding. I'm capable of holding it." She gestures to the open doorway. "Go in."

"I wasn't …" He shakes his head. "Forget it, I'm not arguing with you." He crosses the threshold into the lobby and takes a deep breath. "That coffee smells good," he says. The tone of his voice makes it clear he's letting the little incident go. Good, Sarah thinks, she didn't want to start an argument but Greg is always doing things like this. He thinks he's being a gentleman, or so he's explained. She's not sure exactly how to explain to him that those sorts of things don't make her feel special and appreciated, they make her feel like she's in the way or doing something wrong.

Take the door incident just now as an example. She was standing there, being polite, holding the door for him the entire time he crossed the parking lot. She saw him coming and made a choice to be friendly. That's nice. If he had done that for her she would have thanked him when she got to the door and jogged right through it as quickly as she could so he could let it close. Instead, he'd gotten closer and tried to take the door from her as if she had been wrong to hold it. It wasn't necessary and it wasn't faster. It was annoying.

While Greg fiddled with the coffee pot, preparing himself a coffee, she grabbed her stuff from the desk and set it on top of the counter. Like Alicia had done last night for their shift change, she leaned on the desk from the civilian side. "There's a lost item form in the inbox for whatever officer is handling those today," she says. "Otherwise the only thing going on from last night is whatever Marino is handling."

Greg turns around and he's holding two cups of coffee in his hand. One in a travel mug with a lid perfect for driving and the other in a regular diner-style mug. "What is that?" Sarah asks, her voice tinged with a little of the annoyance from the door incident.

"A peace offering," Greg explains. "I feel bad that what I thought was a nice gesture at the door upset you. I didn't mean it that way. When I smelled that coffee I realized this would be a better way to show kindness." He crosses the space between them and holds the travel mug out toward Sarah. "Just a little of my sweet creamer that you liked last time, no extra sugar."

Sarah feels her annoyance melt away. This isn't a gesture that says she was in the way or doing something wrong. This, like her own gesture of brewing the coffee before Greg's shift, is something that shows consideration for another person. This is sweet. She takes the coffee, flips open the lid, and takes a sip. "Perfect," she says.

Greg takes a sip of his own and then sets it down on the counter. "You were saying, about Marino?"

"Right." Sarah puts her coffee down and leans on the counter. "Something big happened last night. When I got here at eleven there were four uniforms here." Greg's eyes widen appropriately. "I'm not sure what was going on, you know how quiet they can be about it, but they had someone in Interview One and they asked for a few phone record request forms."

"That's pretty standard."

"I know. But they were here for hours. Then when the guy was leaving Marino asked me to give him the phone number for a grief counselor."

"Yikes." Greg lays his hand on his chest as if it pains him to think of that.

"Then I heard Marino on the phone talking about the coroner."

"Oh shit," Greg says. "Someone died then. But that guy who was here must have been a witness or a friend, not a suspect. You don't give a suspect the number of a grief counselor."

"Exactly. But we don't know if it was foul play, of course."

Greg shakes his head. "No way, you said they were here for hours. Something foul is up for sure."

"That's what Alicia thought too. She'll want details so you'll have to keep this relay going." Greg's shift, according to the schedule on the wall in Alicia's nice handwriting, ends at one when Ted comes in. Alicia isn't in until three.

"I'm on it," he says, laughing. "In other news, how was that date you went on last night?" Greg asks.

Sarah rolls her eyes. "Does everyone know about that?"

Greg reddens and drops his eyes. "I asked about your situation and that's what Alicia told me."

Sarah feels mildly guilty watching his embarrassment grow. Greg is a nice guy. Maybe she owes him at least a little of the explanation she would normally give people who express an interest in dating her. "Ok, do you want to have this conversation?" she asks.

Greg's blush deepens. "What conversation?"

"About my," she uses her fingers as quotation marks "situation".

"Sarah, you know I'm interested in you. I'd like to take you out sometime. I thought I was clear about that. You haven't exactly been clear about how you feel. That's why I was asking around. If you aren't interested, I respect that."

"Sorry, it just feels weird to have this sort of conversation at work where anyone might walk in. I probably should have been more upfront with you when I realized what your intentions were," Sarah says. "But let's get to it. I do like you, I think you're a nice guy and you're definitely cute." Greg's blush deepens again. "There are a few things you probably should know. First, I'm absolutely not looking for anything serious. I do not do relationships. I do casual dating for fun."

"Ok." He looks skeptical.

"In fact," Sarah continues. "I'm currently seeing two people. One of them was my date last night. They've both had similar versions of this same conversation in the past. I date and I have fun, but I'm not looking for labels or exclusive dating."

"At least you're clear with people," Greg says, still looking unsure of where this is all going.

"I try to be. One last thing, do you consider

yourself to be straight?" Sarah asks.

Greg nods.

"I thought so. I'm bisexual, which means I'm queer. I'm not sure how much it would bother you to be dating someone who was queer and only casually dating you and two other people. Only you can decide that." She smiles. "I've given you a lot to consider. But you have my cell phone number. I think you should call me sometime and let me know what you're thinking. No hard feelings either way." Sarah picks up the coffee and her belongings.

"Sarah, would you like to go to dinner with me sometime?" Greg asks.

Sarah turns her attention back to Greg's face. She wasn't kidding about him being handsome. He has brown hair that he keeps trimmed up but long enough to style. His brown eyes have hints of green and his looks are classic enough that she could picture him as the leading man on a popular television show. Right now, he's smiling at her in a way that would make anyone watching that TV show swoon. It's working for her a little too if she's being honest. "I didn't scare you off?" she says.

"I'm not easy to scare."

"Good to know. Use that phone number. Call me. We'll schedule something. I have to check my calendar first." By that, she really means she'll have to consider whether Greg is a lunch date, a coffee date, or a dinner date. There are levels to this whole thing that she can't properly consider with his smoldering smile sitting directly in front of her. Time and space are the best ways to get that information. Plus, it's been a long night and she could use a little cat nap before class. "I'm going to get some sleep. Talk soon." She winks at him and heads out of the building.

The parking lot is emptier than it was when Sarah arrived to work last night. Normally by this time of the morning officers would already be showing up, collecting forms, and following up on cases. Now that she thinks about it, it's strange that she and Greg were able to have a private conversation for a bit without anyone coming into the room. Again she can hear Marino's voice asking about a coroner and she wonders if that could possibly be where everyone is. In movies, it often looks like only one or two cops are working on a situation but the reality is nothing like the movies, she knows that. So is it possible the entire force is working on this case?

She turns and looks at the quiet building again. Is there a murderer in her sleepy little town?

Suddenly she doesn't know, but she does move faster to get to her car and she does lock it as soon as she is safely inside.

CHAPTER 7

The sky is still dark when Sarah pulls her car into a parking spot outside of her apartment. She sleepily makes her way up to her front door and manages to get the key into the lock on the first try. Normally, Sarah can make her way through anything the day throws at her without a problem, but for some reason the second she gets home after this shift she feels the entire day catch up with her. It's always a struggle to get in the door without falling asleep. She doesn't sleep much, but when she does it's always intense.

She gets in the door, drops her things right there in the entryway, and pushes the door shut behind her. Then she collapses on the couch, which is a lot closer than the bed she can see through the open doorway. Still dressed from her date and wearing her shoes, she slips into a deep sleep.

Two hours later another preset alarm on her phone goes off. Sarah stretches for the items she dropped on the floor but her arms simply aren't long enough. That, she supposes, is just as well. If she could reach the phone to silence it she would be at risk of sleeping here all day and she can't do that. Today is Thursday, which means she has two classes to get to before she has to be at her second job. On Tuesdays and Thursdays she only has two classes, on the other three weekdays she has three. Usually, that means she can get more homework done on days like today, which is a good thing since she got interrupted a lot more last night at work.

Sarah makes her way across her bedroom, shedding clothes as she goes, into her bathroom where she turns the shower on as hot as it will go and steps in. She washes her hair with something that claims to be specially formulated for curly color-treated hair. While the matching conditioner sits in her hair she scrubs at her face and body with a facecloth, imagining the long day from yesterday sloshing off her body and down the drain. By the time she rinses the conditioner out, she already feels revitalized and ready to do it all again.

She dresses quickly, pulling on something simple from her closet selection since there are no planned dates today that she needs to worry about. Checking the time on her phone, she hustles her way into the little kitchen on the other side of her unit and fills her hand with easy-to-eat food: an apple, a granola bar, a single croissant she brought home from a coffee shop yesterday, and a chocolate bar. She pinches the lid of a plastic water bottle between her pinky and the rest of her hand and walks quickly to the place where she abandoned her belongings last night.

After dropping all her food preparations into her bag, she leaves the apartment again and makes sure to lock the door behind her. In the car, she notices she's left herself less than ten minutes to get to campus, find a parking spot, and get to class. She curses herself for taking too long in the shower and decides she'll have to resign herself to sitting in the back of the lecture hall in hopes that no one will notice she's late.

It's a beautiful autumn day now that the sun has decided to join them. One of Sarah's favorite parts of this town is the weather. In the fall the evenings have a crispness to them that lets you know cooler days are coming. Not cold enough to remind you that snow will be falling someday, but cold enough to remind you that it's not always one hundred and humid. Then, during the day time they have what can only be described as perfect weather. Sunny, seventies, and air that just smells fresh and clean. It's nothing like the capital city two hours south. Flagstaff is beauty incarnate. Sarah drives the short distance to campus with the windows of the car down to fully appreciate the perfect day.

Luck is on her side, there's a parking spot relatively close to the building she needs. She makes no apologies as she hustles past people standing around talking or moving from one class to another. When she gets to the lecture hall, she allows herself a quick second to pause and take a deep breath. It wouldn't look great to pop in late already breathing heavily from hustling across the parking lot.

The door to the lecture hall opens at the top of the row of seats all pointed toward the professor standing at the bottom. Sarah's eyes spot an empty seat on the aisle three rows up from her. She hustles to it, thankful she won't have to pass people to get from the aisle to something open. The professor, who was talking when she walked in, pauses mid-sentence but doesn't call her out. Sarah silently thanks him for his kindness and pulls out her belongings as quickly as she can.

Then, she centers herself and focuses completely on what he is saying. In elementary and high school Sarah was always a straight A student. Even when she was being bounced around to foster homes, even when her mother showed up again and she was trying to do homework in a drug user's house, even when she was left alone in that house for weeks at a time and had to get herself to school. Her plan to get herself into a better life started with doing well in school and Sarah never let herself get derailed from that plan. It was literally the one thing she could control and that hasn't changed. For the remainder of the ninety-minute class, Sarah takes copious notes and commits a multitude of facts to memory.

She doesn't notice Keith until after the professor releases them.

Two rows up from Sarah, Keith turns around to head up toward the door Sarah came in earlier and she spots him. She recognizes his face immediately and wonders why he didn't look familiar last night when he was at the station. She's probably seen him before. Then again, she reminds herself, there are about three hundred seats in this lecture hall and most of them are full. She tries to recall his name and can only pull a last name from her memory bank, Armendariz. Did she even hear his first name last night?

He walks past her, never noticing her sitting there, and Sarah follows him out. She tells herself that she's not really following him, just moving with the flow of people exiting the classroom. But when he takes a right out of the building, she goes in the same direction. Her next class is on South Campus, whereas this one was on North. Sometimes she'll drive down there. Today she is going to walk. She tells herself this is her own decision and not one made out of some morbid curiosity about the events of last night.

About ten yards in front of her, Keith pulls out his cell phone and slips in a set of earbuds. Sarah is close enough to catch snippets of conversation. She hears him tell someone he's "sorry for their loss" and ask about a "memorial service". She thinks she hears the name "Craig" but it could also be "Greg". Then she hears an answer to a question she also has herself. "Honestly, I just needed to pretend things are normal today. I went to class this morning hoping I could put off making this feel real. Is that stupid?"

She wants to tell him no. She wants to hug this poor guy. Clearly, someone close to him died last night. Would it be weird to stop him and ask him if he's safe? Does he know what happened? She knows that would be weird. She would never do something like that.

Ahead of Keith and to the right Sarah spots a coffee shop. The same one, in fact, that she visited yesterday. The sad croissant sitting at the top of her bag suddenly seems unappealing. She can get something different. A fresh scone, maybe. Plus the coffee shop has the added benefit of not being where this guy is headed, which means she can stop creepily following him through campus.

She tries to send literal good vibes Mr. Armendariz's way before she turns toward the coffee shop. This poor guy deserves his week to get immeasurably better. She can't imagine trying to power through her plan if someone she cared about turned up dead.

She turns into the coffee shop and hops in line. She orders a large black coffee and a warm blueberry scone. Ordering the coffee reminds her that she left the travel mug full of coffee from Greg somewhere, likely in her apartment. She'll have to remember to dump out whatever is left, wash that, and get it back to Greg.

Sarah checks her watch. She has just under two hours until her class on South Campus. Two hours is plenty of time to get some work done. She claims a little round table by the window and sets up her little workstation, a small laptop claiming center stage. Two refills and ninety-five minutes later, her paper is done for her class tomorrow and she's completed a smaller assignment for the professor she has just left.

She leans back in the chair, finishing the last bite of scone and stretching her fingers. Beside her, two girls have dropped into a table exactly like hers. "His name was Craig," one girl says. "They live in the apartment right under mine. I'm not even sure it's safe to keep living there, or whatever. There's like police tape and they wouldn't even let Keith back in."

"Keith is the roommate?" the other girl

asks.

"Yeah. He's the cute one and the more friendly one, but I've met Craig at least once."

Police tape around an apartment in this town has to be related to whatever Marino was handling, Sarah knows. Police tape that is still there the next morning combined with talking about Craig, a name she thought she heard the guy from the station last night say over the phone, means he is likely the dead guy. Sarah hides her lean closer to the table under the guise of putting her head in her hand.

"So, wait, he died? You know for sure?" the friend asks. Sarah likes this question. If it's possible to listen more carefully, she does so now.

"Yes. For sure. There was a coroner van in the parking lot just outside my apartment sometime early this morning. All the police lights were coming right in my bedroom window, I slept like total shit. I was watching the whole thing."

Coroner van. That confirms Sarah's suspicion that this is related. Officer Marino mentioned the coroner, a rare enough word for her to hear in the office that she knows this is the same case. This is insider information she couldn't even get at the police station. Sarah practically holds her breath waiting for more information.

"Did he, like, use drugs or something? Was there a party? What happened?" All good questions, again. Sarah immediately likes the girl in charge of questioning.

Apartment girl throws up her hands. "I have no idea. No one is telling us anything. My mom even heard about it on the news down in Phoenix. She called to ask if we are safe. I mean, I said we were. But we're on the back of the unit. Seriously right outside my door is like trees and forest and stuff. What if someone, like, broke into their apartment and killed him? I'm not safe. Would they have to let me move to a new unit or something if that's what went down?"

"Maybe that's not what happened. They'd probably tell you if that's what happened."

The barista calls out a name and the girls stand, pushing in their chairs. Sarah almost calls them back. She's pretty sure the girl would be happy to continue gossiping about this with her. She could get them to stick around and ask them a few more questions.

Her eyes fall on the laptop and she sighs. She didn't get enough work done last night because of this distraction. Now here she is wasting what is left of her study time listening to more gossip about the same case.

She opens a file for a group project she needs to review and rate her group on. She will focus. Nothing, not even a murder in her college town, will keep her from good grades.

CHAPTER 8

When her class on South Campus is over, Sarah is one of the first people out the door. She opens her phone and frantically texts the boss for her retail job, her thumbs flying across the keyboard. *Class ran a little late. I might be like two minutes late, depending on traffic.*

At her car, she pops the trunk open and drops in her bag, snagging the apple and granola bar out of it and setting them on top. Then she pulls off her tee shirt, exposing her entire bra and a lot of bare skin to anyone paying attention. She quickly throws on the approved polo shirt from her trunk, the one every employee of the little store in the mall is required to wear. It's a terrible color for her, the fire engine red does nothing for her reddish hair.

She slams the trunk shut, slips the granola bar into the pocket of her jeans, and holds the apple in her mouth so her hands are free to tuck the shirt in. Then she hops into the car and drives slightly faster than she probably should through the college town.

There are a lot of people in Flagstaff who walk everywhere. Honestly, when she first enrolled at the university, Sarah didn't have a car. Adding the little used car to her life helped her expand her radius for possible second jobs. This job, working retail at the mall on the far east side of Flagstaff, is something mostly locals take. The university is the heart of western Flagstaff. As you drive further east, things change. There are more houses and older businesses. Everything on this side of town has a more lived-in small-town feel and Sarah loves it. If she were able to afford an apartment on this side of town and justify that longer drive to class, she'd live out here. As it is, she lives in the cheapest place in town. At least it's her own place, she tells herself. That's something.

She parks in the employee section of the parking lot, which is the last ten spaces farthest from the door no one would use anyway if they didn't have to. Then she literally runs from her car to the employee entrance. She tosses the apple core into the trash can outside as the doors whoosh open. She scans her badge into the machine. Only then does she slow down and take a deep breath. Once she clocks in, she's on company time which means she can't get any later.

Sarah was recently promoted from women's wear to hardware. This, in her opinion, is a brilliant decision. In hardware, she gets to work with people who know exactly what they came in the door for. She doesn't have to empty fitting rooms. She doesn't have to wrestle with hangers.

She checks her cell phone one last time before slipping it into the little bag she's required to keep her personal belongings in. She sees a reply from her manager, *No problem, see you soon. Drive safe!*

Sarah rounds the corner of appliances, waving at a few of the nicer employees as she passes, and enters into familiar territory. Somehow the store even smells different on this side: more grease, more paint, and less perfume. Sarah takes a deep breath of the air here. This is the smell of a low-stress job where time moves slower. She waves toward the handsome, tall brunette leaning on the counter, a good signal for Sarah that it hasn't been a busy day.

He waves back, his entire face breaking out in a grin. "Technically, you're late again," he says, laughter tinting his voice.

"Fire me, Assistant Manager man."

Dan rolls his eyes and gets off the counter to allow Sarah to stash her little company-approved bag where customers can't see or reach it. "Who would I casually date from the company pool if I fired you?" he whispers.

Sarah laughs out loud. "I'm the only female here and you're straight."

"Doesn't casually dating a queer girl sort of make me queer by extension?" Dan asks.

"Are you thinking of playing around with boys?" Sarah makes a big show of looking around the department. "Because I have to admit there aren't many good options here. But there are a few I could introduce you to if you're willing to expand your radius just a little."

Dan's laughter rings out over the empty department. "Seriously, how are you? Did your class run long again?"

"I'm good," Sarah says. "That professor always runs long. I swear she became a professor just to listen to her voice drone on and on about her topic. It's exhausting. I should really just start leaving at the prescribed end time."

"But you won't."

Sarah frowns. "But I won't. You're right. I just don't have it in me to be that rude." She looks around the department again. There's noise coming from a few aisles over, possibly near hammers. Otherwise, there is no sign of anyone here who isn't an employee. "Been slow today?" she asks.

Dan nods and leans back on the counter between the registers again. "Been like this all day. I'm supposed to remind you to handle your small tasks whenever it's not busy and to not stand around lallygagging in between customers." He crosses his ankles as if proving he intends to not take his suggestions.

"Is that what you have to remind me of because you were promoted?" Sarah teases. Sarah was promoted to this department six months ago. In the women's department, everyone is eager to prove how important they are to the company. Everyone moves quickly, everyone does their small tasks without needing to be reminded, and people short themselves on lunch breaks. When she was transferred it was a breath of fresh air. The guys here do what needs to be done and literally nothing else. They clock in exactly on time, clock out exactly on time, and do the small tasks when they need to be done. They don't waste their time doing things just to appear busy. Somehow they still get everything done and keep the area clean.

Two weeks ago, Dan was promoted to Assistant Manager. That position comes with a dollar-an-hour raise and, according to their Manager, was intended to motivate the other employees to exceed company expectations. Instead, it's shown them all that you can move up in this business by perfectly managing expectations and not burning yourself out.

"That," Dan says, "is exactly why I have to remind you. This is why they pay me the big bucks." He pushes off the counter and takes a step toward the entrance door behind Sarah. "Speaking of big bucks, this guy looks like he's ready to spend them. Excuse me a second."

Sarah turns around to see a guy in a company shirt everyone in the department would recognize. These guys, a local mechanic shop, regularly drop a lot of money buying replacement tools or sets for new employees. They usually come in with purchase orders, meaning they have to spend every last cent of it and know exactly what they want. Everyone jumps to help them because helping them usually just means taking their armfuls of items from the shelves to the register until they're ready to pay. When you work on commission, customers like that are gold. "Damn," Sarah mumbles. She should have been watching that door.

The customer Sarah heard banging around in hammers curses. Sarah decides they're likely someone who needs help. She moves around the corner and spots a shorter woman with dark hair pulled into a ponytail kneeling on the ground by sockets. "Can I help you find something?" Sarah asks.

"I can't find the size I need," the woman says. She holds up a bolt. "It has to fit this."

Sarah smiles and takes the bolt from the

lady. "No problem."

"You'd think it would be easy since I brought the damn bolt but none of these fit. I tried every single one. It's closest to the ⅜ but that's not quite right."

"Maybe metric would be better," Sarah offers. Sarah considers the benefits of showing this lady the metric sockets. Likely, she'd need a ratchet. That seems like a lot of things to help her find. Sarah thinks of alternatives. "Or we have adjustable wrenches instead of sockets. Are you trying to put the bolt into something or take it out?"

"Metric? What the hell is that? I'm trying to put them in. The stupid table I bought didn't come with the tools to assemble it."

"Table legs usually have a little more room. You can probably get an adjustable wrench in there. Let me show you." Sarah walks her over, grabs the right tool, and demonstrates how to use it. All in all, she probably spends ten minutes with the lady before she finally gets her to the checkout counter. When the customer leaves, Sarah knows she helped someone and she knows it's appreciated. But she also knows she made a total of like four cents commission for that small sale. Not the best use of ten minutes. Of course, the department is practically empty so it's not like she had much of a choice.

As if on cue, Dan pops up and drops three more items onto the large pile he's got going on the floor beside the register. "This is a big one," he says. "Dinner is my treat tonight." He winks at Sarah.

Sarah frowns. "Wait, no …" but Dan is already gone, back to hold arms full of items for a guy spending company money with little self-control. She didn't have the chance to fully object, to tell him that she got no studying done last night. Come to think of it, she didn't even get the chance to tell him about the murder in town. Isn't that important information someone should have? Dan lives on the west side and takes a few classes at the University. Maybe someone dying should have more widespread appeal. Did it warrant a spot on the local news? Sarah doesn't know, the news isn't something she's found a way to incorporate into her time.

She reaches under the counter and frees her phone from the little bag. Having your cell phone out during your shift is one of the company rules Dan does actually feel strongly about. Typically, this is one she would never break. No one in their department would. But Sarah has a strong desire to check on the news and this seems like a perfect time to do it.

She opens up a news webpage and waits while it loads the impressive amount of video clips and bars that contain all the information anyone might need for the day. This page is news for the entire state of Arizona. Phoenix area weather is on the top. Sarah she uses her thumb to scroll down a little. She glances over her shoulder to check that Dan is still occupied and sees him in the drill aisle, his back turned toward her. She returns her attention to her phone and sees a headline that looks promising "College Student Found Dead in Flagstaff Apartment." Sarah clicks and speed-reads the article, looking for important phrases that she may not have already known.

When she hears footsteps, she pushes the button to turn her screen black. "Are you seriously on your phone right now?" Dan asks in a whisper. "I know it's slow in here but the cameras will catch me not catching you and you will get me in trouble."

Sarah scrambles to slide the phone back into her purse under the counter. "I was checking the news. I have to tell you about something that happened at the other job."

The customer Dan was shopping for appears at the checkout counter. "If my Math is right, that's everything," he says.

Dan adopts his perfect retail employee smile, the one Sarah is convinced actually got him the promotion. "Excellent. Give me just a second to get this all rung in for you." He casually chats with the guy about his line of work, doing a really convincing job of acting like he cares about the mechanic shop. Then he reads a total that makes Sarah blink too rapidly. Did this guy really just spend $800?

Sarah watches the purchase order change

hands and Dan key in all the valid information. She helps drop everything into the large bags only found in this section of the store, the ones with the extra reinforcement on the handles, and then the customer is gone. She sighs. "Seriously, I'm sorry about the phone. I had to check on the news. I think someone was murdered in town last night."

Dan holds up his hand. "I want to hear all about it. Honestly, I do. But we need to table this discussion for dinner."

"I can't do dinner tonight. I didn't study at all last night because it was so busy at the station. I have to get some things done."

He takes a step closer to her. Dan is about six inches taller than Sarah, so when he steps closer he has to look down a little. Something about the way he looks down at her makes her heart flutter. She closes her eyes, willing herself to not focus on how cute he is when she opens them again. It sort of works. "You are stressed and running yourself ragged at these two jobs. You need a night without studying, just eating with a casual date. We're having dinner. My treat."

Sarah wants to argue, sort of. But she also wants to talk to Dan about everything she just read in that article and dinner seems like a good time to do that.

She relents, the arguments and plans for the night leaving her in a rush that already has her feeling more relaxed. "Fine. But right after our shift and not staying out too late."

Dan winks. "Exactly."

CHAPTER 9

When their shift ends, Sarah and Dan walk side-by-side to the time clock, all the employees they pass heading in the same direction. A few nicer coworkers wave or call out cheery "good night" calls. At the time clock, Sarah purposely steps behind Dan. Will the extra three seconds actually mean even a penny more? Probably not, but it's worth a shot.

Dan stands off to the side while Sarah swipes her card, ending her shift. Then he offers up the name of the restaurant one storefront over in the mall, "Reds?"

In answer, Sarah starts walking in that direction. "So, last night was weird and we need to talk about it," she says.

"I'm listening."

They take the long way around the store, enjoying the cool air and the empty parking lot. Sarah manages to get most of the major facts out before they even reach the restaurant. Keith's interview, the phone records requests, Officer Marino's mention of a coroner, and the article Sarah saw online today when she checked the news.

At the counter, Dan holds up two fingers to the host who immediately grabs menus and starts a path through the mostly empty space. Sarah and Dan follow. All three of them are quiet as they cross the restaurant to a small round table near the window. When the host leaves, Dan turns concerned eyes to Sarah. "So this article you found confirmed the kid was killed?"

"Yeah, and kid isn't the right word. I mean he was a college student. Our age, Dan. The article mentioned a roommate. That has to be the guy coffee shop girl called Keith, who I think is the same guy I saw in Interview 1 last night. Someone who goes to college with us was killed in their apartment. How is that not huge news spreading through the town like wildfire?"

This is the exact moment the waiter emerges from somewhere behind Sarah. "What can I get you two today?" he asks, all smiles. He was either not listening to their conversation or he isn't at all bothered by the thoughts of a murder in town.

"I'll just have the salad bar and a diet soda," Sarah says.

"Chicken wrap with the salad bar instead of fries and an iced tea," Dan orders.

"Perfect. Help yourselves to the salad bar and I'll get those orders in." The waiter is gone again without writing anything down. Sarah stands up, realizing she's incredibly hungry and the fresh veggies on that salad bar are calling her name.

On the way to the salad bar, Sarah tries to remind herself that she signed a document keeping her from spreading privileged information to the public about the police department. Of course, that's intended to be something that keeps them from calling the press but she supposes it's also to keep people like Dan from calling the press after Sarah spills her guts. She has to be careful not to give him more than he would find if he read this news story on his own. She has to keep her personal knowledge of things out of this. If the information she has was obtained at work, she has to pretend not to know about it.

As much as she prides herself on being better than a town gossip and above all that drama, she's shocked to find how quickly she's dissolved into just another rumor hound in the wake of a single murder. She let herself get sidetracked from studying last night, got distracted at her study session in the coffee shop today, and agreed to another dinner with someone when she should be trying to squeeze in a little more studying and sleep before her shift. All those changes to her routine could cost her the future she's dreamed of. She cannot allow herself to turn into one of those sad girls who never finished college and didn't become all they wanted to be.

By the time both Sarah and Dan have returned to the table with full plates from the salad bar, she has stubbornly decided she will talk about something else. "So, how's life been for you?" she asks, taking a bite. Some time while they were at the salad bar their drinks and Dan's chicken wrap were dropped off. Sarah takes a huge swig of her soda.

Dan shakes his head. "No way are you changing the subject. Did the article say how this kid died?"

"Stop calling him a kid and no, it didn't. Plus, I really shouldn't be talking about this."

"You brought it up."

"I know." She grimaces. "I shouldn't be as obsessed with this as I'm being. Let's talk about something else."

"Sarah, what if one of us knew this guy? We have classes on campus. We know people," Dan points out.

Sarah has a strong memory of seeing Keith

in her class this morning. She'd passed him daily for months and didn't recognize him when she saw him at the station last night. What if the same is true about the victim who was killed? Craig, she thinks his name was. Dan could be right. He could be a regular at the store, someone she has a class with, someone she saw at a party once, or the person who sometimes serves her at the coffee shop. There's no telling how many people you interact with daily or whose life yours intersects with. She shakes her head to clear out that unproductive line of thinking. "I can't think about that, not right now."

"Ok, fine. We can talk about something else," Dan agrees. They both lapse into silence, eating food without any conversation flowing from either half of the pair. It's as if, despite their promise to stray to other topics, both of their brains keep coming back to the one taboo topic they agreed not to discuss.

Finally, his wrap almost gone, Dan gives in to the temptation. "Did the article at least say if it was like a break-in or something? I live in an apartment too. Should I be doing something to be a little safer?"

Sarah sighs. "It didn't say. But that's what the girl at the coffee shop was worried about too. That seems like something I can ask an officer about. Maybe they can make some kind of statement to the news about the security angle of this whole thing. I'll ask. I promise."

"It just seems like it's ok for us to take this seriously. I mean, someone died."

"I know," Sarah agrees. "I just can't let this derail my focus. I can't keep obsessing about this."

"Got it." Dan waves his hands over his mostly empty plate. "Consider it done." He smiles and Sarah has no choice but to smile back. Something about the dimples that appear on Dan's cheeks when he smiles at her has a way of tugging her own smile right out of hiding. "Seen any good movies lately?" Dan asks.

Sarah laughs. "I haven't made much time for movies."

"Maybe we should. We can see something together." Dan taps her foot with his under the table. "We can see whatever you want. Sit next to each other in the dark, hold hands, snuggle in, and share some popcorn." He winks at her. "Somehow that seems like a fun little date."

Sarah can imagine the scene he's painting; drawing close enough to smell that woodsy cologne Dan always wears, feeling the heat from his hands, their fingers brushing in the tub of shared popcorn, maybe even a goodnight kiss that would have just the right balance of sweet and heat. "That sounds fun," she agrees. "Just not a scary movie," she adds.

"Right, totally a romcom or something romantic," Dan agrees. He picks up his iced tea and downs the rest of the glass. "What do you think, are you having more salad?"

Sarah eyes the salad bar and her empty plate. The salad bar is intended to be something you visit more than once, that's what makes it the best deal. But right now she's suddenly feeling tired, which never happens. If she makes a second trip up there and puts more food in her stomach, the sleepy feeling will just increase. That, combined with the knowledge that she has to go into the police station tonight, spells trouble for her getting through her schedule. She shakes her head. "I shouldn't. I need to pop home and get a little nap before my other job, I think."

"What time do you have to be there?"

Sarah checks her watch. "My shift starts at eleven." She was hoping to get a nap in. She has just under two hours until she has to clock in for her shift. "Soon enough that if I want to squeeze in that nap I can't have more salad."

"How about this," Dan says, standing up, "I'll drive you over to that side of town so you can sleep in the car. I'll even let you sit in the parking lot of the police station, sound asleep, while I play some mindless game on my phone. That way you can maximize your time and I can spend a little more time hanging out with you. Plus, this has the bonuses of letting me keep you safe and letting me spy on who comes and goes from that police station."

"That is a tempting offer," Sarah answers, a yawn snatching up the end of her sentence. "But what would we do about my car? It will be here and I will be stuck at the police station tomorrow morning."

Dan grabs the paper check, which the waiter must have dropped on the table when he dropped the wrap, and the pair head to the front to pay. "So give me your car keys. My roommate and I will coordinate the car pick up and drop it for you at the station. Easy."

"That's not easy." At the checkout counter, Dan pushes Sarah's debit card out of the way. She rolls her eyes. "Let me pay for mine."

"They didn't charge us for yours. Check the ticket, I'm telling you the truth. He charged us for one salad bar."

The waiter, now behind the cash register, smiles. "It seemed easier. The salad bar is unlimited and you guys never eat a lot of refills. This way is cheaper and the restaurant doesn't care. Trust me."

"Fine." Sarah slides her debit card back into her wallet. "But I'm paying next time."

"That just means there will be a next time." Dan winks at her. "You just keep throwing yourself at me."

Sarah laughs. Then a yawn slips out again. "Seriously, why am I so tired?"

Dan signs the check with a flourish and slips out the door Sarah holds open. The wind has picked up and a little chill is in the air now. Involuntarily, Sarah shivers. Dan steps closer and puts his arm around her shoulder. As much as she wants to protest, his body heat feels amazing beside her and he smells exactly like she imagined in her daydream about the movies earlier. She melts into his side, curling her face into his chest. "Let me do something nice for you, Sarah," Dan says. "Let me drive you to work. We'll figure out the logistics of your car later."

Despite the logical side of her brain finding fault with this argument, Sarah lets herself be led to Dan's car. She drops into the passenger seat and is asleep before he's even out of the parking lot for the shopping mall.

CHAPTER 10

Sarah wakes up peacefully, becoming aware of her surroundings slowly before opening her eyes. She's sitting up and something smells amazing. A woodsy sort of smell that instantly makes her think of the forest or camping, something she's not altogether too familiar with thanks to how she grew up. Somehow her brain associates it with being safe and secure. She takes a deep breath and sighs it out.

She opens her eyes to find herself sitting in the front seat of Dan's car in a dark parking lot.

Beside her, his phone is in his hand and he's tapping away. He smiles at her, clicking his phone screen dark. "How was the nap?" he asks.

Sarah stretches her arms out, arching her back to work out those kinks, and takes stock of how she's feeling. "Amazing, actually. I was exhausted. I'm not sure I would have made it through this shift if you hadn't offered to drive me here."

"I'm not sure you would've safely made it across town. I was just looking out for the rest of the citizens." He smiles. "Seriously, I'm glad I could help."

Sarah looks around the parking lot, which Dan seems to have parked in the back of. There are the normal amount of cars here tonight, which makes her feel a little better. Chances are this is going to be a quieter night than last night turned out to be. "What time is it?" Even as the question leaves her mouth, she finds herself reaching for her purse to grab her phone and check for herself. Clicking the side button to bring the phone to life she sees that she still has half an hour before she has to be inside.

"You've got time. You could probably snag a little more sleep." Dan laughs a little. "You are a deep sleeper, did you know that?"

"I've heard it a time or two, yeah. It's the reason I don't have a roommate. People think it's weird that I can just flip a switch inside myself and fall asleep anywhere. As soon as I decide it's time to sleep, I'm out."

"Clearly." The laugh builds until Sarah can't help but join him.

"I feel really good right now," Sarah says. "Ready to get some work done, I think."

"Well, you can't go in early. What are you going to do for the next half hour? Do you want to go grab a drink or something?"

Sarah leans her body over the center console between them. "Actually, I have a better idea." She reaches out her right hand and wraps it around Dan's neck. He lets himself be led forward until their lips touch. It's a light kiss at first, but Sarah isn't planning on a light kiss. Her brain is filled with that scent she woke up with and that sense of comfort it brought her. Suddenly what she wants is a very intense make-out session in the front seat of this little sports car with the boy who took time out of his night just to let her sleep. That is easily the nicest thing anyone has ever done for her and Sarah can think of no hotter way to repay that kindness than deep sensual kisses.

She feels his hands roaming over her back, up her shirt to graze her skin and she marvels at the warmth of his hands. It's chilly in the car. Not cold, but crisp. His hands radiate warmth everywhere they touch, making her want them on more parts of her body. As if he can hear her thoughts, Dan continues moving his hands slowly up all over her skin. Sarah brings herself up off the seat and leans even further into him, deepening the kiss with an almost animalistic longing.

Dan suddenly pulls back, separating them. "Hang on," he says, his voice hoarse and almost distracted. "We're in a parking lot."

Sarah leans closer to him. "So what?"

He puts his hand on her shoulder, stopping her from coming any closer. "We're in the parking lot of a police station where you work. There are probably cameras here."

That pulls her back to reality. There are cameras. Cameras all over this entire lot. Cameras she watches as part of her job. She looks up at the building. Sure they're far enough away that things are probably blurry and someone would have to be actively looking, but Dan's right. This isn't the way things should go down. "Right. You're right." Sarah flops back to her side of the car, pulling her shirt down. She can't help but be a little disappointed.

"Hey, you know I want to …" Dan trails off, letting Sarah fill in that gap however she wants.

She offers him a little smile. "Right. Yeah, I know." She reaches down to her feet and frees her car keys from her purse. "Do you really want these or should I just Uber over there tomorrow morning?"

Dan shakes his head. "Give them to me. I already talked to my roommate. We're going to go get your car right after I drop you off."

"Great." Sarah drops the keys into the cupholder between them and reaches for the door handle."

"Hey, c'mon you don't have to go," Dan says. "You have half an hour. Sit, let's talk or something."

Sarah pops the door open, letting in a burst of air that makes goosebumps rise on her arms. "No, I think I'm going to just get inside there and get a cup of coffee or something. Thanks for doing this though, I really appreciate it." She can hear him protesting but she jumps out of the car and slams the door.

She cannot believe she just embarrassed herself like that. He probably thinks she's a total slut, ready to make out with him just because he did her a favor. He shouldn't have any respect for her. She's better than that.

The truth is, she's mad at herself. Because if Dan hadn't stopped her that was exactly what she had planned to do. Something about this guy is dangerous to the future she has planned. She's not herself around Dan. She can't seem to keep herself focused around him and she keeps finding herself breaking her rules for him.

"Sarah." She hears a voice behind her and hates that every particle of her body reacts to the sound. She stops and turns around to find Dan has jogged right up behind her in the parking lot. He holds out his hand. "I'm sorry if I offended you."

"You didn't," she says honestly. "I'm embarrassed. I can't believe I just did that."

"Hey," he steps closer, touching the side of

her cheek. Her eyes slip closed and she leans into the touch. Then she forces her eyes open, hating her instinctual reaction to him. "I loved it. I just didn't want you to regret anything when you got inside. If someone was watching on those cameras I wanted you to remember that."

"Yeah, and you're right. Someone is always watching."

Dan smiles. "I'd hurt your casual dating vibe. Wouldn't want anyone getting the wrong idea."

That stops any self-hatred Sarah had been hurling. Does he think this is about him not being good enough? Is it possible he stopped her not because he didn't want to make out with her or because he thinks she's embarrassing but because he's worried about her reputation? Does he think he is, somehow, beneath her? That is interesting. She takes a step closer to him now, closing the last of the space. His hand, which had been on her cheek, drops to her shoulder. "I don't care who sees us together, you know," Sarah says. "I actually think you're quite the catch. You're incredibly handsome. Did I ever tell you that?"

Under the parking lot lights, Sarah can see his entire face redden. "I don't think you've mentioned that."

"Right, well, you are. You're also generous and kind. I like that about you and we are absolutely going to do this again." She closes the rest of the space between their lips and holds them together until his lips part enough to let her tongue snake in. It's not quite the make-out-in-the-car scenario she had in mind, but it's hot enough to whet her appetite.

When the kiss ends, Sarah winks at him. "I'll talk to you later."

The front door buzzes as soon as Sarah gets near it, which means Dan was right about Alicia watching. Sarah enters the bright lights of the lobby, blinking against the harsh bulbs. "Hey lady," she calls to Alicia.

"You're early. Who is that dish out there?" Alicia tips her head toward the monitor.

"That is Dan, the casual date from last week. He works with me at the other job." Sarah crosses behind the counter and goes immediately to the coffee pot. "Should I make a whole pot?" Sarah asks, hinting at finding out if anyone else is hanging around tonight.

Alicia shakes her head. "They seem to all be holed up at the main police station downtown tonight. They keep calling to ask me to push things through but they're not here much. I'd say make what you'll drink and call it good."

Sarah goes through the motions of making a small six-cup pot, the smallest she knows she can make on this old machine without losing quality. Then she stands behind Alicia, checking the monitors. Dan is already gone from the parking lot, which means she can't check the quality of the video way out there to see what

Alicia might have seen from the car. She already knows, however, that Alicia would've seen the entire kiss in the center of the lot. The thought makes her blush a little.

"So what's new tonight?" Sarah asks. "Any new gossip?"

Alicia spins in her chair. "The phone company called about the records requests. Apparently, they have to get the signature of the account holder for the victim's phone records and the account holder wasn't him. So I filled out another form with the parent's names and sent that along to Marino so he could get a signature. At some point that might come back signed and you'll have to forward it along."

"Got it," Sarah says, pouring herself a cup of black coffee from the only partially finished pot and taking a sip.

"Otherwise, nothing has changed."

Sarah nods. "I saw an article about the case online," she admits. "They're saying he was murdered."

"Right, that reminds me. There have been reporters showing up all day asking for statements. I don't think anyone will show up tonight, but if they do we are supposed to say the department has no comment at this time."

Sarah can feel herself start to sweat at even the thought of talking to reporters. "I have to say that?" she squeaks.

"Like I said, I don't think you'll have to do

anything. They're not going to come by at night when the department has closed looking for statements. I'm just telling you what I was told." Alicia lays a hand on her arm. "It's not going to be needed, relax."

"Right." Sarah takes another sip of the hot coffee. "Let's talk about something else. Didn't you have a date last night or something?"

Something in Alicia's face darkens. She shakes her head. "No, it was a few nights ago." She turns back around in her chair, fiddling with the monitors.

"What's up?" Sarah asks. "Are you upset that I didn't ask sooner? I'm sorry, I forgot."

"No, that's not it. The guy was just a little intense. He thought it was a bit more serious than I did." Sarah watches as Alicia logs out of her email and closes a few windows. "It's fine. I'm handling it. I just don't want to talk about it."

"Ok, sure." Sarah can understand not wanting to talk about bad dates. She'll let it go. Maybe in another week Alicia will change her mind and want to let someone in, get some advice. Sarah hopes she has someone she can get that advice from, even if it's not her.

"I'm gonna duck out a little early," Alicia says, "since you're here."

"Right. Absolutely."

"I'll see you tomorrow. Remember, no comment."

"Got it." Sarah nods. "No comment."

CHAPTER 11

Alicia was right. Everything is quiet around the station. It feels more normal, which Sarah realizes allows her to act like it's normal. The phone rings three times, but it's for typical things she's used to answering. Things that you'd find in the script.

Just before midnight, Sarah sees her car pull into the parking lot and Dan steps out of it, stretching. She smiles involuntarily at the camera as if he can see her. A few minutes later his car pulls in and he jumps into the passenger seat. She grabs her phone from beside her on the desk. *Saw my car arrive, where did you stash the keys?* she texts.

He answers right away. *Under the driver's seat. That ok? Should I have brought them in?*

No, you've done enough. Thank you.

Anytime.

Sarah sets her phone down and focuses her attention back on the essays she's trying to write. Nothing pulls her attention away from the essay again until she notices a person on the monitor a little after four in the morning.

She squints at the person, wondering if there's a reason why her heart is suddenly racing and her palms are sweating. The guy steps into the light and rings the bell. Sarah hits her button to allow him in, trying to calm herself with deep breaths. Keith pulls the door open and comes into the lobby.

"I wasn't sure someone would be here," he says.

"The desk is monitored twenty-four hours a day," Sarah answers. "What can I help you with?"

"They asked me to drop off this paper for Craig's phone. His parents signed it," Keith says, coming up to the counter. "Is that something I can just leave with you or do I need to call Officer Marino?"

This must be the form Alicia warned her was incoming. "You can leave it. Let me just make sure everything is correct on it." Sarah takes the form, which is the records request she was expecting. She scans for any blank lines or incomplete sections. Everything looks good. "This all looks correct," she says. "It's not for your phone, right?"

"Right. It's Craig's. He's my roommate." Keith winces. "Was my roommate. Craig was my roommate. Officer Marino asked me to bring this by."

"Well, it looks like it's been all filled in correctly. There are no missing lines. I can pass this along to Officer Marino for you. Is there anything else you need?" Sarah sets the paper down on her side of the desk. She'll move it to Marino's inbox in a minute.

"I don't think so. You don't need the passcode, do you? I assume the cops have the actual phone. My friend says this is just a records request. I figured they'd probably want to get into the phone too."

Sarah shoots him a confused look. "I thought this wasn't your phone. Why would you have the passcode?"

Keith reaches up a hand and rubs the back of his neck. "I just happen to know the passcode. It's the same damn code he uses for everything. I haven't checked but I'm sure it's the right one."

"Have you ever unlocked the phone before?" Sarah asks. Asking these kinds of questions isn't at all in her job description. She's supposed to take the forms. An officer will handle everything else, including calling the person who filled out the form, during normal operating hours. This conversation should be left to Marino but Sarah finds herself drawn to this conversation and this sad-eyed boy who experienced something he never should have. What if talking about this is good for him? She tells herself that his mental health is her primary concern, which sounds much better than her secret thought that she was getting more information for the local rumor mill.

"Yeah, shit. Was I not supposed to admit that?" Keith rubs his eyes hard. Sarah wonders if he's slept at all. It is, after all, four in the morning. "Does it make me look guilty or something that I know his passcode? I didn't do anything with it. Shit, I haven't even been back to my apartment. For all I know, his cell phone is still there."

Sarah's heartbeat picks up. "Did you …" She trails off, swallows, and tries again. "You didn't try to access anything from some other device, right? Like the cloud or something?"

"What? God, no. I'm not stupid." Sarah sighs with relief. "I almost wish I could see his stuff, you know? I want to be prepared for what's going to come next. If the cops know then the reporters will know and there are just things out there about Craig that aren't the best. He wasn't perfect. Fuck, who is? But, like, none of that should matter. He didn't deserve —" Keith raises a visibly shaking hand to his mouth and wipes at his lips, unable to finish the sentence.

"I'm so sorry," Sarah says, really meaning

it.

"It's fine." He shakes his head. "I mean, it's not but it's also not your fault at all." He tries to offer her a smile but it's more like a puppeteer is pulling at the corners of his mouth, the rest of his face does not cooperate. "This is so fucked up," Keith says in a quieter voice. "You didn't know Craig, right?"

Sarah is shocked by the question, she pulls back a little from the counter. Does Keith recognize her from class? Does he know her? "I don't… I don't think so." She stumbles over the answer.

"Everyone else seems to. He's always been really popular. He had a few girls he was seeing at the same time."

Sarah thinks about her own casual dating and is tempted to throw out some comment about how that is perfectly acceptable and isn't something someone should be judged for. She holds back, not wanting to stop whatever else this guy is going to offer her from spilling out.

"He sort of sleeps around a lot and makes promises to all of them. They have no idea how many of them there are. They're going to be pretty upset when they all find out about each other in the next few weeks or whatever." He closes his eyes and sighs. "I suppose I'll have to deal with all of that. God, I hope they don't all show up to the apartment at the same time." He shakes his head. "What am I saying? They won't let me back in there."

He looks up again, his eyes falling on Sarah. It almost seems to shock him to find her standing there. She's struck again by how tired he looks, large black circles that look like bruises are rimming the bottom of each eye. "Will they let me back in?" Before Sarah can even answer, tell him she has no idea but she will ask, he answers himself. "It doesn't matter. I don't think I want to go back there. I'll have to find somewhere else."

Sarah looks down and her eyes fall on the paper, reminding her of the reason this exhausted man is here instead of sleeping. "I can pass on this form and whatever information you want me to give Officer Marino in the morning. If you think it's alright to give me the passcode, I'll have you write that down too." Sarah gets a yellow sticky pad from the desk and sets it between them.

"It's Craig's mom that's giving them permission to get the records or whatever and if this just makes it easier, I guess she wouldn't care. I didn't specifically ask her about the passcode, but I can't imagine she'd care." On the sticky pad, Keith writes four digits. Then he sets the pen down beside it and sighs with finality. "I guess that's all I came here for." He smiles at Sarah, this one a little closer to genuine but not quite. "Thanks for letting me vent."

"Hey, no problem. I'm really sorry for what you're going through. Did you call that grief counselor we gave you the number for?" She takes the sticky square and attaches it to the form, pushing down hard in hopes it will stay in place.

"Not yet. I will."

"I think you should. It's unreasonable to think you won't be affected by losing a roommate." She lays a hand on his arm, which is resting on the counter between them. "Seriously, call them and open up about all of this."

"It's going to get harder, isn't it?" Keith asks. "Once all this comes out about Craig? They're going to make him out like some bad guy who slept around and was sort of an asshole like that excuses the fact that someone fucking killed him."

"I hope not," Sarah answers. But the truth is, they both know that's how this ends. The news will want to reassure the rest of the college community that they're safe. How better to do that than by making it seem like this guy was his own worst enemy? "Don't worry about the future until you have to," Sarah offers. "Take it one day at a time. For now, go home and get some sleep. You have a place to sleep, right?" She remembers what he just said about his apartment and, for a beat, worries that's why he's here in the middle of the night.

"Yeah, I do. A friend is letting me crash with him. I just can't seem to …" he trails off, his meaning pretty clear.

Sarah, who has never had a problem sleeping in her life, doesn't know what to say.

Even when her childhood was dangerous and sleeping was sketchy at best, she was always able to sleep when she wanted to. She doesn't need much of it, that's something she's trained her body for, but she can get it when she needs it. How can someone like her advise someone like Keith about falling asleep? She doesn't even know how it works for normal people. "I'm sorry," she says again. She's saying that a lot.

"Not your problem," Keith says. He pushes off the counter and rolls his shoulders. "I'm going to go try again. Maybe the weight of that form off my to-do list will let me get some sleep." He turns and heads for the door. "Thanks again," he calls.

"Goodnight," Sarah calls back.

When the door closes behind him, Sarah flops into the chair with a huge sigh. That was substantially harder than it should have been. "That poor guy," Sarah says into the quiet of the station.

She rolls her chair to the set of cubicles on the side of the room, drops the paper into Marino's inbox, and then wheels herself back to her essay. That was quite the distraction. It's time to focus.

CHAPTER 12

Sarah eyes her empty coffee mug as she submits the last of her pending assignments. Then her eyes flick to the time on the bottom of her computer screen. It's after five in the morning. If she makes coffee now, it will keep her awake for the rest of her shift but it might screw up her schedule for the rest of the day. That thought reminds her to actually look at her schedule for the day. She pulls up the calendar app on her phone and scrolls. Today she'll have three classes to get to, which means no study time in between classes. That's fine, as the task board on the side of her calendar app shows her she has nothing else due today. That means she'll have the weekend to get anything done before next week's due dates start. After her last class today she'll have her shift at the mall but nothing else is on the schedule. If this keeps up, she'll be able to get some sleep this morning, get through all of her classes, and then actually relax going into the weekend. This is shaping up to be a perfect day.

That decides for her. If today is about recuperating and resting, she doesn't need coffee right now. What she needs is to curl up with a book that's explicitly not for classes and just enjoy herself. Sarah swipes the calendar app closed and calls up an ebook app instead. She selects a short story anthology she's been meaning to get around to and settles in to read a little.

As it always does, Sarah's cell phone alarm chimes at 5:45, alerting her that it's time to get ready to clock out for the day. Some days this alarm is completely unnecessary, as Sarah has been doing nothing but watching the time tick along and waiting for her shift to end. On other days, like yesterday, she has become entranced in some assignment and needs the alert or she will keep working right up until Greg arrives. Today, she feels the heavy limbs and eyelids that tell her exhaustion is catching up with her. She was practically asleep in the chair, despite the good stories vying for her attention. She needs to get home and get some sleep.

Sarah sets her phone down and follows her routine. She packs up her belongings, runs through the steps of logging herself out of the computer programs, and makes coffee. She's careful to only make six cups, hoping the half-empty pot will keep Greg from making her a cup she'll only dump down the sink when she wakes up from her sleep to a cup that's gone cold.

This time when she goes around to unlock the front door, Greg is nowhere in sight. She curbs her irritation. He's not late, she's just unlocking the door early. So why is she quick to internally blame him for keeping her here longer? She returns to the rolling chair, dropping heavily into it. On the monitor, she sees when Greg pulls in and parks his truck. Again she feels the prickle of irritation at seeing how far back in the lot he parks. Is he being polite to the officers who will be on shift today? Of course.

But he's also making it a further walk for him and a longer wait for her. She checks her exhaust-driven irritation while she watches him walk up, he's obviously noted the time and he's moving quickly to get to the door. Sarah grabs her stuff when Greg gets closer. That way, when he walks in the door, she's already standing with her items in hand.

"Am I late?" Greg asks, a little winded from hustling up the walkway.

"I don't think so. I'm just exhausted so I'm

in a bit of a hurry." Greg comes around the desk to settle himself in for the day and Sarah rushes to get through the housekeeping things, her words rushing out quickly. "There's a records request Marino was waiting on in his inbox, he'll want that as soon as you see him this morning," Sarah explains.

"What's the form for?" Greg asks, the playful uptick in his voice telling Sarah she's piqued his curiosity just by mentioning Marino. Is seems everyone is obsessing about this murder case, not just Sarah.

Normally that would be a perfect time to spill everything she's learned about this case with someone else who has an interest in it. Today, Sarah just wants to go home. She keeps her answer brief. "The person who died two days ago's cell phone records, which Marino requested. The roommate dropped it off early this morning."

Greg's eyes widen. "Is the roommate the same guy from Interview 1? Did we confirm for sure this guy was the roommate? That's intense."

"Yeah, it was definitely the same guy. His name is Keith. When he was here this morning he mentioned he was the roommate, at least I think that's what he said. Anyway, there's also the note about reporters —"

"Why'd he have to bring the request?" Greg interrupts. "Can't you just mail those things in or send them by fax? They don't normally need to be walked in. Do you think they have the physical phone? Do you need a records request to access apps and things?"

Sarah lets her irritation show in her sigh, drawing out the sound and making it deeper than usual. When she answers, she speaks slowly as if Greg may not be picking up on the signals she's trying to throw his way. As much as she considers him a friend and appreciates that he shares her interest in this stuff, she's seriously exhausted. She just wants to go home. "I have no idea. I just know Keith, the roommate, said Marino asked him for the form so he brought it by." She waits for a beat, clearly communicating her wish to move on to another topic. Greg squeezes his lips together to show he doesn't plan to interrupt again until she's done.

Sarah rushes on. "Anyway, Alicia also said if reporters show up at the door we're merely to tell them no comment. Nothing more. I didn't see any reporters last night but Alicia said a few showed up during the day yesterday. Now that we're open you might see some. Until an officer gets here to make the statement for you, you're just to say no comment."

"Got it," Greg says with a nod.

Silence follows the comment for one second. Then Greg rushes to fill it. "But the guy who was here, he talked to you?"

"Yes," Sarah keeps the word clipped, harsh. "He talked a little."

"Did he say anything interesting?"

"Just that he was asked to drop off the paper. He seemed a bit worried that people might get the wrong idea about his friend when they saw how he behaved. Apparently some women think he's an asshole or something. But he was very clear that his love life is no excuse for what happened."

"Why would some women think he's an asshole?" Greg pushes.

"Greg, how would I know that?" Sarah says, letting her irritation leak through to her tone of voice.

"But it's interesting, right? That could be a clue or something. Maybe one of them —"

Sarah jumps in before Greg can finish the thought. "It's not our job to solve it." She holds up her finger, in a wait-one-second gesture. "We work the front desk and pass information on to the officers. Don't go playing Junior Detective here. Stick to the job."

"Right, sorry." Greg smiles at her. "In other news, did you do any more thinking about that date?"

Sarah wants this conversation to be over. She's very tired and the thought of driving back to her apartment this tired has her mildly worried. The fastest way to get this conversation out of the way would just be to schedule something. She does want to go out on a little date with Greg, she decides. He's nice, he's funny, and he's pretty cute. She's not sure how he compares to the dinner date style person she normally goes out with. He's not as put together as Mariana or Dan, for example. Quickly, her brain settles on the perfect solution. "How about if we have coffee at the place on central campus tonight sometime around eight-thirty between my two jobs?"

"That would be great," Greg says. "Coffee sounds perfect."

Coffee sounds safe and small. Coffee gives you an excuse to leave whenever you want because the cup is disposable and can be taken with you. Coffee also usually comes with the added bonus of being surrounded by other people, giving you plenty of other people to watch and talk about if the conversation lulls. Coffee is an underrated first date when you aren't sure how you'll mesh with the other person. Plus, Sarah has already checked her schedule and knows she has nothing else going on tonight. If she's planning on getting some sleep, she'll simply get something decaf. It's perfect. "I'll meet you there." Sarah smiles. "Right now, I have to get home and get a little sleep before class. I can feel my body starting to shut down. If I don't get home, I'm going to fall asleep in the car. I'll see you tonight."

"Sleep tight," Greg calls.

Sarah waves at him over her shoulder on the way out of the door and walks quickly to her car. The sun hasn't come up yet so Sarah uses her flashlight to check the backseat of the car before opening the driver's side door. She's sure that looks strange on the monitor where Greg is likely watching her, but it feels weird getting into a car that hasn't been locked. Of course, she was also watching her car all night so she already knew it would be empty. Good habits are not something she'll apologize for, even to herself.

She gets in on the driver's side and fishes her keys out from under the seat where Dan promised they'd be. Then she starts the car, turns on the cold air to keep herself awake and alert, and drives herself home.

In her parking lot, Sarah remembers to get everything out of the trunk and lock the car before heading to her unit. She unlocks the door and tosses everything in. Then, her thoughts full of thoughts of murder and roommates who are too scared of their apartments to live there, she remembers to lock it from the inside before dropping onto the couch to get some much-needed sleep.

She kicks off her shoes, falls onto the couch, and tucks the small throw pillow under her head. Then, before she can even think about getting up to put on some more comfortable clothes, she drifts off to a peaceful, dreamless sleep.

CHAPTER 13

On the other side of town, Andy Salinas prepares for his morning run. He props his leg up on the chair by his desk and pulls back, stretching his hamstring. Just as he switches to his other leg, his cell phone rings. He looks down at the screen, spotting a phone number he doesn't recognize from their local area code. He hits the red button, sending the caller to voicemail.

Next, Andy spreads his legs shoulder-width apart and does some side lunges to open up his hips. Despite not being on the track team anymore now that he's in college, his habits from running in high school have stayed with him. He'll stretch properly and try to get a run in every morning. It keeps him healthy and gives him something to focus on.

Beside him, the cell phone screen lights up again. He squints in confusion. That's the same area code. It might even be the same phone number. The number is not in his phone, but who calls the same number twice by accident? Maybe it's an emergency? He grabs the phone and clicks the green button. "Hello," he says into the phone. Silence. "Hello?"

He pulls the phone away from his ear, checking that he is still connected. Then he puts it back to his ear and listens. When he hears only silence and static he hangs up. Stupid spam calls are getting out of control.

He drops the phone back on his desk and resumes the side lunges. When he finishes the side lunges he checks the time and realizes if he plans to get this run in before he is supposed to meet the cute girl from his study group, he needs to leave now. He grabs his water bottle and keys off the table on his way to the front door. Then he stops to check the windows on the patio, making sure they're closed enough to keep strange people or animals out of his apartment. On the patio, he turns around and uses the keys to lock the door behind him and twists the handle to make sure it locked like it should. Then he zips the key into the special pocket on his running shorts, slips his phone into the holder on his arm, and starts his jog.

Andy's feet follow the same path they normally take, across the apartment complex between buildings, then out through the woods between his complex and the Department of Motor Vehicles office. The woods here are dense enough to dull some of the noise from the town but thin enough to allow ease of motion and to keep Andy from getting lost. Plus, since he's still near major landmarks his phone maintains his GPS coordinates in case he does manage to get turned around.

Just as he gets into a good rhythm, he feels the phone vibrate on his arm. He pulls his arm around and sees what is likely the same phone number on the screen. He turns his frustration into a speed increase, moving his legs just a little faster as he continues west through the trees. The sun has only been up for about half an hour and it's not fully reaching this part of the forest yet. There are dark shadows here that would likely make anyone nervous if they weren't the kind of person who ran through them daily. For Andy, this is typical. With the exception of the one time he almost stepped on a homeless man sleeping in a makeshift tent, he's never encountered anything that would make him worry about this route. Remembering the homeless man and how nervous he'd been when he noticed him makes Andy chuckle a little. You see some crazy things in this little town.

Twice more before he reaches the main road outside the DMV Andy feels his phone vibrate. He doesn't look at it to verify the phone number. He does, however, make a mental note to run that number through a quick search online and see if it's already been flagged as spam. He's pretty sure if he puts the number into his app it'll stop him from receiving calls from that number. Of course, if it is a spammer, they'll likely spoof a different number and keep trying. You can't keep them all away.

At the main road, he takes a right, which will bring him back to the road that runs down to his apartment. If he had more time for a longer run, he could keep going in this direction and come the long way back to his apartment. There are routes he's taken for his morning run that are two miles, three miles, or even five miles depending on how much time he has. Judging by what time it was when he left the apartment this morning, he doesn't have that much time. Instead, he will have to take the one-mile loop straight back to his apartment.

A few cars are buzzing past him on the road as he runs up the sidewalk, the woods now on his right-hand side and his apartment complex looming up in front of him. He jogs straight past the main entrance, since he's not in a car, and crosses through the landscaping to get to his building, back a little from the main road. He keeps up his speed, jogging up the stairs. Even when he pulls his key out and unlocks the door, he keeps jogging in place to keep his muscles from seizing.

He slams the front door and the curtain flutters in the breeze from the open window off the patio. He pulls his phone from the case and checks the call log. He has missed nine calls and they all came from the same phone number. He clicks on it, intending to block the call. The phone rings in his hand. Same number. He hits the green button, "Who is this?" he asks. Silence. "Fuck you," he yells into the phone. He slams the end call button and tosses the phone down on the couch. If he's hoping to get a shower in before he goes to this meeting, he needs to get in now.

He sheds his clothes on his way to his shower, holding them in his hand until he gets next to the laundry basket. The habits his mother instilled in him simply won't let him throw them on the ground, although he does think that would be easier right now. He turns the water on in the shower and jumps in while it's cold. He washes everything quickly and rinses, hopeful that he won't be late for this study meeting. The girl he's meeting is hot. She's in his psychology class, a class he otherwise hates because it's down on South Campus in a building he normally doesn't have to go anywhere near. They sat next to each other a few times in class. The first time was accidental, fate if you could call it that. After that, Andy was careful to plant himself near her. By the third time they sat together, he was brave enough to introduce himself. When it became clear she was nervous about an upcoming test, Andy immediately offered to help her study. She told him that she was already part of a study group. But, mistaking his interest for fear of his own, she'd invited him to join the group.

The group had been relatively harmless. It was good to run over the information again before a test. But the only person he'd been at all interested in seeing again was this girl. So, he'd asked if it would be possible to get together one more time before the test. Today is the day. The test is this afternoon and they're meeting this morning to go over the notes. Does he actually need to go over the notes? Not particularly, although he can't imagine it would hurt. But this is a good opportunity to see this girl again without the distraction of the other people in the group. Who knows? Maybe they'll get along, maybe they'll decide they want to hang out when it's not for class. It's worth a shot.

Andy jumps out of the shower, dresses quickly, slaps on some deodorant, and runs his fingers through his short hair to comb it back. Then he grabs the bag full of things he carries to and from classes. He actually can't remember if the laptop in the bag is even charged so he grabs the charger from the table in the living room, slipping it down the side of the bag as he walks.

In the living room, he walks to the windows to make sure they're closed, his routine when he's leaving the house. The one to the left of the door is closed. But the right one is open, curtains blowing in the breeze and giving it away. Andy freezes, looking at the window with confusion. Didn't he check the window before he went on his run? He always checks the windows, it's a habit from growing up in a more populated city. You always check the windows and doors before you leave the house. He can't imagine he would go on his run and leave that one open like it is.

He crosses to it and inspects the frame. Nothing looks scratched. The screen is still in place, the little black pull tabs pointed inward so the only way to get the screen on or off would be to do it from inside the apartment. He must have just forgotten to close it. He won't make that same mistake again. He pushes the lower half of the frame down until it closes with a click. Then he turns the lock mechanism at the top of the frame, keeping it in place. There, he will remember doing that. If it's open when he gets home, he'll know someone has been messing with him.

He grabs his phone and sees that he missed another call from the strange number. This time, he remembers to open the call list and block that caller. He pockets his phone and hustles out the front door, turning to lock and check the lock on the door behind him. The apartment is secure. Time to focus on this study session.

He uses his phone to text the girl he's meeting as he walks. *On my way now. Should be there in about five.*

He doesn't wait for her response, just jumps in the front seat of his SUV and peels out of the parking lot. Andy drives as fast as he runs. Always keep moving, always a little faster than the flow of traffic. He should have no problem getting to the library on this side of campus in the five minutes he just quoted his study partner. Assuming he can find a spot to slip the car into, he'll be flopping into a chair and dropping his first flirtatious line exactly on time.

Perfect, just the way Andy likes things.

CHAPTER 14

When Sarah wakes up to her morning alarm, she decides to forgo the shower in favor of stopping for a breakfast sandwich at the little takeout diner on campus. Today is, after all, the official end of the week, which also means it's practically the start of the weekend. She's caught up on schoolwork, just got a great little nap in, and plans to have a relaxing and stress-free day. That calls for a breakfast sandwich.

She changes clothes, puts on deodorant and

a little spritz of body spray, and brushes her teeth. Then she pulls her long hair into a ponytail, tying it off with a rubber band specifically designed for thick hair. She notes the length in the mirror and thinks it might be a decent idea to get a haircut this weekend if she has time. Her locks are getting long.

Then she grabs her stuff and heads out. The on-campus diner doesn't have a long line this morning, which feels like fate. Sarah steps up and orders her favorite, a potato egg and cheese burrito with a side of hot salsa. Then she grabs a cup and fills it at the fountain with something caffeinated, just in case that tired feeling comes back.

She unwraps enough of the burrito to eat it as she walks up to the building where her morning class is held. This class is one that she has to go to every day of the week, which is unusual. Most of the classes Sarah is enrolled in are either two or three days a week. This one is five, which is stupid except for the fact that it earns her more credits overall.

She pushes her way into the classroom and takes a seat in the last row at the back of the lecture hall. She's not late but she also doesn't particularly want to call attention to her breakfast spread. She sets her drink between her feet, unwraps the rest of the burrito, and hurriedly tries to finish it before the clock ticks off the last two minutes before the start of class.

She doesn't remember to take a look around and see if Keith might have made it to class until after the last bite of the burrito is sliding down her throat. She scans a few rows, mostly the backs of heads because of where she's sitting, and doesn't immediately spot him.

Then the time for looking is over because the professor is opening that side door and making his way to the front of the room to begin class. Sarah slips her laptop out of her bag and sets herself up to take notes, careful not to dislodge the sugary drink from its hiding spot between her feet.

Today's lecture feels redundant. Sarah pulls up her notes from the previous week and looks them over, even using a search command to find the exact line she's looking for. Yes, they've definitely talked about this before. She wonders why they're going over it again. Is it important? Does the professor think they didn't get it the first time? Maybe he forgot they already talked about it.

Sarah decides she'll give him five minutes. If he hasn't moved on to new material, she'll raise her hand and ask. Maybe she'll even slip out the back door and disappear into the hallway like the ghost of a good student who can't bring themselves to leave the school halls and spends their afterlife roaming. She shakes her head. No, if she were a ghost she definitely wouldn't only wander the halls of her college campus. She could find something more productive to do with her time.

She checks the clock on the bottom of her screen again. He's got two more minutes and she's calling him out or leaving. She uses the time to look around again for Keith. At this point, she's feeling confident she can find him. He's been consuming so much of her time lately, at the police station making a statement and then in this class with her. Then he showed up at the station again. She got a good look at him when he came in this morning. She should be able to find him.

A noise draws her attention. Is that a quacking duck? She looks around the room, trying to see if anyone else is reacting to the noise. A few of the kids near her are smiling as if they're sharing a secret with her. But the people further down are not. That means the noise must be coming from somewhere up here. Where has she heard that before?

After two sets of quacks, it stops. Sarah shakes her head, trying to refocus herself on the lecture. At the front of the room, the professor has not moved on to new material. Instead, he appears to be cycling through the information that he already covered. Sarah wonders if he just grabbed the wrong lesson plan this morning and thinks this is something he's supposed to be teaching today. The thought makes her have to choke down a laugh.

The quacking starts again. This time Sarah

is pretty sure the noise is coming from the hallway. It's faint, if the classroom was any louder or if she was sitting any further away from the door she wouldn't be able to hear it at all.

Something in Sarah's brain tugs at her. There's a memory tied to that sound, but she just can't seem to grab the thread that it's linked to. It's like she's blocked from untangling the noise from all the others she's heard.

Then, with a click, she remembers. Keith had that ringtone when he was at the police station giving a statement. Sarah had thought it odd at the time and now she's hearing it again from the hallway outside the class they normally have together. Maybe that's why Sarah can't find Keith. Perhaps he's standing out in the hallway, letting his grief over the loss of his friend overcome him.

Sarah decides she doesn't need this repeat lecture. What she needs is to help this guy through whatever he's going through. He's a nice guy, he could use a friend. Sarah quickly packs up all her things, using small movements to make it a little less obvious. Then she slips out the door and into the hallway of the building.

She has never left class early before in her life. Her heart thuds away in her chest, an obvious sign that she is worried about getting caught. Really, the thought is laughable. Even if the professor did notice her leaving, he has no idea what her name is. He would have no way of holding her accountable for leaving early.

The sound of the quacking duck comes again, definitely closer to her now. It echoes up and down the little hallway, but it sounds like it is originating across the hall. Sarah follows the noise. There are restrooms here. Women's on one side of the hallway and Men's on the other. The door to the men's room is propped open a little, Sarah can see light spilling out into the slightly dark alcove.

Her eyes trail down the door and find a head of hair wedged into the door at the bottom. Is someone passed out in the men's room doorway? Sarah reacts quickly, rushing to them and dropping onto her knees. She pushes the door open further and taps the person on the chest. "Are you okay?" she asks. There's no response.

She taps again, harder. "Hey, can you wake up?"

When there is still no response, Sarah calls out her next intention. "I'm just going to check for your pulse to make myself feel better." She pushes the hair out of the person's face so she can get to their neck. Her breath catches in her throat and she jerks her body back from them. Keith. What happened?

She reaches in with two fingers, finding the spot on his neck that will tell if he has a pulse. She closes her eyes, focusing on the feeling of the skin beneath her fingers. She's not feeling anything. She tries to tell herself that she needs to calm down and focus but her panic is rising and making everything else harder.

She sits back on her heels and pulls her phone out of her pocket. Shakily, she dials the emergency number and waits. "What is your emergency?" the voice asks.

"There's a boy here passed out in the men's bathroom. I can't find his pulse and he's not responding," Sarah says, her voice shaky.

The operator walks her through giving the exact location and tells her someone is on the way. Then she asks if Sarah can perform CPR. Sarah stands, pushing the door open the rest of the way. She almost drops her phone when the rest of Keith's body comes into view. Instead, a strangled sob escapes her lips. "Ma'am, what's happening?" the operator says. "Ma'am, are you safe? Ma'am, talk to me."

The increased tension in the operator's voice snaps Sarah back to reality. She tries to take a deep breath but can only get shallow ones. Now that the door is fully open she can smell what she can only assume is blood. It smells like the piggy bank she used to keep under her bed, a powerful overwhelming smell similar to metal coins. It makes her want to vomit. "There's so much blood," Sarah whispers. "I got the door open and there's blood everywhere."

"Ok," the operator says. "I'm going to ask you to back up out of that restroom. Are you somewhere safe?"

"Yeah. I'm in that little alcove with the

water fountains. I'm the only one here right now. Everyone is in the classrooms."

"Someone is on the way to you. They'll handle the rest of this. You did well. You just sit tight."

Sarah looks down at her free hand, which is shaking. She blinks her eyes and realizes she's actually crying. She's not sure when she started that. She closes her eyes and tries to breathe.

"Honey, they're on the way into the building right now. Can you wave them down if you see them?" the dispatcher asks.

"Yeah." Sarah backs up into the hallway and waves when she sees two paramedics in navy blue polo shirts holding all kinds of life-saving devices that Sarah is terrified they won't need. Somehow seeing them makes her cry harder until she's having trouble catching her breath.

"Do you see them?" the dispatcher asks.

"They're here," Sarah whispers.

"Alright, then I'll leave you in their hands. Thank you for calling. Good luck, honey."

The younger of the two paramedics stops beside her. "Are you Sarah?" he asks. "You're the one who called it in?" Sarah nods. "Ok, why don't you have a seat right here." He points to a spot on the floor, against the wall. Sarah follows his directions and takes a seat, her back to the wall. She sets her cell phone in her lap, face down. "Try to take deep breaths in through your nose and out through your mouth. Do you need some water?"

From somewhere beside him he produces a bottle of water, which Sarah takes. "Good. You drink that. I'll be right back."

He steps away toward the bathroom. It takes Sarah three tries to get her shaky hand to open the little plastic top on the bottle. When she does, a little of the lukewarm liquid sloshes out over her hand. She raises it to her mouth and takes small sips. The task gives her something to focus on, which calms her a little.

Down the hallway, two uniformed officers appear. Sarah doesn't recognize either of them, which is odd considering they are on campus so the officers from the on-campus building would usually respond first. No one pays any more attention to Sarah, which is fine. She hears lots of noise coming from across the hall but tries hard not to focus on any of it.

She sits there so long that the police tape goes up. Important people from the University come and dismiss classes. Police show up and question people. Officer Marino shows up, although if he's surprised to see Sarah he doesn't show it. A few detectives in suits instead of uniforms arrive. Still, Sarah sits up against the wall, sipping from the bottle of water.

Eventually, someone remembers she is there. "You're the lady who called the police?" a detective asks.

"Yes, I'm Sarah." Her voice comes out strange from disuse. She clears her throat. "What do you need from me now?" she asks.

"I think we'll go ahead and take you someplace away from all this chaos and let you give your statement. Do you have someone you can call to meet you at the station after you're done with the statement?"

Sarah picks up her phone and opens her recent call logs. Recently, she's called Dan, Greg, and her boss at the mall. If she adds in text messages, she's also connected with Mariana. "I can find someone."

"Great. I'm going to have an officer take you to the station and get you all settled." She waves at some uniformed officers standing nearby and gives them general commands. Sarah gets up off the floor and follows the officer on weary legs.

Halfway down the hallway, someone calls out "Wait," and footsteps are heard jogging in their direction. Sarah and the officer turn to find Marino coming their way. "I'll take her." He offers her a smile. "Is that alright, Sarah?" She merely nods and lets herself be led away toward Marino's patrol car.

CHAPTER 15

Officer Marino holds the door open for Sarah, guiding her through by laying his hand on her upper arm. Vaguely she's aware that she should tell him he doesn't need to hold that door. But she just walks through, as if in a trance, into the familiar glow of the building she's been in countless times before.

On the other side of the desk, Greg stands up. Sarah registers in her shock-addled brain that this means it is still before 1:00 in the afternoon. She wonders how it can simultaneously feel like so much time has passed and yet still feel as if time has trapped itself in a bubble and refuses to move. "Sarah?" Her name leaves Greg's lips on a question as if he's confused by this person before him. In reality, she's sure he's confused by what she's doing here when her shift is perhaps long over. He's wondering why she appears to be being escorted by a police officer.

"I'm going to need an open interview room," Marino says. "What's available?"

Greg blinks too rapidly as he tries to process this. "They're all available," he finally answers.

"Why don't you bring a witness statement and a clipboard to room 1 for us." Marino turns his attention to me. "We'll head in there and get you all settled. You can give your statement and then we'll get you home safely. Does that sound alright?"

Sarah wonders if she has a choice. She doesn't ask, choosing instead to nod her agreement. Her feet start the path to the Interview room which she has wiped down, vacuumed, sprayed air freshener in, delivered papers and water bottles to, and taken trash out of. When she pushes the small door open she's shocked the room doesn't look any different than normal. She's never been in here for its intended purpose. It shouldn't feel like a normal day in a room she's been in a hundred times. It should feel heavier than it does.

She takes herself around the table and drops into the stiff chair. They're not folding chairs because folding chairs are flimsy. Plus wrestling has taught us they are useful as weapons in a pinch. Instead, these are a heavier wooden chair with no padding like the kind Sarah remembers elementary schools having in their libraries. Incredibly uncomfortable but sturdy enough for any amount of weight you might put on them. She tries to adjust her butt to a more comfortable position before giving up and deciding comfort isn't going to happen here today.

Sarah has left the door to the room open. Normally Officer Marino would escort the people he brings into the station into the room himself and he would then leave the door open if he needed to step into the hallway, especially with a witness who isn't considered dangerous. She wonders if he merely broke this protocol because of their history or if it's a sign that he isn't taking this statement seriously. She didn't think of that until right this moment in an uncomfortable chair under the harsh lighting. Is there a reason why she was ignored at the school and is now being treated differently? Are they not planning on taking this seriously? Sarah feels her body get hotter, her anger rising. Someone got hurt. She's pretty sure someone died. If that isn't serious, she's not sure what is.

Marino appears in the doorway. "Sorry about the wait, I just had a message about something really important that I'm handling. I'll be right with you."

Sarah watches her vision darken as her eyes narrow at him. She wants to tell him to take this seriously but he ducks back out into the hallway before she can.

In his wake, Greg pushes his way into the room. He's holding two sheets of paper and a pen in one hand. The other arm is being used to press a bottle of water, a can of soda, and something that might be an energy drink up against his body. He sets the paper and pen down. "I brought some drink choices," he says. He displays each one to her before setting it on the table. "Take your pick."

Sarah reaches out and snags the energy drink, pulling it toward her. "I'm just a witness to something awful," she says.

"You probably can't talk about it."

Sarah shakes her head. Her vision blurs a little as her eyes well with tears. She takes a deep breath, trying to hold them back. "I think I found a body," she whispers, hoping the cameras in here are not turned on until the police officer is present. "But don't tell anyone."

"Holy shit, are you serious?" Greg's hand flies to his mouth. "Of course you are. Who jokes about that?" He shakes his head. "I'm sorry. Shit. That's scary." He pushes the soda her way. "Take this too, for later. It's your favorite."

Sarah wraps her hand around the can.

"Yeah, I think I will."

"Drink them. You might need the energy and I'm sure you need liquid. Try to stay calm. Marino will be right back and he'll get this all sorted."

"He needs to take this seriously," Sarah says, remembering her anger.

"I'm sure he is. You saw how he was about the other victim. He's a good guy, Sarah. He's got this." Greg picks up the water. Then he holds it toward her. "Do you want me to leave this one too?"

Sarah shakes her head. "No, this is enough. I'll ask for it if I need it."

"Right. Shit, I'm going back up front. Let me know if you need anything." True to his word he leaves the room with the door to the hallway hanging open.

Sarah takes a deep breath and pops open the can of energy drink. She takes one tentative sip, making sure it won't make her want to throw up. Then Marino enters the room, shutting the door behind him.

"Sorry about that wait," he says. "Let's get this down." He grabs the pen and the paper and straightens them in front of him. "I'm going to record this in case we need to get the details of your statement later, is that alright with you?"

Sarah nods, again wondering if she has a choice. Marino clicks a button on a remote he's brought in with him then sets the remote control on the table between them. He picks up the pen. "Why don't we start at the beginning? Why were you in that building this morning?"

"I have a class at 9:30 Monday through Friday in that building."

Marino nods and writes something on the paper in front of him. "What class?"

Sarah gives him the room number, class name, and professor's name. "Keith, I think that's his name, is in that class with me." Her voice hitches a little and she clears her throat. "I didn't know that before I met him here at the station. But after I met him the first time, when you asked me to give him the number of a grief counselor, I noticed him in the class."

"Was he there today?" Marino asks.

"I didn't see him. But I remembered that ringtone he had, the one that sounded like a quacking duck." Marino nods as if he also remembers. "Well when I was sitting in class, near the back door, I heard that duck noise."

"You heard it through the door?" Marino asks.

"Yeah, it was pretty quiet in the room. No one except the professor was talking and he was way at the front. Plus, I was sitting in the back row right near the door. It was quiet but I heard it. At first, I couldn't figure out why it sounded familiar. Then I heard it again and I remembered. So I got up to go check it out."

"Why?"

Sarah tries to remember her thought process, mentally walking herself back to this morning before everything changed. "Honestly, the professor was going over stuff I already knew and I was sort of annoyed. I decided I wanted to get out of there anyway. I figured my curiosity about Keith and what he might be doing in the hallway with his phone was a good excuse."

Marino again writes on the paper, this time for a little longer. When the pen finally stops moving he returns his attention to Sarah. "So you got up and went into the hallway. Walk me through what happened next."

"I heard the quacking again," she starts.

"So it was three separate incidents of the phone ringing?"

Sarah tries to remember. "I'm not sure. I think so."

"Right, keep going."

So Sarah does. She explains about following the noise near the bathrooms and finding the door propped open. She tells him she noticed a person was passed out on the floor. She knelt to check on them. They weren't responding to her taps. They didn't have a pulse.

"At this point did you know who the person was?" Marino asks.

Sarah closes her eyes, remembering the pressure of her knees on the hard floor, the feeling of the skin under her fingers not pulsing with the heartbeat. Her eyes snap open again. "No, not right away. I had to move his hair out of my way to check for a pulse and that's when I noticed who he was. It didn't seem important before that who he was, just that he needed help."

"When did you call for help?"

"I think I called when I couldn't get them to wake up."

Marino writes more on the paper, his hand tracking left to right quickly. "Tell me about opening the door. When did that happen?"

Sarah thinks back again, fighting the desire to not take this trip down memory lane. She remembers the voice of the operator, asking her questions and guiding her. "The person on the phone asked me if I knew CPR. I had a CPR class years ago and I figured I could probably do it if she just walked me through, but I knew I had to get access to the chest for compressions. So I sort of threw my body into the door. It took a few tries, but it moved enough for me to get my head in." Here Sarah has to stop to take a few deep breaths and get herself under control. "It was really bad in there," she says. Her voice comes out raspy and she sees the tell-tale blurring of her vision that tells her the tears are building. "There was a lot of blood and it smelled like —" her nose wrinkles as she tries to remember "—like the way your hands smell after counting change."

"Like the copper in pennies, yeah I've heard that before," Marino says. "Tell me what happened next."

"The operator told me to step out of that area and wait for help. That's what I did. I went across the hallway and sat on the floor and waited."

"Did anyone come by besides the officers or the paramedics the entire time you were in the hallway?" Marino asks. "Think hard."

Sarah does. She walks herself through listening to the ringtone, kneeling to help Keith, and sitting in the hallway as if she's watching the replay on a sped-up recording. "No," she says after watching the mental replay again. "No one came by at all except for police officers and paramedics escorted some official looking people by to evacuate students, or something. They must have taken the students out another door."

"Alright. Do you mind showing me your call log on your cell phone so I can get the official time the call was placed? Obviously, you don't have to do that. I can get the information from the operator."

Sarah is already slipping her phone from her pocket and swiping it unlocked. She opens the recent calls tab and slides it, face up, toward Marino. He can see the only call she made all morning was to the emergency line around 10:15. She hasn't made any calls since.

"Thank you," he says. "You can put that away." Marino stands up from his chair as Sarah slides the phone back into her pocket. "Alright, I'm going to quickly get this form copied and I'll be back to have you review and sign it. You sit tight. I'll be right back."

He leaves and Sarah is alone again with her torment and the memories that he has unlocked. She wants to know how the body of Keith ended up bloody in a bathroom on campus. She wants to know if it is related to what happened to Keith's roommate. Right now, she's not sure how it could not be related and, for some reason, that terrifies her.

CHAPTER 16

Writing an official statement takes a long time. Sarah has, obviously, seen people come and go from the station for this exact purpose but she's never watched the entire process happen from start to finish which means she's surprised to find how long it takes. She reads over the typed statement and clarifies two questions Marino brings back into the room, then she has to sign and date the document. She waves off the offer of the name and number of a counselor since she knows where to find the information if she changes her mind. Lastly, she makes sure he has her current phone number on the form in case anyone has a follow-up question.

By the time Marino is escorting her back out to the area behind the desk, Alicia and a tall man who Sarah assumes is Ted are both back there sharing the space. Sarah recalls the schedule she's been given well enough to know this means it is now sometime after three in the afternoon. Her entire day has officially been spent dealing with this death and she's officially late for her shift at the mall.

She pulls her cell phone out of her pocket and unlocks it, seeing she has missed three calls from her manager. "Shit, I'm late for work," she mumbles.

Marino frowns at her. "Do you need me to call someone?"

"No, I'll do it." Sarah turns her back on the group, trying to score a little privacy by turning toward the wall. She hits the button to call her boss and waits.

The call is answered after one ring. "What's going on?" her boss asks. "Is everything ok?"

Sarah sighs. "Yes. I was a witness to something awful at school. I had to go to the police station and give my witness statement. It took a lot longer than I thought it would. I'm actually still here. I can probably be there in —"

Her boss cuts her off. "Oh my God, are you ok? Like you weren't hurt or anything, right?"

"No, I'm fine. I swear. I just witnessed something." She won't let herself talk about the details. She doesn't want to. She just wants this to be over. She doesn't need more people thinking she might be connected to or affected by this death. She didn't even know Keith.

"Wow, ok. Obviously, take the rest of the day off. I can cover your shift."

"No, you don't have to do that," Sarah says. Even as she says it her mind is already thinking of how nice that would be. She hasn't eaten anything today since the burrito this morning. How long ago was that? Shouldn't she get something in her stomach? Plus she could use a little more sleep. Her body feels suddenly heavy.

"Nonsense, I'm already here. It's fine. I'm just glad you're alright. We heard something about a police presence on campus and we got really worried when you didn't answer. My mind just assumed the worst."

"I'm sorry I worried you." Sarah sighs. "I am hungry from being here all day. If you're good with covering for me, I think I'll take the time off so I can go home and eat something."

"Absolutely. I'll see you tomorrow. Be safe."

"Thanks, you too." Sarah hangs up the call and turns around, feeling already lighter knowing her day just got a lot more open. Ted is standing at the desk, guiding someone through filling out a form. Officer Marino is hovering nearby as if waiting to make sure Sarah leaves. Alicia, however, jumps up from her chair and comes their way.

"Sarah, I heard you were in here." Her eyes flit to Marino. "Is everything alright?"

"Everything is good," Marino answers. "Sarah was just giving me a statement because of something she witnessed this morning."

"This morning? You've been dealing with this all day?" Alicia shakes her head. "You're probably exhausted. Why don't you take the day off? I'll get the desk covered."

Sarah considers arguing. With the time off from the other job, she could handle staying here tonight without a problem. But she saw a dead body today. A chill runs up her spine and she finds herself nodding. "Yeah, if you're sure."

Alicia smiles at her. "I'm absolutely sure. Take the day. Call me tomorrow and let me know if you think you need more time. Ok?"

"Yeah, thanks." Sarah turns to Marino. "Are we good?"

"We're good. Call me if anything changes or if you remember something you may have left out. Do you need a ride?"

Shit. Her car. Her car is on campus outside of the building where her class was being held. She sighs. "No, it's walking distance back to my car. I'll get there safely."

The walk back to her car out in the bright sunlight makes Sarah feel lighter. Nothing out here looks any different. The campus is crammed full of students hustling along to their classes, completely unaware that someone has died. Actually, she corrects herself, two people have died. She wonders how many of these people have heard the rumors.

Halfway to the car her phone rings. She has the number programmed into her phone as Greg. She answers. "Hello?"

"Hey, it's Greg. I hope it's alright that I'm calling. I was just checking to make sure you're ok after this morning."

"I don't know what I am," she says. "I'm sort of numb to it right now if that makes sense. I just can't think about it."

"I get that."

"Alicia gave me the night off. I'm going home to get some food and maybe some sleep."

"Are you ok to be alone?" he asks. "I mean, you're not worried or scared or anything, right?"

Sarah shakes her head. Then she realizes he can't see that and answers out loud. "No, I'm good. I mean, I have nothing to be scared of."

"Sarah, someone died."

"Right, true. But I only found them. I'm not connected to all this. I'm just a witness."

Sarah hears Greg draw in a slow, measured breath. "I don't know. I didn't even witness anything and I'm a little shaken up. This is all so weird, isn't it? This kind of thing doesn't happen here and now it's happened twice. It seems like a big deal."

"I don't want to think that way," Sarah says. "I want to go back to normal."

"Alright, normal it is. How about we get that coffee sometime after your nap?" Greg says. "I mean since your evening just opened up."

"Shit, the coffee." Sarah completely forgot about the coffee date with Greg in all the chaos of this morning. But, honestly, it sounds like a perfect way to relax and let things feel normal. It's not a bad idea. "That's a great idea. What time is it right now?"

"3:20."

"Let's plan for like 7 tonight. Does that work? I'll meet you on campus like we planned and we'll get some coffee and be normal."

"See you there," Greg agrees.

Sarah thinks she can hear the smile in his voice and it coaxes hers out. "Alright, I just got to my car now. I'm heading home. See you later." She hangs up the phone before he can answer. They've already made plans, she doesn't need to drag out the goodbye. Besides, she suddenly feels like it's important to take a look at the vehicle she's getting into.

Feeling silly, Sarah takes her time walking around the outside of the car and checking for anything out of the ordinary. The tires all appear full of air, there are no scratches or marks that weren't there before, and nothing unusual is showing through the windows. When she pulls on the handle of the driver's door, she's relieved to find she remembered to lock it this morning.

She unlocks her car, practically melts into the driver's seat, and takes herself home. Despite the bright sunshine and the carefree attitude she projected on the phone, Sarah does notice her nerves are kicking in as she parks her car in the parking lot of her apartment complex. She notices more of the shadows than she normally would, her eyes snaking along all of them as if searching for some hidden danger. Mentally, she chides herself for being ridiculous. No one is here waiting to jump out of the shadows and hurt her. She is safe. She was always safe.

A voice in the back of her mind tells her that, at some point today, she was close enough to a murderer to be worried. Keith didn't kill himself like that, at least probably not. That means at some point today a killer was in the same building where Sarah has her morning class. Maybe they were even there at the same time as her. She may have even been in the hallway while Keith took his last breaths. She walks faster through the parking lot and makes sure to lock her apartment door behind her after she enters. Then she leans on the door and sighs.

The apartment looks completely untouched. All the windows are closed and the lights are off, just like she left them. She flips switches as she crosses the little apartment, leaving everything glowing with warm lighting as she checks out every corner and nook in the place.

Satisfied when she finds no one behind the shower curtain or hiding in the little closet, she makes her way to the bedroom where she kicks off her shoes and strips off her pants. Then she climbs under the covers of her bed and nestles herself on the pillow. She knows she should eat something and probably set an alarm. But right now this seems like the best idea. A little rest. Then she'll eat.

It feels like it's been only five minutes when Sarah's phone rings beside her. She blinks in the brightness of the apartment and grabs the phone without checking who is calling. "Hello?"

"Hey, it's Dan. Are you good? Heard you're not coming in today. Maybe you got mixed up in whatever was happening on campus. I thought I should check."

Sarah lays back on the pillow, the phone still to her ear. "Yeah, I'm good. Actually, I haven't told anyone the details of what happened yet. Got a minute?"

"For you? Of course."

"Remember Keith, the guy I was telling you about whose roommate died?"

"Yeah," Dan answers, his voice tipping up as if it was a question.

"I found his body outside my class this morning in the science building. I thought I heard his phone ringing, he has this distinctive ringtone, and I went out in the hallway to see what was going on. I found him, dead, on the bathroom floor. His body was sort of stuck in the door, kind of propping it open," Sarah says, her voice catching on the last sentence. "It was terrifying."

"Jesus Christ," Dan grunts. "Fuck, I'm sorry. What do you need?"

Despite the terrible situation, Sarah smiles. "I'm ok. I just want them to figure out who did this and get them off the streets before someone else gets hurt." She sighs. "Plus, I'd like to go back to normal." She sits up. "Speaking of which, what time is it?"

"Around 6, why?"

"I'm supposed to meet a friend for coffee." Sarah sits up and swings her feet out of bed. "Plus, I really could use a shower." She thinks about the smell of blood earlier and shivers. Now her entire body feels slimy and gross. She can't believe she slept like that, without showering in the hottest water her little apartment can provide. "I don't think the shower can wait now that I'm thinking about one. Can I call you later?" She heads for the bathroom, hoping he will understand if she hangs up on him even if he says no.

"Of course. Call me whenever. Even if it's in the middle of the night. I want you to be safe."

"I am. I just need to shower. Talk soon." She hangs up the phone with one hand and flips the water on with the other, turning the dial up to hot. New plan, one very hot shower to get the feeling of this morning off of her skin and then she'll go have coffee with Greg and forget about all of this. Keith and his roommate got themselves tangled up in something, which is sad but entirely not her fault. Her life will resume normal activity as soon as today is over.

CHAPTER 17

The coffee shop on campus is busy at all hours of the day. Sarah knows this from previous experience. It seems that college students will consume cups of caffeinated sugar from sun up to down if given the opportunity. Today is no exception. Every chair in the little building is packed and people are standing around the outside edges, clearly waiting for their orders to go. The noise of the foamers and workers is high as they try to pump out enough drinks to keep people satiated.

Sarah spots Greg at a table for two in the back corner. He already has a paper cup of something in front of him and another paper cup is sitting in front of the empty chair across from him. A tall, fit, brunette guy in jogging clothes is standing beside the table. Sarah considers giving the men time to finish their conversation by ordering herself something. Still, she wonders if that other paper cup is actually for her. That seems like something Greg would do since he already knows what kind of coffee she likes. She decides to make her way through the crowd to them and find out. When she's close, Greg looks up and catches her eye. "Hi," she greets with a wave.

Greg smiles. "Sarah, you made it. This is my friend, Andy. He's just waiting for his coffee."

"Is that for me?" she asks, dropping into the chair opposite Greg and gesturing to the cup in front of the seat.

"It is. Vanilla latte ok?"

"If it's not, I'll drink it," Andy offers. "I'll drink practically anything if it's free, you know what I mean?"

Immediately, Sarah doesn't like this guy. Something about his attitude comes through as cocky and condescending, two things she doesn't like. She tries not to let her annoyance show. First impressions can be wrong. She takes a sip of the latte. "It's perfect, thank you."

Andy's cell phone, which is currently in his hand, rings. He hits a button, silencing the call.

"This is getting fucking ridiculous," he mumbles.

Sarah notices a band on his arm, the kind made for runners, designed to hold his phone. She figures that, along with the jogging clothes, means Andy was out for a run. She wonders why the phone is out of the pouch right now. "That's the third one since you've been in here," Greg says. "What's up with your spam filter?"

"I have no idea," Andy answers. "I can't seem to block the numbers fast enough. It's been two days of this nonstop calling from unknown numbers. Even if I answer it, there's no one there."

Sarah assumes that's the reason the phone is out. She frowns in his direction. "They're all unknown numbers? Are they local?"

"Sometimes they don't say but the ones that do are the right area code to be local. Fucking spammers are getting out of control," Andy answers.

"Try this call filter." Sarah pulls out her phone and shows Andy an app. "It's a bit stronger of a filter than the one through the providers. I have the free service but if that's not good enough you can pay like $5 a month and they'll filter even more."

Andy nods. "I might have to do that. Thanks." He sighs. "I don't know. It's just annoying."

"Maybe it's just that girl who wouldn't give you the time of day," Greg says. His tone of voice makes it clear to Sarah that this is supposed to be a joke told to lighten the mood. She doesn't get it.

Apparently, Andy doesn't either. His body language becomes instantly angry, his shoulders roll forward and his hands clench tight around the phone in his hand. "Bitch should've just taken the second date," he says in a dark voice.

Sarah flinches back from him. What the hell?

From the counter a barista bellows, "Tall toffee latte for Andy".

Andy turns and looks that way. When he turns back to them, he's put his anger away again. He laughs a little, but it sounds forced. "You're probably right though. Could just be someone pranking me. It's possible to spoof numbers with a good enough knowledge of computers, I'm sure. Anyway, that's my order. I'll see you around, G." He turns to Sarah. "It was nice to meet you. Thanks for the spam blocker tip."

"Don't mention it." She takes another sip of her latte to give Andy time to walk away. Then she widens her eyes at Greg. "That guy was intense. What the hell was that thing about a girl?"

"Nothing really. A few months ago Andy and some girl went out on a date. Andy says it was a good time but he wasn't happy with the way it ended."

"Why? What does that mean?" Sarah pushes, even though Greg's body language is looking a little closed off as if he doesn't want to talk about this.

"He just thought they connected better than she thought they did."

Sarah can feel her anger bubbling. She has a feeling she knows exactly what Greg means here. Andy wanted a goodnight kiss at least, sex at most. He didn't get it. She wants to be wrong. She wants it to be something else. She wants it to not be a story of an asshole who tried to push a girl and couldn't. She wants Greg to not support this behavior or joke about this behavior at a coffee shop full of people. She tries to take a calming breath. "What I'm imagining is pretty bad. Why don't you tell me what actually happened?"

Greg sighs. "It's not my story to tell. Andy just said she was giving him signals all night but then wouldn't even let him kiss her. He tried to call her later for a second date or to find out what went wrong, but she wouldn't talk to him. She blocked his calls or something. It was really extreme. So he went to her apartment to talk to her and she sort of flipped out."

Sarah sits in silence for a few seconds while she processes this. She wasn't wrong about Andy, clearly. How is it possible she was able to get a read on that guy's red flags so quickly and yet Greg calls him a friend? Greg jokes about this girl who, it sounds like, was harassed at her home after a first date that didn't end the way she wanted. A girl who Sarah would've suggested make a statement down at the station if she felt unsafe. "That's fucking terrible," she says, anger making her voice sound harsh. "You're telling me he showed up at her house when she wouldn't take his calls? Not a public place where they can talk safely but at her private residence? How the fuck are you excusing that?"

"Sarah, I had nothing to do with it. Andy's just a guy I know from a few classes."

"No, you called him a friend. You sat here and made a joke about that girl. Did you see how angry he got? That kind of guy is fucking dangerous. You're going to tell me if he saw that girl in the middle of the woods at night she'd be safe? No. I can tell you right now she wouldn't be. None of this is a funny story."

Greg runs his hand down his face. "I didn't say it was funny. I shouldn't have tried to make a joke. That was stupid. Can you just take a breath and calm down?"

Sarah closes her eyes. "Did you really just tell me to calm down?" she asks, her voice dangerously quiet. She opens her eyes again to find Greg looking resigned. It's not enough to calm her anger.

"You're getting worked up about this. It was at least a month ago. It's not a big deal," he says in a voice that sounds like someone trying to calm a spooked animal.

"So let's find her," Sarah says. "Let's ask her if she thinks it's a big deal. Because if it were me I'd be planning my classes and routes around campus to avoid your friend. I'd be trying my best to make sure we didn't accidentally come into contact with each other. I'd be thinking about it every single day. I'd be locking my apartment door because he clearly knows where I live and has no boundaries. I can't believe you don't see this for the problem it is."

She stands up and slowly pushes her chair in. "I don't think this is your fault, by any means. But I also don't think it's something to joke about and I can't just pretend like it is. I'm sorry. We're just not on the same page. This isn't going to work."

She hears Greg get up behind her. She hears him calling her name and following her. But she just can't stop walking out of the coffee shop. She can't be another person who excuses these behaviors and makes them socially acceptable. Stalking, that's what Greg's friend Andy did. Whether they want to call it that or not, he stalked that girl to her apartment to demand a second date. What was he prepared to do if he didn't get it? She remembers the anger that clouded his face when he said she should've taken the second date. No, no matter how nice Greg seems, he saw that same anger and still said it was "no big deal". Fuck that. Andy is dangerous. Sarah sees it and she can't believe Greg excuses it.

In the car, Sarah hits a button to call Dan. The sound of ringing fills the car. Sarah flinches when she realizes what time it is, Dan is probably trying to run closing procedures. Before she can decide to hang up, he answers. "Hey, what's up?"

"Shit, sorry. You're probably busy at work. I just had a disaster of a coffee date and I was gonna ask you a weird question. Call me when you have time?"

"I left early today. It was slow. I'm starving though. Meet me at the buffet place?"

The buffet place is located on the south end of campus. Sarah can take the car down to a closer parking space, get some food, and vent about this entire situation. "You read my mind. I'm like four minutes away. See you there."

Dan is waiting for her when she walks up to the small building. Sarah wastes no time getting into it, starting the story of the coffee date while they're still in line. They shadow each other around the buffet, alternating who fills their plates at random intervals along the options. Then, by the time they select a two-top table near a window, she wraps up her story and gets to the point. "Am I making too much out of this? I've known Greg for a while. I shouldn't judge him so harshly for who he associates with, right?"

Dan takes a forkful of something with noodles, chews, and swallows. He looks contemplative. Sarah likes that he takes time to think about this before answering. "You weren't wrong," he says. Immediately, he digs back into the food.

Sarah drops her fork. "That's it?" She

gestures toward his plate. "You looked like you were giving it so much thought and all I get is three words?"

"One of them was a conjunction," he says. Then he laughs lightly as if to prove that was a joke. Sarah doesn't smile. Dan puts his fork down. "Fine. You want more? Guys like Andy are dangerous, you're right about that. If Greg wants to excuse the behavior of his friend or pretend he's an acquaintance that's bad enough. I'd even support you yelling at him for that." He picks up his fork again and uses it to gesture at Sarah. "This dude did worse than that. He supports it because he made a joke about it. I wasn't there but I get the impression Greg is just as dangerous as Andy. He's just pretending this behavior is a problem now because you called it out." He dips the fork into some mashed potato and brings it closer to his mouth. "I think you need to put some space between you and Greg."

Sarah blows out a breath. "Wow, ok. Thank you for agreeing with me." She picks up her spoon and loads it up with applesauce. Then she pauses, a thought occurring to her. "Wait, this isn't jealousy talking, is it? You're not, like, being gross by convincing me all other dateable people are assholes who should be ignored?"

Dan smiles. "No way. Date whoever you want. In fact, I'll call that Mariana girl for you right now if you want, she sounded cool. But you need to be safe and those two guys give me bad vibes. They're not safe."

Sarah nods and resumes eating. She wonders what unsafe people Keith and his roommate got tangled with to end up dead. For the few seconds she lets herself think about it, the world is a terrifying place.

CHAPTER 18

Sarah's legs seem incapable of carrying her past the building where the body was found to the place where her morning class is being held on Monday. The building where Keith was found is closed for at least the rest of the month and professors have had to find open buildings where they can put their classes. But to get to where this class is being held, Sarah has to walk by the building where she found the body.

She spent the weekend at home, relaxing and enjoying some much-needed time off. She cleaned her entire apartment, washed all her laundry, did some grocery shopping, paid bills, read a book, and tried not to think about the body she found. It mostly worked. But the second she got on campus this morning her legs just froze. Now she's the girl standing outside the building blocking the traffic flow like an idiot.

She noticed this weekend that focusing on menial tasks made her feel more normal and let her forget about the sight and smell of blood coming from the bathroom. Apparently walking to class is not enough of a menial task. She'll need something else. Something stronger.

A guy walking and talking on a cell phone narrowly avoids crashing into Sarah. "Why are you standing there?" he yells as he moves around her. "Bitch."

That does it. Sarah propels herself in his direction, anger letting her legs move past the building. Why do people like this think they can intimidate whoever the fuck they want? Sarah won't stand for that. "You got a problem?" she yells.

The guy turns his head and narrows his eyes at her. Then he rolls his eyes and continues on his way. The message is pretty clear. He doesn't think Sarah is worth the time. She could keep arguing and get out some of her frustration on him. But then she notices that she's past the building she was avoiding and drawing closer to the one holding her class. She smiles. Saved by an asshole. What a weird day.

In the classroom, which looks remarkably similar to the one they normally hold class in, although newer, Sarah considers where to sit. Part of her wants to take a seat in the back for ease of leaving the room if she becomes uncomfortable. But her body won't allow her to do that again. She sees the seat, considers why this is the best idea, and then her feet carry her three rows up to an entirely different seat. Even as she feels herself grow annoyed with her body's reaction, she takes the seat.

The professor for her class is visibly nervous, Sarah notes. He keeps things short and simple today and makes a point of talking about the number for a grief counselor if anyone requires it. He spends the last ten minutes of class talking about what it's acceptable to feel. How it's normal to feel grief for the loss of your own safety because something like this happened so close to your life, even if you didn't know the young man. He tells them not to downplay their grief, but to get help dealing with it. He also reminds them to stay safe and be vigilant in their interactions with surroundings that feel dangerous.

Sarah is proud of herself for not telling him that the campus didn't feel dangerous before that incident. He's making it sound like Keith did something wrong by ignoring the signals or something. It's not like he was doing some shady drug deal in a back alley somewhere in the dark.

He was using the restroom in the building they would all be in if the class hadn't been moved. Keith was doing something they've all probably done a thousand times.

No. This is not productive thinking. Sarah grabs her belongings and follows the rest of the class out the back door and into the sunshine of a beautiful fall day. She will not think about this death and let herself enter that thought spiral that could take her to a dangerous place. She is safe. Keith and his roommate might have been into shady things. Maybe that was a drug deal in a bathroom. That could happen. She doesn't know.

What she does know is that she is safe. She won't let herself think otherwise.

"Good morning, beautiful."

Sarah turns toward the voice, expecting to see someone on the phone or something. She's shocked for a half second when she sees Mariana smiling at her from the grass beside the walkway. Stuck in her own head, she'd almost missed her. "Good morning." Sarah stops, stepping out of the flow of people to stand beside her. "How are you?"

"I'm alright. I tried to call you yesterday. You didn't answer."

Sarah remembers the screen on her phone lighting up while she was paying bills. She remembers ignoring the call. Why didn't she call back? "Sorry about that. I was getting some bills paid and I must have forgotten to call you back.

What's up?"

Mariana shrugs. "Nothing important. I just wanted to chat." She rakes her fingers up through her hair, pulling it off her face. "Did you hear about the kid that was killed?" Mariana asks, tipping her head toward the closed building. "It's all anyone can talk about this morning. My professor went on and on about grief counseling for anyone who knew the victim. It's so crazy."

Sarah feels a lump in her throat that she can't seem to move. She doesn't want to talk about this but can't find the words to stop Mariana. Mariana, for her part, seems not to notice. She rushes on, now using the hand that had been in her hair to gesture around her as she speaks. "I heard there were actually two people that died. Someone said they even knew each other like they were best friends or lovers or something. It's so crazy. I hear there's even a film crew on South Campus somewhere talking to students."

Film crew? That's not good. Sarah makes a mental note to avoid the south end of campus at all costs.

"Then I heard some poor girl even found one of the bodies," Mariana continues. "Can you imagine? You're just going about your life and all of a sudden —"

That does it. The one thing that Sarah has managed to avoid all weekend. She feels her chin wobble and before she can even think about stopping it, she's crying. Right here on North

Campus in front of everyone and Mariana.

"Oh, shit. I'm sorry." Mariana wraps her arms around Sarah and tries to pull her close.

Sarah puts her hand on Mariana's shoulder and pushes her away. Then she uses her other hand to wipe away the tears. "Shit. I'm fine."

"I didn't mean to upset you. I probably scared you. I'm sorry, I talk when I'm scared or nervous or something." Mariana reaches for Sarah again and this time Sarah literally swats her hand like a bug. "What the hell, Sarah, I'm trying to be nice. You can't let me comfort you when you're upset?"

"I'm not upset." Sarah wipes at her face again, making sure she gets all the tears. She puts on a fake smile. "I'm fine. I'm just tired and I don't want to talk about this. I have to go to class." Really, only one of those things is true. She doesn't want to talk about this. Not with Mariana, not with a grief counselor, not with anyone.

Mariana puts her hands on her hips. "Fine. Whatever."

Sarah rolls her eyes. "You're mad now? I don't want to stand on campus and cry so you're mad?"

"You don't want to let me in on whatever is going on with you. We're supposed to be friends, maybe even more. But you have to do this 'I'm independent' bullshit where you handle it all by yourself even if it breaks you. I'm not mad you don't want to cry I'm mad that you're obviously cracking and you can't admit it. Whatever. You do you." Mariana throws her hands up. "I'm not gonna change you so I don't know why I even try."

Sarah should feel bad that it came to this. But she is independent and the fact that Mariana just admitted to trying to change her, instead of accepting her for who she is, rankles. She shakes her head and just walks away. Mariana doesn't call her back and, honestly, Sarah is glad it worked out that way. Better for them both to know where they stand before this thing between them goes any further. They were doomed if Mariana wanted to change Sarah from the start. If there's one thing Sarah can't stand for, it's people not accepting her for who she is. She thought Mariana was different but, apparently, she was wrong.

Sarah is walking by the buildings at the center of campus before she realizes Mariana may have helped her. With anger coursing through her at this change of heart, she hasn't thought about the body she found for at least five minutes. That was a nice break.

CHAPTER 19

The discovery that anger is enough of a menial task to get her through the day helps Sarah with her second class, lunch, and traffic. She finds herself inwardly angry at everything and sometimes even lets outbursts escape through her lips. Someone cuts her off in traffic and she hollers into the empty car "No problem, asshole, come on over." It's not her typical behavior, but at least she's not remembering the smell of blood in the bathroom or that fear she felt when she had to walk by the building this morning. She's not thinking about Mariana, the girl who decided Sarah's inability to let people in was a problem. For those few seconds she's angry, she's not thinking about any of that.

She parks her car outside the employee entrance of the mall and locks the doors before standing and surveying the building. She can do this. She had a weekend off, that's why it feels strange to be standing here. It's not because it's the first time she has had to stand here since she found a dead body. No. She shakes her head and forces herself to reshape the unproductive line of thoughts into something more logical. She's just had an entire weekend to herself, which allowed her to see how easy trust-fund babies who had college paid for without having to work must live. That's why it's hard to come back. There's that anger now, simmering under her skin. This world is not equal and it's not fair. She leans into the anger and stomps her way across the parking lot.

The other employees must notice her attitude right away because everyone gives Sarah a large berth as she makes her way through the store. She yanks on doors harder than she needs to, has her teeth clenched, and slams things down on counters without provocation. No one says hi to her as she marches through departments.

When she reaches the counter in hardware, she throws her bag below the metal top. There's already a line and another employee is logged into register one, working their way through. Sarah logs quickly into register two, mashing her fingers on the keys, and waves over the next person in line. The old man plops his things down on the counter and Sarah scans them. She reads his total, takes the money he is already holding out, counts back his change, and drops his things in a bag.

"Next," she calls.

A lady steps up and puts her things on the counter. "Is this the best drill?" the lady asks.

Sarah sighs. "The best drill ever in the history of drills? Probably not. The best drill under $30 that we sell?" Sarah's eyes flit down to the drill noticing which one the lady has selected. "Yes."

"You don't have to be rude, I was just asking."

Sarah's eyes flame with anger. I do have to be rude, she wants to say. I have to be rude to keep my mind right here and right now. I have to be rude to stop myself from thinking about how a girl I was dating dumped me this morning publicly in the middle of North Campus. I don't want to think about how the girl called me out on not sharing my emotions and refusing to let her in, which are both true. I don't want to think about how what upset me the most was her saying the girl who found the body had a right to be upset because I really, really don't want to think about what that means.

Instead, Sarah offers her a smile. She's pretty sure they can both tell it's fake. "I'm sorry, would you prefer me to walk you to the drills and try to talk you into something better but more expensive?"

"Just ring this one up. I hope there's a survey on my receipt."

Sarah rings her up, takes her credit card, and runs the payment. Then she throws everything in a bag. "Have the day you deserve," she says.

The lady freezes. "Was that supposed to be an insult?" she asks.

Sarah smiles again. "Why would you ever think that?"

When the woman snatches the bag from her hand and stomps away down the center aisle, Sarah's real smile surfaces. "Next," she bellows.

The line of customers continues for the first hour of Sarah's shift. It's endless. She realizes, when she actually stops to think about it, that this is likely the start of what is projected to be a very busy holiday shopping season. Sure, they're only in November right now, but a lot of people get their shopping in early. She makes a mental note, between customers, to check and see if she's scheduled to work on Black Friday. The store offers double rates for employees on Black Friday, something the police station absolutely cannot match. It might be a good idea, she muses, to request off from the police station and ask for a double shift here.

After an hour, sweat beading on her brow,

Sarah finally gets a moment to breathe. There are no customers in line. "Been like that all day," the employee on her left tells her. "I haven't logged off this computer for more than ten minutes. Sorry about the big stack of go-backs. I gotta run."

Sarah turns and looks behind her. In the box that forms their register counter, the employees have a medium-sized plastic tub where they drop anything that needs to be put back on the shelf. It can be a customer return or something someone changed their mind about at the last minute. Normally this gets emptied frequently. Right now it's completely full. If a customer decided to return a wrench Sarah couldn't fit it in that box. "Are you kidding me right now?" Sarah barks.

"Sorry, my shift ended fifteen minutes ago but I didn't want to leave you with that line. I can't put it away." The girl is already grabbing her bag from under the register.

"I'd rather have the long line," Sarah mumbles.

"Whatever," the girl responds.

Sarah blows out a frustrated breath and grabs a few things from the box to put away. She stomps around the aisles, slamming everything into the appropriate spots. She counts seven customers shopping in their section, which is a lot for this time of the week. She doesn't offer to help any of them.

When the box is half empty, she hears

footsteps approaching the register. Assuming a customer is ready to check out, she spins toward the register with her new scowl firmly set in place. Instead of a customer, she finds Dan holding a plunger up near his chin. "Don't shoot," he says. "I come in peace."

Despite herself, Sarah chuckles.

"Or, if you really need to fight, en garde." He flips the plunger around so the handle is pointed in her direction.

"Am I being that awful?" Sarah asks, already knowing the answer.

Dan sets the plunger down on the counter and leans his hip beside it, angling his body toward Sarah. "Not awful. Defensive. You get like that sometimes." He shrugs. "Usually it gets you what you want."

She feels the now familiar anger bubble up under the surface and readies herself for another conversation like the one this morning. She wonders, briefly, if she'll handle this one any better than the last one. "Oh yeah, what do I want?" she barks, her voice clipped and harsh.

"I assume you want to be left alone," Dan answers. "Am I wrong?"

"I hate you," she lies.

Dan smiles. "No, you don't. Is it working? Is being left alone making you feel better? Because I can walk away if it is."

"Yes. It's working." She hates that her throat burns like she might cry in a public place …

again. For the second time in a single day. She needs her anger right now. "Go away," she orders.

Dan stands up fully and throws his hands up. "I'm going. But if you want to try something different, I'm available. That's all I'm saying." He grabs the plunger and saunters off again, disappearing around the corner he came from.

Sarah manages to stem her tears and focus on work for the next three hours. She snaps at customers a little too much, slams around objects, and even manages to type her own password wrong a few times because she's trying to type it in anger. When the phone rings, she relishes the feeling of slamming the handset down on the cradle.

At the treadmills she watches Dan talk to an older woman. Despite her best efforts, it makes her smile watching him with the customers. He's got a natural ease with people that comes out in a retail setting. He chats with everyone like they're a friend, like he truly cares what happens with them. It's inviting. Sarah knows that too well, she supposes.

What if he's right about there being a better solution to dealing with whatever she's going through than just losing herself in anger? She doesn't like who she is right now. She doesn't like who she's been since she first learned about Keith's roommate dying. She was one of those obsessed people, looking for details about this death everywhere. Now she's even closer to it and that's not acceptable. She has to get back to focusing on her plan. She has to get back to living her life. She can't walk around angry all the time. What if one of the customers from the start of her shift does call in a survey? Can she afford to be written up at this job when she's trying to get double shifts on holiday pay at the end of the month? She's completely letting herself derail her future.

Oh, she realizes with a pang, she's turning into her mother.

That thought pushes her to leave the little box for registers and make her way over to Dan. The customer is walking on the treadmill now, her back to both of them. The sound of the treadmill running isn't loud, but this isn't a top-of-the-line treadmill so the noise does exist. Sarah can use that to give them a little semblance of privacy.

She stops beside Dan and leans toward him a little so he can hear when she whispers. "Maybe we should try it your way. Do you maybe want to get dinner after this shift?"

"That depends," Dan whispers back. "Are we going to try talking about whatever is bothering you?"

"Yeah, I think so. I'm not sure how long I'll be able to talk about it, but I want to try."

Dan nods. His head turns a fraction closer to her before he whispers again. Sarah can smell him now and almost hates how her body instinctively reacts to that smell. "Is this a date?"

he asks.

She loves the feel of his breath on her cheek as he whispers, which is probably why she nods before she can stop herself. "Yes."

"Then I wouldn't miss it," he says. Then he straightens again and immediately assumes his retail persona. "What do we think, Ann?" he asks in a louder voice. "Is this the one?"

Sarah turns and walks back to the register, little butterflies fluttering around in her stomach.

Sarah swipes her badge near the machine, clocking herself out for her shift. "Same place as last time?" Dan asks.

"Sounds good." Sarah leads the way, marching along the concrete and listening to her steps bounce off the building.

"Are we gonna talk about what's going on?" Dan asks. "Does this mood have to do with finding Kevin, or whatever his name was?"

"Keith," Sarah mumbles.

"Right, Keith. Is this mood related to that?"

He puts his hand on her back, right between her shoulder blades. It's a comforting hand as if he wonders if Sarah needs that support. She pulls away and hears his hand slap back down on his jeans. "Or maybe," Dan continues, "this is more of an angry-at-men-like-that-douchebag-who-showed-up-at-your-coffee-house-date kind of thing."

"I forgot about that," Sarah says. She pulls open the door to the restaurant and lets Dan slip in first. He holds up two fingers for the host who Sarah recognizes from the other times they've been here. She falls in step behind Dan who is following the host, making a little line to the table near the salad bar.

She notices the waiter didn't bring menus. "Anything to drink or add to the salad bar tonight, guys?" he asks.

"Iced tea for me," Sarah says.

"Just water for me tonight," Dan says.

The waiter walks off and Dan resumes their conversation. "So if it wasn't the coffee house douchebag, since you forgot about that, I'm guessing I was right the first time. Should we get some food before we dive into a complicated conversation about dead bodies?"

Sarah sighs. "Yes, I need food." She uses the opportunity of walking to the salad bar to let herself contemplate how much to tell Dan. She really doesn't want to dig back into the whole finding a body thing. He already knows about that and she doesn't want to get into it again. Instead, she decides, she'll vent about Mariana and how that whole thing went down. Dan is curious why she was slamming things around and her anger with Mariana is the answer to that question.

Back at the table, she takes a few bites before launching into the prepared explanation. "Remember that girl I went out to dinner with, Mariana?" Dan nods. "Right, so I didn't tell her about what happened with Keith. I mean, I didn't tell anyone. It wasn't about her. I just haven't spoken to her. I didn't call or text or whatever. I was processing what I went through. It wasn't like I was leaving her out on purpose. I just didn't tell her."

Dan holds up a hand. "That's a lot of words to say you didn't tell her yet. I get it, you don't have to defend yourself to me."

Sarah appreciates that he doesn't point out her obvious lie. She did tell someone. She told him. She rushes on. "Right, well I didn't tell her. But then I ran into her on campus this morning. All she wanted to do was talk about it."

"A murder on campus is a pretty big news story. That's an expected reaction."

"Right, but I didn't want to talk about it."

"Understandable." He takes a large forkful of salad, chews, and swallows. "Did you tell her that?"

"I didn't get a chance. She was babbling on and on about it and then she says that she heard someone on campus found the body. She told me she couldn't imagine how devastating that would be for that person."

"It would be devastating," Dan says. "It would be scary and traumatizing."

Sarah shakes her head. "Why does everyone keep telling me I should be traumatized and upset?"

"You're not upset?"

"Obviously I am. This was scary and I feel bad for Keith. I can't stop thinking about it, even when I want to. But there's nothing I could have done differently to stop what happened."

"I agree," Dan says, setting his fork down.

"There's nothing I could've changed that would have kept him safe."

"I agree again." Dan reaches across the table and touches Sarah's arm.

"There's nothing about this situation that says I'm in any danger."

"I hope that one is true," Dan says.

"Well, you're being rational about it, at least. Mariana cornered me on campus and wanted me to cry about it and be comforted right there in front of all the people. The worst part is she didn't even know the whole story, so she wouldn't even know why she was comforting me. I didn't want to be a basket case right then. I wanted to be strong. I wanted to not think about it and she just wasn't getting it. Then we got into this huge fight because I told her I wasn't talking about this and she said I always do that."

Sarah moves her arm, dropping Dan's hand to the table where a second ago her arm was. "Whatever, I just want to eat." She's not sure if he knows the snapping at him now is a signal that she was feeling emotional again or not. She's not sure if she cares what he thinks. She just wants to fill her stomach and stop talking about all of this.

He lets her finish her plate in silence. Then he stacks their plates together on the edge of the table and stands up. "I'm getting more. You coming?"

Sarah stands and follows him back to the salad bar. She fills her next plate with only things that she feels like eating, regardless of whether they make any sense on the same plate. Two hard-boiled eggs, a scoop full of red gelatin squares, a bunch of grapes, three carrot sticks, and one chocolate chip cookie. She smiles when she notices Dan's plate is a similar conglomeration.

Back at the table, Sarah tries the talking thing again. "I just don't like being vulnerable in public places," she admits.

Dan chuckles and Sarah's eyes fly to his face. "Are you laughing at me?" she snaps.

"Not at all." He smiles. "Sorry. I was laughing at the lie. You don't like being vulnerable at all. It has nothing to do with public or private."

Sarah wants to be offended. She wants to tell him he's wrong. But he's not. She shrugs instead. "Whatever."

"Between finding Keith's body, which I agree would traumatize anyone," Dan says, "and this girl pushing you, you've had a rough week."

"Don't forget finding out my friend Greg also calls a total asshole a friend," Sarah adds. "That guy was seriously giving creep vibes."

"It's a lot to unpack," Dan says. "I'm not sure where to start."

Sarah laughs. "That will be on my tombstone. Here lies Sarah, she was a lot to unpack." She rolls her eyes. "I'm feeling better. Venting helped. I'm done talking about this. Distract me with something else."

For the rest of their dinner, which for Sarah is two more trips to the salad bar, he does exactly that. Dan talks about a class he's taking that has his interest, a class he's taking that bores him right into fighting sleep, and his roommate who has a habit of leaving socks lying around the apartment in weird places. Sarah finds herself relaxing more as the evening goes on.

When the bill comes Sarah pulls out cash for her half. Dan does the same, which makes paying incredibly simple. They just tuck the bills into the little black folder and stand up. "Well, it's time to make that drive back across town," Sarah says. "It's been a long day."

"Are you tired?" Dan asks.

"A little."

"Do you have to get to the other job?"

"Nope. I took one more night off mostly to

avoid an awkward confrontation with Greg, although I'll have to face that at some point or another," Sarah says. "The schedule tonight involves getting myself home and getting some sleep. Or maybe watching a mindless show before drifting off to sleep on the couch." She pushes the door of the restaurant open and steps out into the cool night air. "Unclear which path I'll choose at this point."

At the employee parking lot, Sarah stops. "I guess this is where we part," she says. She can see Dan's truck a few aisles over from her car. "Drive safely and sleep well."

"Can I admit something?" Dan asks. Sarah nods. "I'm mildly and irrationally worried about you being alone in your apartment."

"I've been alone all weekend."

"I know. I was irrationally worried all weekend."

Sarah rolls her eyes. "Are you telling me you're worried that whoever killed Keith knows where I live and plans to come to my apartment and finish me off even though I don't know anything?" Her voice drips with the obvious sarcasm of her statement. Even in her darkest moments this weekend when she worried about her safety this one was stupid. She has no idea who did this to Keith and they don't know anything about her at all. She found the body after the killer was gone. End of story.

"No." Dan reaches out and touches her

arm. "I wasn't even thinking about that. This Andy guy makes me nervous. We already know he's shown up at some other girls' apartment before. I'm worried about him."

"Oh, shit." Sarah hadn't thought about that. If Greg complains about her leaving their date to his friend Andy, would Andy show up to reason with her the way he had done to the other girl? Sure, he doesn't know where she lives, but would it be that hard to find out? She feels her pulse quicken. She was relaxing. Now she has to drive home to her empty apartment in the dark to be alone all night in the fucking dark. Shit.

"I'll follow you home," Dan offers. "Then I can at least see if there's anyone at your place before you go in."

"You'd do that for me?" Sarah asks.

"It's the least I can do after I can tell how much I just freaked you out."

"I'm not going to lie and say you didn't. Follow me." By the time she reaches her car and unlocks it to let herself in, Sarah is worried she made the wrong choice. Has admitting she might be a little afraid of the dark made her weak? She doesn't want to be weak. She isn't weak. She contemplates texting Dan, calling off the follow. She decides to head toward her apartment since Dan lives near her. If they get closer and this feeling keeps up, she'll call him off.

As she's winding through the dark backroads in the forest, she tells herself she may have made the right call after all. Her pulse races and she jumps at movements in the shadows. This situation she's found herself in is seriously damaging her independence and she's going to need to work on that. Because right now she'd much rather pull over to the side of the road and leave her car here to ride with her eyes closed in the passenger seat of Dan's truck than keep driving.

Instead, she continues, watching him in the rearview mirror to make sure he stays behind her the entire drive. She parks her car near her apartment building in a spot with another one directly beside it. She's happy when Dan takes the hint and pulls into the empty spot. He shuts off his car quickly and jogs to meet her at the front of their vehicles.

"Everything look normal in the parking lot?" He asks.

Sarah takes a second to look around. She isn't exactly familiar with all the cars in the complex, but nothing seems obviously out of place. She nods. "But come with me to the front door, just to be sure." She doesn't pause to consider how ridiculous this makes her sound, just follows the advice of her beating heart and spits it out. Then she grabs Dan's elbow and drags him toward her stairs. They make their way up, side by side. Sarah doesn't let out her nervous breath until she sees the porch is empty and the door firmly closed. Her shoulders sag. "I'm being so ridiculous."

"No, you're not."

"I am. Thank you for doing this. Come inside, we'll pour a drink and watch mindless TV or something."

Dan reaches up and touches her face. "Are you sure?"

The intimacy of the small gesture hits Sarah in the stomach and settles it down. For a heartbeat, everything else slips away except for Dan and the warmth of his hand on her face. "I'm absolutely sure," she says. She grabs Dan's hand and holds it while she unlocks and opens the front door. A bit of her fear tries to trickle back in as the dark, empty apartment greets her, but she holds tight to his hand and lets the warmth chase it away.

She drops her bag and flips on the overhead light. Dan closes the door behind him and flips the lock. Sarah squeezes his hand before dropping it and heading for the kitchen, flipping another light along the way. "I probably have a bottle of iced tea, I definitely have half a bottle of whiskey, and I have water from the tap. What would you like?"

"If you have ice I'll take some of that whiskey," Dan says as he makes his way in the other direction toward Sarah's bedroom. She watches as the lights flick on and then back off. Dan reappears in the doorway. "All good in there. Do you mind if I turn this on?" He holds up the remote to indicate that he means the TV.

"Turn it on. Find something." She grabs

two short glasses from the cabinet, drops four ice cubes into each, and pours a generous amount of the whiskey into the glasses. Typically, if she drinks at all, Sarah will mix this with something else, usually ginger ale or cola. But she's out of both so it's a straight whiskey kind of day.

Sarah kicks off her shoes and settles herself on the couch beside Dan, handing him his whiskey. He takes a small sip and winces a bit. "Strong stuff," he says. Then he takes a second sip. This time he smiles. "Good finish though."

"You sound like you know what you're talking about," Sarah says. "I never know how alcohol is supposed to taste." She takes a little sip of her own and feels her cheeks spasm in response to the burn. "I just know how it's supposed to make you feel when you drink enough of it."

Dan chuckles. "I try not to drink that much but my parents own a bar so I know the differences."

"Is it a local bar? Someplace I might have stumbled upon by accident?"

Dan laughs now. "No. I'm originally from Prescott. The bar is on Whiskey Row. Unless you were doing the tourist thing in Prescott you probably missed it." He tips his chin toward the TV. "What are we watching?"

"I told you to pick."

"Any suggestions or rules?"

"Something we won't miss too much of if we fall asleep. Something light. No murders."

"Got it." Dan selects an older sitcom, one that would likely run on over-the-air channels as reruns with a laugh track behind it. Then he settles back on the couch, letting his right arm rest on the back.

Sarah takes that as an invitation and snuggles up next to him. "Is this ok?" she asks.

Dan lets his arm drop off the back of the couch along Sarah's arm and adds a little pressure, like a side hug. "Perfect."

Sarah rests her head on his chest and sighs, letting herself relax. She's asleep within ten minutes.

CHAPTER 21

A ndy rolls over in bed and reaches for his ringing phone in the dark. His hand closes around it, and he answers it automatically while raising it to his ear. "Hello," he mumbles.

The sound of silence greets him. Frustrated, he punches the end button and sits up a little in bed, rubbing his eyes. According to the time on the phone, it's just after one in the morning. This phone number, which he adds to the growing recently blocked list, is another one that appears to be local. Again, there was no one there. He knows he shouldn't have answered it. Had it been a normal hour of the day, he might not have. But instincts win out at this time of the night.

He flips the phone onto silent mode and puts it face down back on the table beside the bed. Then he flops back onto the pillow and stares at the ceiling. Now he's awake. "Shit." He throws off the covers and stands up, intending to head for a suddenly much-needed restroom break.

As soon as he's on his feet his eyes land on a strange shadow on the ceiling of the hallway just outside his room. He squints at it, slowly stepping closer as if being drawn to it. With each step he expects his eyes will focus and he'll know exactly what it is. Instead, he gets more and more confused and feels his heartbeat start to pick up. "What the fuck is that?" he mumbles.

In his bedroom doorway, standing almost directly underneath it, he finally realizes what he's looking at. The little hatch that leads to the attic of this apartment is open. "How the hell ..." he mumbles, staring up at it. He has never been up there. He knew it was there. He remembers telling his parents and friends that it wasn't weird to have an attic in an apartment and explaining how he fully intended to use it. He thinks he even told people it was "free space", which in this market is practically unheard of. But since then he's never been up inside that area once.

He reaches up and pushes the drywall

hatch, it moves easily. He sets the hatch correctly back into position, sealing off the dark line he'd been looking at on his way to the bathroom. Then he shakes his head and turns, intending to finally make that restroom trip. But, he wonders, how the hell did the hatch get offset in the first place? Are there raccoons up this far north?

Shit. No way he's sleeping now that he's imagining creatures rustling around up in his attic. Maybe it was a bad idea to take a unit with free space he didn't plan to use. Andy moves across the room and snatches up his cell phone, flipping on the flashlight. He looks around for something he can use as a ladder to lift himself into the attic opening. His eyes fall on the bookcase standing along the wall in the hallway mostly underneath the opening but a little to the right. Andy knows he has decent upper-body strength. He can make that work.

He tests his weight on the first shelf, being sure to keep his feet to the outer edges of the shelf. It seems like it will hold. Carefully he steps up onto the second shelf, leaving the ground behind. When it again holds, he pushes the hatch door open and makes his way up.

Andy's first impressions of the space are that it's a bit cooler up here and it smells faintly like mildew, which worries him. He pauses, bare chest up in the attic and feet precariously planted on the top of the bookshelf, long enough to listen for scurrying or movement. Hearing none of that, he uses his arms to pull himself all the way up into the attic.

The attic seems to run the full length of the apartment, which makes sense. He can see the sloping of the roof and a partition that must indicate the unit behind him in the glow of the flashlight, but most of the outer corners are dark shadows to him. Andy has been in attics before, mostly the one above his parent's house in Phoenix. He's familiar with the basic rules: keep your feet on the boards and out of the insulation if you don't want to fall through the ceiling. Also, watch your head on the roof beams.

He carefully steps deeper into the attic toward the direction that would be above his bedroom. Here a piece of wood that has been laid flat over the beams allows him more walking space. Someone before him did use this unit for storage, judging by this larger flat surface. It's sturdy wood and supports his weight so his further steps are more confident. He stands on the platform, holds the flashlight over his head, and turns in a circle taking in everything.

In the corner, he spies a box and some other items that someone before him must have left behind. He makes his way to it. There's a heap of clothes or something fabric beside it. Maybe a blanket someone was leaving behind? He wonders how many previous tenants made use of this space the way he always promised he would.

Halfway to the box, he starts to notice trash

and wrappers scattered about. "What the fuck?" he whispers. Someone was hanging out up here making a mess. It's a wonder he doesn't have raccoons or bugs at this point. Gross. He makes a mental note to come back up here with a trash bag in the light of the morning.

He reaches the box and kneels before it to see what's inside. It seems to be full of papers and maybe printed photographs. He uses his flashlight to illuminate the innards of the box. The first printout he snags his hand on looks like a screenshot of a text message stream. He squints at the page, expecting an autocorrect fail joke or something similar.

Instead, his blood runs colder than the attic temperature. The blue bubbles on the right side of this screen are his messages, he's pretty sure. He sent these. According to the icon at the top of the screen, he sent these to "Bar Chick". He remembers this exchange, although reading over it now he almost feels ashamed. It doesn't look so good out of context.

Him: Hey, remember me? Wanna hook up later?

Her: Uh … like for a coffee or are you asking for a booty call?

Him: Don't gotta be booty. You can suck my <eggplant emoji>

Her: ? Were you an asshole last night too?

Him: Nevermind. I'll find someone else.

Ok, not his finest moment. Who the hell

had this screenshot? Wouldn't it have had to come from his account to show him as the blue-colored boxes? Andy puts the paper in his left hand with the phone and digs back into the box. This time his hand closes around four photographs. He holds them up to the flashlight one at a time. The first one is a picture of him running his normal path around the neighborhood. The second one is a picture of him and some girl with reddish hair at a table for two somewhere. He doesn't immediately recognize the girl or the restaurant but shoves it to the back of the pile anyway. The third picture is Andy at a bar somewhere dark and smoky. He's leaning on the bar, chatting with someone on a bar stool. This someone is blonde, thin, and hot. He doesn't remember her, but this could be any night of the week. He spends a lot of time in bars. The pictures aren't unusual but why, he wonders, are they up in his fucking attic and who took them?

The fourth picture he grabbed out of the box looks like it may have been taken by a security camera. It's grainy and taken from a high angle above him, looking down. It's also in black and white. This image shows a very angry Andy, hand raised as if he's pounding on the door in front of him. He's on a porch he doesn't recognize and his face is contorted in a way that makes him look dangerous and a bit scary. "What the fuck?" Andy whispers. He looks down at the box, which is full of all sorts of things. He wonders how many of these are text messages or photographs of him.

"Where the fuck did this all come from?" he asks the attic.

He hears the footsteps behind him too late to do anything about it. The knife point touches his neck first, almost hesitating as if the killer wants to make sure Andy sees who has been the cause of all this. In that heartbeat, Andy understands how it all fits. The phone calls, the pictures, the text messages. "I fucking knew it," he says.

It is the last words Andy Salinas ever speaks before his throat is cut clean through.

CHAPTER 22

When Sarah's eyes pop open the next morning the first thing she realizes is that she has fallen asleep in her living room. That in itself is not unusual, it's part of the downside to her ability to fall asleep quickly and anywhere. The second thing Sarah notices, however, is that her head is resting on something warm that is rising and falling with the consistency of even breathing. Her heartbeat quickens, signaling her panic even as her nose recognizes the smell of Dan.

She tries to calm herself, taking deep breaths and telling herself that Dan is a good friend and that's all this is. A good friend was comforting her after a bad day. That is normal. It doesn't mean anything.

Still, her panic rises. She changed her plans for him last night. She let him come to her house. She let him sleep at her house. She didn't sleep in her bed or follow her routine. These might seem like small things, but Sarah has to wonder if she's standing on the top of a very slippery slope precariously balanced to fall into the kind of future she swore she would never have.

Her anger wins and she puts her hand on Dan's chest to push herself up to a sitting position. She's not careful and the aggressive pushing motion wakes Dan. "Can you move your feet?" Sarah barks. "I have to pee."

Confused, Dan scoots his feet off the couch until they hit the floor, letting Sarah squeeze out beside him and rush away. She slams her bathroom door and collapses onto the top of the toilet seat. There, she drops her face into her hands. "Shit," she mumbles. This is not good at all. If she comes at Dan too hard, she could lose a good friend. But if she doesn't push him away she's in danger of letting him get too close. "I'll just have to let him down easy," she decides.

She stands and then realizes she still needs to use the restroom. She quickly does her business, washes her hands, splashes her face, and heads back out into the living room. Dan hasn't moved much. He's standing beside the couch, arms crossed over his chest. "Hey," Sarah says, trying to sound friendly. "I think we should talk just to be clear about what this was." She gestures between the two of them.

"Alright," Dan says, drawing out the word to show his hesitation. "I thought we did that already. I was just here as a concerned friend, remember?"

"So, we're clear? This is not a thing. We are not a couple."

Dan shakes his head. "You keep feeling like you need to say that. Am I missing something?"

"Jesus, Dan." Sarah points to the couch. "We fucking slept all curled up together on my couch last night. This isn't some romcom. I can't do that shit."

His voice rises to match hers. "What, exactly, are you afraid of? Me sleeping here last night let you relax enough to stop being worried about your safety and get some sleep. I didn't have to spend the night tossing and turning in my bed worried that some asshole was going to come after you. It was just logistics. What are you so worried about?"

Sarah throws her hands up. "I have to keep doing what I've always done, don't you get it? I have to go to class. I have to go to work. I can't call in sick and change everything just because you're worried about me. I have to keep the plan going."

He takes a small step closer to her, his hand out in her direction. He takes a deep breath and intentionally lowers his voice. "Why? You took one night off work to get some rest after you went through some seriously bad shit. You hung out with a friend you could trust because you were worried. It's normal. Also, you already took the night off before you even talked to me. How is this my fault?"

"You're not getting it. Behavior like this isn't me. Behavior like this is how you end up dropping out of college, chasing someone else's dream, and raising kids you never fucking wanted."

Dan drops his hand to his thigh with an audible slap. "You're projecting a lot of bullshit onto this conversation right now, Sarah. We're friends. I was worried about you. That's it."

She plants her hand on her hip and tilts her head. "So you're saying if I threw myself at you right now, you'd turn me down?"

Dan groans. "That's not fair."

"It is fair. If I told you I wanted to drop out of college right now and run away with you somewhere, you can't honestly tell me you wouldn't consider it for a second."

"I'd say no, Sarah. We both need to finish school. We're not running off."

"But you'd consider it for a second before you answered. Worse, if I slept with you first and then offered, you'd consider it longer. By the time we'd slept together for months, it'd be harder to convince you to stay. That's what happens. It's small at first and it doesn't seem like a big deal. Then you're raising children in some really shitty conditions and wishing you'd had the strength to chase your dreams."

Dan opens his mouth and then snaps it closed again. He reaches behind him and grabs his jacket off the back of the couch. When he looks at Sarah again, she sees sadness on his face. He shakes his head slowly. "You have a lot of baggage," he says in a quiet voice. "I'd love to help you with all of it but you'd have to realize I'm not the enemy. We are friends. I care about you, Sarah, and that's not a bad thing."

He spins to the front door of her apartment, putting his hand on the doorknob. "Call me when you decide you need a friend again, alright? Because I'm going to be there for you whenever you're ready to work this shit out. I'm not that easy to push away."

He pulls the door open and steps onto the porch. Then he pauses like he's waiting for Sarah to tell him to stop, waiting for her to apologize. She almost does. She can feel the urge to do it tugging at her. But, in the end, Dan pulls the front door closed and Sarah remains frozen right where she was.

Sarah stands in the living room, forcing herself to not move to the window. She wants to be sure he'll drive away but she also doesn't trust herself not to fling the door open and yell at him to come back in. She wants to apologize for being ridiculous but also tell him that she has every right to be ridiculous. Frustrated, she lets out a grunt and stomps her foot. "Enough," she tells herself. "Back to the plan."

She shakes off the stress of the morning, promises herself she won't think about Dan, and locks the door to her apartment. Then she heads into her bedroom to strip off her clothes and get in the shower. She cranks the water up as high as she can stand it and uses it to wash away all the thoughts she promised herself she wouldn't think about Dan. Then, thoroughly cleansed but still frustrated, she gets dressed and grabs food.

Today the plan will be simple: stick to the schedule, don't think about Dan, don't think about Keith's body.

She locks the door on her way out of the apartment and takes her car to class. Today luck is not on her side, forcing her to park in the back of the lot. She slams her door and starts walking toward the building, moving fast so she's not late to class. There are a lot of people milling about today, almost enough people to take her mind off the last thing she saw inside the building her class used to be in before they moved it.

She shakes her head. No, she will not think about Keith or the metallic smell of blood. Shakes her head again. No. Focus. Back to normal.

Things in class feel comfortably normal,

which is a huge relief. Sarah loses herself in the careful notes and lecture. For the ninety minutes she sits in the hall listening to the professor, she finds she doesn't have to keep reminding herself what she's not supposed to be thinking of. Instead, her brain is consumed with science. So much so that she's sorry when the professor puts down the marker and brushes his hands together declaring that "all for today" and dismisses them.

She packs up everything she had brought out of her bag and stands, more determined than ever to focus on her day and ignore anything else that might get out of her way. Today is all about sticking to the schedule and keeping everything normal.

On the walk to her second class of the day, she keeps her head up but ignores everyone. If someone were to ask her twenty questions about the people she passed on the way to class, Sarah is pretty sure she'd get exactly zero of them right. She is in her own head, which she's been finding herself doing a lot lately. Everything is spiraling out of her control and the only thing she knows how to do is put herself back into her routine and get herself back on the right path. No more distractions.

The second class turns out to be a lot more boring than the first. She takes the notes but her brain wanders in between each careful line. Slowly her page fills with random doodles and sketches that have nothing to do with the subject matter.

When the professor dismisses them, she grabs the edge of the notebook to slam it closed. That's when she notices she's managed to doodle Dan's name in the margin of the notes. She grabs her pen and scribbles it out so hard that the paper tears.

In her third class, she uses the notepad app on her phone to keep herself from being capable of doodling.

When the third class ends, Sarah stops at the trunk of her car to switch into her work polo shirt before jumping into the driver's seat. She reaches into her purse for a granola bar and cannot find one. Irritation floods her body as she checks the digital clock on the dash and realizes she won't even have time to stop to grab an alternate snack. She is staring down the barrel of a five-hour shift with no food. The last thing she ate was the bag of dry cereal she grabbed from her apartment this morning on the way out.

She parks in the employee lot and practically runs to the building where she swipes her badge to clock in. Then, following the routine she's carefully cultivated, she slows down for the walk to the section. For the first time, she realizes she will have to face Dan again today. What are the odds that he was so embarrassed by her outburst this morning that he would call in? Not likely. Fine, she will face him like a big girl. They can be friends but last night went too far. No more dinners, no more dates, no more sleeping on her couch.

When she gets to the hardware section, there are no people at all. No employees in their obvious polo shirts, no customers milling about. Sarah stashes her purse under the counter and logs into the computer. She pulls up the sales history for this morning and sees two things in the report. One, it's been a slow day. Two, Dan is definitely at work. As recently as fourteen minutes ago he was ringing up customers at this terminal. She logs out of the report and looks around, almost expecting him to pop around the corner again wielding some sort of weapon or shield.

Instead, her eyes fall on a small piece of paper on the counter with her name on it. She picks up the note, finding a bag of chips underneath it. "Friends don't let friends starve. Did you even eat today? You don't eat when you're stressed."

Sarah laughs and tosses the note in the trash can. She opens the chips, takes one out, and pops it in her mouth. Only then does Dan appear, as if by magic, from an aisle across from her. "You didn't eat, did you?"

"I'd love to tell you that I did and you don't know me as well as you think you do," she says. "But no, I did not."

"Well, then you're welcome."

"Thank you," Sarah says. But Dan is already gone, back into the aisle he came out of.

CHAPTER 23

"I'm so glad you're back," Alicia greets, reaching up to pull Sarah into a hug. Sarah lets herself be hugged, feeling the squeeze of Alicia's arms around her shoulders. When she pulls away, there's concern on Alicia's sweet face. "Are you sure it's not too soon for you to be back here?"

"It's not too soon," Sarah assures her, dropping her bag behind the desk. "I need to be here. I need to be working." She looks at the monitor, checking to make sure her car is parked in a visible section of the screen, even though she knew it was. "What have I missed?"

Alicia leans on the counter beside Sarah. "Not much. We think Marino went on a date because he was acting really weird about this girl who called him. Greg has been asking about you a lot, he seems to think he pissed you off and he won't tell us why. Oh, and Rocky arrested the guy who was stealing bikes from the campus bike racks."

Sarah nods along to the gossip as if she cares. She can tell Alicia is avoiding talking about the murders. It's practically humming off her body, the need to spout this particular juicy piece of gossip, whatever it is. Sarah doesn't want anyone walking on eggshells around her. That always succeeds only in making her think about the thing she's not supposed to be thinking about more instead of less. So when Alicia says "Is it ok if I fill you in on what's been happening with the big case or is that something you want me to avoid?" Sarah simply says, "Go for it. Tell me all about it."

"Alright. Craig, the first victim, was sleeping with a married woman." She claps her hands together. "That means the woman's husband is an actual suspect and he's supposed to be coming in for questioning tomorrow or something. Can you believe this? The whole case could come down to the jealous husband."

Sarah rolls her eyes. "That sounds like a

crime show plot."

"Exactly. True crime. The shit that really happens. Our little town is becoming real news. I heard it was on the local stations in Phoenix last night. It's all anyone can talk about."

"Great," Sarah says. "Just what we want to be known for."

"Whatever, the news dug up something we didn't know. Keith was also accused of sexual assault twice while he was in high school. So both of these guys aren't as squeaky clean as they seemed."

"Accusations don't mean anything," Sarah points out. "They could've been false or it could be a lie now. We shouldn't be saying these things. We have no proof. Plus, I thought you liked the husband for the first murder. Why would the husband kill Keith?"

"I don't know," Alicia whines. "Maybe Keith saw something or knew something about the killer."

"Then why would it be relevant to the fact that Keith was accused of sexual assault in high school?" Sarah pushes. "This is why we should leave the actual detecting of clues to the officers and stay the heck out of it." She spins her chair to face the computer screen.

Alicia jumps to her feet and sighs. "Whatever, I'm just saying they're not the good people everyone thought they were at first. I mean this third guy —"

Sarah spins her chair back so quickly that it stops Alicia mid-sentence. "Did you say third guy?"

"Yeah, you didn't hear?" Alicia covers her mouth. "Oh, shit. I'm sorry. I thought you would've heard the news. There have been radio and TV reporters calling all day. I figured you'd heard somewhere."

"I didn't." Sarah suddenly feels like there's not enough blood in her head. Her eyes are unfocused and she's very glad she's sitting down. "When? What do we know?"

"Are you sure you want —"

"Tell me," Sarah barks.

Alicia kneels in front of Sarah on the floor so they're closer to eye level. "Right, ok. Stop me if it's too much." She pushes her hair out of her face and focuses on Sarah. "A man was killed last night in his apartment. A neighbor heard a commotion that sounded like it was in the ceiling so he called the police for a well check. They entered the apartment and found the attic hatch open. When they went up into the attic they found the body."

Sarah's eyes close and tears leak out of the corners of her eyes. Alicia continues in a softer voice. "He lived alone. I don't think they know how anyone got access to his apartment yet."

"Oh my god," Sarah whispers, "Why does this keep happening?"

"I'm not sure." Alicia rubs Sarah's arms. "Are you alright, sweetie? You seem hurt by this.

Do you need to talk to someone?"

"It's too much. These people just keep dying. I mean, shit, I found one of their bodies. This is too much." She shakes her head. "I can't even explain why this feels so heavy. I just … I just need it to stop."

"I know, honey. I know." Alicia keeps up the rubbing motion on Sarah's arms. "If it's any consolation, this Andy guy sounded like a real asshole. I don't think anyone thought he was a good guy."

Sarah's head snaps up. "Andy. Did you say Andy?" It has to be a coincidence. There are probably hundreds of Andy's on campus. Certainly, there's another Andy who happens to be a total asshole. Greg's friend can't have the market cornered on that. Fuck. Greg. "Did anyone call Greg?" Sarah asks. "Does he know?"

Alicia seems shocked by the question. She pulls her hand back and rocks back on her heels. "I have no idea. Why would we do that? What am I missing?"

"He has a friend named Andy. I mean, I'm sure that's a common name but we should probably check, right? That seems like a nice thing to do?"

"Yeah, I can. Would that make you feel better?"

Sarah imagines Greg laughing about this, telling her that it's awful someone died but his friend is fine. She nods. "Call him." She waits while Alicia looks up a phone number and uses the handset from the office to dial. Alicia is very adept at using a quiet voice when she's on the phone to keep conversations private. Sarah hears none of the conversation. When Alicia hangs up the phone and turns her attention back to Sarah, her face is a careful mask, showing nothing.

"Did you know his friend Andy?" Alicia asks.

That's all it takes for Sarah to know the truth. First Craig, who she didn't know at all. Then Keith, who she'd only met a few times even though she had a class with him. Now Andy, who she had interacted with. They were getting closer to her and they weren't stopping.

Sarah pushes herself out of the chair and walks out of the building. She stands in the cold, crisp air and breathes. When that doesn't calm her down, she grabs her phone and hits a number almost on autopilot. It only rings twice before he answers. "Sarah? What's up?"

"Dan, fuck, there's been another murder. When we were snuggling on my couch last night someone killed Greg's friend Andy. I can't …" her voice trails off, dissolving in the tears that are suddenly falling.

"Where are you?" he asks. When she doesn't immediately answer, he repeats it in an angrier tone. "Sarah, where the fuck are you?"

"Work."

"Don't move. I'll be there in ten."

By the time Dan arrives at the police station, squealing his tires into the closest parking spot he can find and running the rest of the way, Sarah's tears have stopped. She's pacing up and down the sidewalk, her cell phone in her hand. She's also shaking from the cold but she doesn't appear to notice that. Dan holds out his hands like you would approach a stray dog, afraid to spook her. "Sarah?"

"Oh my God, did you hear about it before I called you?" She rushes to his side, tugging on his arm. "Did you hear about the murder on the news? I've been thinking about it and I didn't turn on the radio or anything all day. Even when I got in my car to drive to the mall I only listened to the music on my phone when it connected to the car. But the store usually has the radio on, right? Why didn't I hear anything about it there?"

Dan reaches for her hand, squeezing it in what he hopes is a comforting gesture. "The news we listen to at the store is national. They try to keep things light and upbeat. It's why retail establishments all use it. I can't imagine them talking about a murder. Hey, can we go inside or something? It's cold out here and your fingers feel like ice cubes."

"Yeah. Sure." She makes no move to head into the police station. Instead, she continues to stare unfocused out into the parking lot, her mind working overtime. Dan uses his hold on her hand to steer her toward the door. She follows as if on autopilot.

Alicia buzzes them in without Dan having to hit the button. Once inside, Dan points to a chair in the lobby. "Sit," he says.

Sarah does, again without really focusing on anything. Dan turns his attention to Alicia. "How long has she been sort of unfocused like this?" he asks.

"Maybe five minutes," Alicia says. "I didn't mean to freak her out. I thought she knew about the third victim and I didn't know he knew Greg."

She looks like she might burst into tears herself at any second. "I didn't mean to hurt her. Is she ok? Did she know that Andy guy or whatever?"

"Not really. I think she met him once."

"They're not, like, friends or anything. Right? I mean, he seems sort of like an asshole."

Sarah's eyes snap to focus suddenly, landing on Alicia. "I'm going to need you to stop saying that. I'm going to need you to stop talking about this case at all." Her voice is a little harsh but Dan hears the pleading edge to it. That edge tells him she's barely holding it together. He sighs and sits down on the floor in front of Sarah.

"Hey," he says in a quiet voice. "This is not good, I think you can see that. I want you to listen to me for a second and remember that I'm a friend, ok?" Sarah nods. "I think you need some serious time off. Call both bosses and take time. Email professors and find a way to work remotely or whatever. My buddy's parents own a cabin out in the woods. We can get away from this news and drama and just reset."

Sarah opens her mouth and Dan holds up a hand. "I know you're going to tell me you can't afford to derail the plan." Her mouth snaps shut because she was about to say exactly that. "I'm not asking you to. I'm asking you to consider how many times in the last two weeks I've seen you completely fall apart. That's not like you. You keep telling me you need to stay the course but this isn't the course. You calling me five minutes into your shift at this station to cry about a guy you met once is not the course. You need a reset. You need to find the path again. I'm just offering to help you. I don't think the way you've been trying to do it is working."

Sarah closes her eyes and takes a deep breath. The names run through her brain: Craig, Keith, Andy. Craig, Keith, Andy. Craig, Keith, Andy. She shakes her head a little, trying to turn them off so she can think. The plan has always been the same. She gets a degree, she gets a job, she works hard, she makes a life for herself. But maybe Dan is right. If she keeps going like this, taking time off and crying on her shift she's going to get fired. That's definitely not in the plan.

Her eyes pop open. "Shit, I'm so sorry. You're supposed to be off already. You can go," she says to Alicia. "I'm sorry."

Alicia waves her hand. "No, don't worry. Oh my god, don't worry. I already called Ted. We're going to cover for you and Greg. Ted's excited about the extra hours. He needs the money. We've got this figured out." She crosses to the little wall dividing the work space she's occupying from the lobby where Sarah and Dan are sitting, resting her arms on the counter. "Honestly, I think maybe the boy toy here has a good plan. Go hang in the forest away from everything. Stay safe. Call me if anything goes chaotic or if the boy toy here turns out to be dangerous. Maybe it has merit, Sarah. I'm just saying you've been upset lately. It's not like you."

Sarah stands up from the chair so suddenly that Dan has to throw his arms behind him to keep from toppling backward. She barely risks a look at him before saying "I'm going to the restroom to think by myself for a second. You two stay here." It stays quiet in the room behind her as she does exactly that.

Once she's behind the closed door, Dan stands up off the floor. He crosses the room and offers his hand to Alicia. "I'm Dan," he says. "In case you'd rather have a name than continue to refer to me as the boy toy, a nickname I sort of enjoy despite it being decidedly false in this case."

Alicia takes the hand, shaking politely. "I'm Alicia, the manager here. I've heard your name before, I think, but only in passing. You think you're important, I suppose?"

Dan shrugs, dropping his hand down to rest on the counter between them. "I don't think that, no. But she is a friend and she does tend to call me in stressful situations."

Alicia nods. "There's been a lot of those lately."

"True."

"Are you the cause of any of these stressful situations, Mr. Dan?"

"Are you asking if I'm killing people in Flagstaff, Ms. Manager lady?"

Alicia shakes her head. "I don't think that's the case. I'm just wondering if you've caused

Sarah any unnecessary grief lately. I don't think it's only the murders doing that. Sarah is a good girl with a good future in front of her. I'd hate to see it getting trashed because of some guy." She leans her elbow on the counter and rests her chin in her hand, bringing her face closer to him. "You know what I'm saying?"

Dan rolls his eyes dramatically. "Honestly an idiot would know what you're saying. Here's what I'm saying. Sarah is a big girl and she can speak for herself. She doesn't need you telling me to treat her right. Thank you for your concern though."

The bathroom door opens again, spilling Sarah back out into the lobby area. She has washed her face, the pink nature of the cheeks showing off just how much she scrubbed. Her eyes are still a little swollen and red-rimmed from the earlier crying, but she looks much more like herself.

"Alright, here's what's going to happen," she announces to the room. "I'm going to take a week off. Just one week. During that time I am going to have my phone but not take work calls at all. I am going to work on my classwork remotely so I don't fall behind. If anyone has any ideas on how to get professors to agree to this particular part of the plan, I'm willing to listen to them. Then, at the end of this week, I will be back and I will no longer be accepting anything in the way of small breakdowns. I will have my shit together, as they say. This is the new plan."

"We're not talking about how you can't will yourself to just stop having breakdowns?" Dan says, quietly.

"We're not talking about that at all," Sarah says. "That is not the point. The point is I'm trying things your way so you need to stop arguing with me. I can't keep doing what I was doing. It's not working. So, instead, we're being drastic."

"If you don't want Dan to take you but you need drastic, say the word. I'll take you myself," Alicia offers.

Sarah smiles. "No, but I appreciate you."

Alicia offers a thumbs-up and moves to sit in the chair in front of the monitor. "I'll take care of the time-off request right now. I'll submit it and approve it before you're even out of the parking lot." She looks up from the computer only briefly to glance at Sarah. "Seriously though, if anything at all feels off while you're there, you text me."

"Promise," Sarah agrees. "Also, thank you."

"No problem, girl. I'm looking out for you." Her fingers fly over the keyboard even as Sarah retrieves her purse and heads for the parking lot.

At the door, Sarah turns her attention to Dan. "Are we really doing this?"

"It sounds like it."

"I didn't even ask you if you can take this kind of time off. Are you sure this is —"

"Don't even finish that sentence," Dan says.

"I'm going with you. We'll be alright. We just need a reset." He grabs her upper arm with just enough pressure to stop her from walking to the car at a fast pace. "Hey, listen, I also want to tell you that this isn't about this morning. This isn't some stupid trick I played to try and get closer to you. I just really think you need this reset."

"I can't believe I agreed to this shit," Sarah said. "I actually let you talk me into this." She smiles. "But I do agree with you." She reaches up and brushes his cheek lightly. "Believe it or not, I can think for myself. This might have been your suggestion but it's my decision and it's made."

She goes up on her toes, bringing her lips so close to Dan's that he can feel her breath on his lips when she speaks again. "I'm going to kiss you now." Then his heartbeat quickens when she does exactly that. It's a small kiss, but the brush of her lips sets fire to him. He realizes at that moment that being just friends with this girl is like bringing a match in your pocket when you go into a fireworks factory. In other words, probably not a good idea.

CHAPTER 25

It takes Sarah the entire car ride to her apartment to convince Dan she will be fine on her own for the night. They agreed to sleep with their phones within reach and that Dan will pick her up first thing the next morning.

Sarah uses her time alone in her apartment to pack, as promised, and to let her mind consider this particular idea again at length. At the beginning of this school year, before all the death, Sarah would never have taken this time off and run away to some cabin in the woods. Never.

Never ever.

But she also would never have found herself unable to get through a day without thinking about dead bodies, the smell of blood, and how much she hated that Andy guy immediately. She realizes that's part of what is making this one harder, Andy was an ass. Of course, that is what Alicia tried to point out to her. But does that excuse his death? No, of course not. He might have been awful but he didn't deserve to die. Not like that.

Sarah's phone chirps with an incoming text message. She swipes it open to see a message from Dan, alerting her that the knock on the door will be him. She laughs a little at the idea that she would need that warning. Then the knock comes and she practically jumps to the ceiling. "OK, maybe I did need the warning," she mumbles.

She wrenches the door open and feels her heart pitter-patter in her chest. Dan has put on a pullover sweater that perfectly matches his eyes and it absolutely works on him. She notices he has stubble across his chin like he could use a shave, telling her he's been distracted in his own routines lately. He's also looking incredibly stern and serious. "Ready?" he asks, his voice devoid of his usual warmth.

Sarah holds up the handle of the bag in her hand. "Ready as I'm going to get."

"Good." Dan turns and stomps down her staircase, leaving her feeling colder than she's ever felt with the weather. She locks the door to her apartment behind her and follows him, tossing her bag in the bed of the truck before jumping into the passenger seat. Dan pulls out onto the road in total silence.

The sun is barely coming up now, bathing the treetops surrounding the area in a beautiful warm glow. Sarah leans her head on the passenger door and enjoys the view for a while. The radio plays softly in the background, something she doesn't need to focus on, but still the absence of Dan's voice starts to feel heavy.

As they pull out of town and onto a main highway, Sarah sits up and looks over at him. She's sure he felt the shift of her weight in the car, something he would normally be in tune with. But he keeps staring straight ahead as if he needs to focus. She glances toward the front of the truck to find minimal traffic and plenty of space for him. Frowning, she looks back at him again. This time she turns fully in her seat, pulling her leg up on the bench seat to get the right angle. He still doesn't react or move.

"You're ignoring me," Sarah points out.

"What?" Still focused on the road. Still refusing to look at her.

"Oh my God, you really are. What the hell did I do? I agreed with your plan. I'm taking time off. I'm here. Are you having regrets about this because if you are you better just pull over right now so we can figure this out."

Dan sighs, the sound loud in the car. "I'm just trying to keep things friendly," he says, his voice the exact opposite of light and friendly.

Sarah blinks rapidly which, in her opinion, would be a perfect way to illustrate her shock if he would just look at her. "Ignoring me is like the opposite of friendly." She smacks him lightly on the upper arm. "I don't think you've ever ignored me a day in your life before this and we've been friends for a long time."

He actually jerks away from her a little. Enough for her to notice. Enough for it to hurt. "Can we talk about something else?" he asks. "I'm still sorting through some things in my brain and I just need to get that sorted before we talk about this." He risks a look in her direction. "Please."

Sarah nods. "Fine, but we come back to this discussion."

"Deal."

Sarah turns the right way in her seat and flips the volume up on the radio. It's quiet again while the song plays but then the song ends and a DJ's voice fills the car. "It's time for our news at the top of the hour," the voice announces. "This morning the investigation into the deaths of three young men from Flagstaff continues. Flagstaff police tell us all avenues are being explored although they have no suspects in custody at this time. They ask anyone who has information related to these deaths to please call the hotline. We've posted the number on our website."

Sarah turns the knob nearest her, changing the station. Then she turns the volume down. "Well, they brought it up. What's your opinion on the murders?" she asks.

Dan takes a slow deep breath as if considering if this is something he'd rather discuss than his strange behavior. "Does it feel like they're getting closer to your inner circle?" he asks.

"What? That's ridiculous," Sarah says, although she had been thinking the same thing when she first heard Andy's name in that police station. "I didn't even know these guys."

"But you'd met Keith and you met Andy. You didn't even like Andy. It's like someone listened to your opinion of him. It's just weird."

"I didn't tell anyone about my opinion of him except for you. Are you trying to tell me you did this?"

This earns her a long, judgmental look from the driver before his eyes snap back to the road. "First of all, you know me better than that. Second of all, I was with you when Andy was killed."

"That's my point. It can't be because they were trying to do me a favor, or whatever fucked up thing you were just trying to say because no one knew. Also, that's a terrible way to get someone's attention." She shakes her head, ready to let the conversation go. She starts to think about other possible topics.

In the cupholder, Dan's phone buzzes. He looks down at it. "Want to see who that is?"

Sarah picks it up and tilts the screen in her direction. "Unknown."

"Ignore it."

She hits the side button, silencing the call. Then she drops it back where it was.

"Greg knew," Dan says.

"What?"

"Greg knew. You told him what an ass you thought his friend was."

Sarah's mouth falls open in shock. Technically, he's right. But is he really saying what she thinks he is saying? "Are you seriously going there? Andy was his friend."

"Hear me out," Dan says. "He works at the police station which gives him information he might not have otherwise, like Keith's phone number and name. Plus being in contact with the officers all the time might help them see him as normal, which will help him stay off the radar. He knew where Andy lived." He points at Sarah. "And he has a thing for you, which he's made clear. The guy's been trying to get you in bed since you met him. He needed something big to draw your attention."

"That's a huge stretch. One, murder would not be OK with me and anyone who has spent even ten minutes with me would know that. Second, even if your bullshit explanation works for Andy he was the third victim. How does this all work for the other two? Again, I'll remind you that I never even met Craig."

"It was just a theory."

"It was just you accusing a guy I work with of murdering people in his spare fucking time," Sarah points out. "Changing the subject, whose truck is this?"

"My roommates. The cabin belongs to his family too."

"What do we know about this roommate? Is he safe?"

"You're worried?"

"Look, your bullshit theory involves this killer getting closer to me. I'm just saying that only one person in recent months has spent the night in my apartment and that guy is about to take some time out in the woods with me with no one else around. Maybe you've been spending too much time worrying about my safety when we should've been worried about yours. I repeat, how safe is this roommate?"

Dan is quiet for a beat. Sarah hopes it's because he's considering what she said. She's not worried about herself, not really. No one is after her and Dan's theory is bullshit. She may have felt some worry about it last night but in the light of the fresh day, she's sure these murders have nothing to do with her. But Dan is exactly the kind of person this killer seems to be targeting. Cute, twenty-something college guys. He should be worried.

"He's safe," Dan finally says. "I've known him a long time and he's never been anything other than nice. Plus, I think we were both home the morning you found Keith."

"Good." Sarah settles back against the seat again. "Maybe this conversational thread wasn't so hot either," she says. "It's done nothing for my anxiety."

"Yeah, sorry about that," he says. "I didn't mean to make things awkward this morning. I think I just realized being friends with you is important to me but sometimes it's difficult to remember that you don't want more than that." He turns his head and smiles at her. Sarah feels her heart melt a little with the gesture. She much prefers it when Dan is not giving her the silent treatment. "Maybe we shouldn't be snuggling on couches or kissing for a bit if what you want is to be friends." He winces and turns back to the road. "I can't believe I just said that."

"We can do that. Thank you for making it sound like it's a respected mutual choice instead of you throwing down the hammer or the ultimatum. I'll think about what I want, I promise."

"That's better than I hoped for," he says. "Thanks for not getting mad."

Dan's phone buzzes again. Without waiting for him to prompt her, Sarah reaches for it and tips it so she can see the screen. "Unknown number again," she says. She hits the ignore button.

"That's weird," Dan says. "I have a call filter, I almost never get those. Here, turn it this way to unlock it." Sarah does as requested and Dan's face unlocks the phone. "Click on recent calls. Are they local numbers?"

Sarah clicks on the button and looks at the two red missed calls. "Yeah, local area codes. Why?"

"Just curious. Maybe I'll answer one later and make sure it's not someone from work or something that isn't in my phone. Don't delete the numbers, just in case. Did they leave a message?"

Sarah looks at the voicemail icon. No red numbers. "Nope."

Dan shrugs. "Whatever. Guess it wasn't important."

Sarah drops the phone back in the cupholder and turns up the radio. "Guess not."

CHAPTER 26

Dan steers the truck down the dirt driveway and parks in front of a decent-sized cabin. Sarah fights her urge to get out of the truck and stretch her limbs after being confined to the cab of the truck for the drive. Instead, she leans forward and looks around. "I want to check every door and window," she says. "Where is the nearest neighbor we could go to in case of an emergency?"

"I saw a house on the way in," Dan says, pointing to the east. "I'm guessing they're the closest.

"Perfect." Sarah opens her door and steps out into the crisp air. She's used to the cold but something about the forest air makes it colder here. Dan heads immediately to the front door, using a key on the same ring as the truck keys to open everything. Sarah notes that there are two locks on the door but they use the same key.

Sarah pulls her bag from the bed of the truck and follows Dan through the doorway. Just inside, she lays her bag down. "I'm going back for my bag," Dan says. "Be right back."

Sarah takes the opportunity to look around. She's entered into a large dining room on a pretty open floor plan. To her right is a big dining table set with six chairs in front of a window. Beyond that she can see through the opening of a door left ajar that there's a bedroom. Straight ahead of her, across the dining room, is a set of stairs leading up. Beyond the stairs is a seating area where Sarah spots a couch. That room appears to have windows on at the length of the back wall. From here she can see an open expanse of forest through the windows. There are no blinds or curtains. "That might be a problem," she mumbles. She knows from the fact that the door was in the middle of the house that there must be more to the left, but a large wall prevents her from seeing that.

Dan comes in, dropping his bag beside hers and rubbing his hands together. "Cold out there," he says. "Brent tells me there's a fireplace in the living room and upstairs. I think I'll get them lit to warm the place up."

Sarah pushes the front door shut with her foot and spins the locks. "How many rooms are there?" she calls to Dan, who is making his way to the room with the couch and lots of windows.

"Um, one down here and three upstairs I think. It's a lot."

"I'm going to look around." The first place she heads to is the bedroom she saw on the other side of the dining table. This room is large. The king-sized bed on the far wall barely takes up any of the space. There's a dresser and a closet, two nightstands, and a bathroom. All of this space is mostly empty of personal belongings. Sarah finds some basic self-care things, like shampoo and a hair dryer, but nothing overly personal. She pulls the door shut on her way out of the room. At the bottom of the stairs, she turns the corner to find Dan. He's on his knees in front of the fireplace, coaxing flames. "Who lives here?" Sarah asks. "It looks empty."

"They rent it out on Airbnb or whatever when they're not using it." He looks up from the fire. "Guess they're not using it right now."

The living room is huge too, Sarah notes. Besides the couch there are two recliners, a coffee table, two end tables, a TV atop a small entertainment center, and the fireplace Dan is working on. "This place is enormous."

"Yeah, he warned me it was a little big for two people." Dan stands, the fire now glowing. He replaces the grate and holds his hands in front of it. "There, that should help. Should I light the one upstairs, too?"

Sarah looks up to the landing at the top of the stairs, which is pretty dark even now. Likely that means the windows are a downstairs problem. "There's a bedroom and a bathroom down here," she says. "I was just in there. It's plenty big enough for both of us. I can sleep on the floor or whatever."

"Let's check upstairs out. We'll make sure it's all safe and sound, close up all the doors, and then we can stay down here the whole time. I don't think we'll have to go up there again," Dan offers.

"Perfect."

For the next fifteen minutes, the pair explores every inch of the house. In addition to the three bedrooms Dan knew were upstairs, all of which are a much more normal size than the one Sarah already found, there is also a bathroom and a cute table and four chairs on the loft at the top of the stairs. All the rooms appear as empty as the downstairs one in terms of closets and cabinets. They make sure all the windows are locked and pull all the doors shut.

Downstairs they find a kitchen with an entrance to a garage and an entrance out onto the back patio. Again they lock all the windows and doors. Finally, they step out onto the back patio. It runs the length of the house. Besides the door into the kitchen there are two others, one into the downstairs bedroom and one into the living room. Sarah checks all of them, jiggling the handle to make sure none of them open.

Satisfied, she drops into one of the many chairs outside. "Seems safe enough," she says. "The windows make me a little nervous but I'm sure it will be fine." There is nothing out here as far as she can see. No houses, no other people. Trees and, presumably, animals. It's quiet and beautiful in a way she didn't even know she craved. Despite the reason they are here, she starts to feel calmer and more relaxed.

"There's a camera out here somewhere," Dan offers. "I'm supposed to ask Brent for the code to log in. He said it has a motion thing and can come to my phone. That would let us know if something weird was going on even when it's dark out here. Want me to ask him for it?"

"Yeah, totally." Sarah stands up. "I also have this app that's supposed to tell you if there are any devices connected to the wifi. I used it once to kick my neighbor off my wifi before I changed the password. We can run it before you call Brent and make sure they're all legit."

Dan dials the number and the screen fills with the roommate's face when the call connects. "Hey man, how's the cabin?" Brent asks. "Everything look good?"

"It looks great. Can you give us the wifi information?"

Sarah connects her phone using his prompting and then opens the app. "OK, so I'm seeing four devices connected. One has TV in the device name so I can figure that one out. One is my phone. One says ZWayz with a number after it," Sarah says.

"Right, that's the backyard camera I told you about," Brent says. "There's an app for it. I'll text you the login information." He appears to be staring directly at them as he uses the device to maneuver to his messages and send off the promised information. A banner on top of Dan's screen shows the message has come through.

"I'll log in when we get off the phone," Dan says. "Thanks."

"The fourth device is a Circle Doorbell," Sarah says.

"Yup, and my parents have the only login for that. If it rings while you're there it will go to them. They can talk to anyone through the app. If you plan to have anyone visit while you're there, you should probably plan to watch for them and just open the door when they arrive. My parents are weird about letting people in."

"That's actually good," Dan says. On the top of the phone screen another call flashes. Sarah sees it says an unknown number but that's all she sees before Dan clicks to ignore it. "No one is coming to visit, man," Dan continues. "We're good. Thanks so much for this. I owe you."

"No problem. If you need anything, just call."

They say their goodbyes and end the call. "You missed a call," Sarah says.

"Unknown." Dan shrugs. "Not worth worrying about."

"Might have been someone from work. You were going to answer one, remember?"

"Oh shit, forgot. I'll get the next one. Don't worry about it. Are you good?" Dan asks.

"Login to that app and I will be," Sarah says.

Dan clicks on the app he downloaded before they left, types in the information Brent sent him, and opens the live video feed. "There we are," he shows Sarah. "Wave to the camera."

Satisfied, they head inside. Sarah locks the doors behind them and heads directly to the kitchen. "I'm starving and there's no food," Sarah whines.

"Oh, I put a box of stuff in the truck. I'll be right back." Dan disappears out the front door and reappears holding a cardboard box. "I didn't bring anything that required refrigeration but I have things we can snack on." He lines the large island with boxes of cookies, chips, and crackers. Then out comes a few cans of food, a can opener, a bottle of whiskey, and a six-pack of soda. "Brent said we can drink the water here so I just brought the other stuff I had at home."

Sarah grabs a can of soup and the can opener. She moves around the kitchen opening drawers until she finds a pan and a spoon. "Perfect," she says. While she busies herself making soup, Dan heads to the living room and flicks on the television for a little background noise.

His phone vibrates. He pulls it out of his pocket to see an alert from the backyard app. He looks out the windows even as he's clicking the notification. There's nothing back there as far as the eye can see. He watches the video, seeing much of the same thing.

He texts Brent. *Motion sensors are sensitive?*

Shit, yeah, sorry. Sometimes the breeze sets them off. I always turn the motion alerts off. Drives me nuts.

Dan looks up at Sarah, who is distracted by the soup. He knows she wouldn't approve of him turning off the motion alerts but, honestly, no one even knows they're here. There's no point in freaking her out every five minutes because it's a windy day and the app keeps saying she should be worried. He clicks the little gear to open the settings and turns off the motion alerts. He'll just have to remember to be vigilant.

Dan wakes up the next morning before Sarah, likely because sleeping on the floor is significantly more uncomfortable than sleeping on a mattress. He folds up the blanket he'd been using and stacks it and the three pillows he'd found on the side of the bedroom near the window. He's careful to do all this quietly to avoid disturbing Sarah who had tossed and turned for a while last night and could probably use the sleep. Then he slips into the bathroom, pulls the door shut as quietly as possible, and takes care of his hygiene needs.

Sarah is still asleep, curled on her side and looking rather angelic when he slips back through the bedroom. He heads for the kitchen where he looks through everything he brought with him. He berates himself for not thinking of bringing a cooler with things like eggs, milk, or butter in it. He's not a terrible cook but when you give yourself nothing to work with you're setting yourself up for failure. He grabs his phone and shoots off a text to Brent, hoping he's not waking him up. *How far is the nearest grocery store?*

Then he pulls up the app he quieted last night and checks for updates. The motion sensor went off at least a dozen times last night. He sighs and opens the oldest one, which went off shortly after they went into the bedroom to get some sleep. He watches the entire thirty-second clip and sees nothing unusual, just trees moving in the breeze.

An answering text comes in from Brent. *About twenty minutes out but there's a freezer in the garage that might have some stuff you can help yourself to.*

"Awesome," Dan says out loud. He opens the door to the garage they found in the kitchen yesterday and looks around for a switch. He doesn't find a regular switch but does find a garage door opener that appears to have a light button on it. Clicking that turns out to bring the overhead light on the opener to life. "Perfect."

As promised, there is a chest freezer up against the sidewall of the garage. "Please don't be empty," Dan mumbles. Then again, he doubts anything he finds in a freezer is going to be helpful. He's expecting meat that would take time to thaw, which isn't very conducive to cooking breakfast for himself and a girl he really shouldn't admit he's trying to impress.

He pulls open the freezer to find it's not empty, it's actually quite full. The top layer of things looks like exactly what he was expecting. Meats of various kinds that look heavily frozen. He moves those out of the way to find things underneath. A few boxes catch his eye, including one that might be breakfast sandwiches. "Don't be empty," he mumbles, reaching for the box. Luck is on his side. The box contains four breakfast sandwiches. He pulls two of them out of the box and carries them inside, flicking off the light and relocking the door on his way into the kitchen.

He finds some coffee grounds in a cabinet and brews six cups, which should be enough for them. Of course, they'll have to drink it black but maybe they can make that work. He reads the heating directions on the little cellophane wrapper of the sandwich, which directs him to pull it apart in order to heat it evenly. He follows the directions and the smell of cooking sausage fills the kitchen area as soon as he pulls open the microwave oven.

He assembles the sandwiches on little

plates just as the coffee machine beeps that it is done. As if called by the sound, Sarah emerges from the bedroom. "That smells heavenly," she says.

"You have perfect timing. Come have a seat. Breakfast sandwiches and black coffee."

She rubs her eyes as she crosses the floor. "How did you sleep?" she asks.

"Fine," Dan answers. "You?"

"I slept great once I fell asleep. Sorry you had to sleep on the floor."

"I didn't have to. I could've slept on the couch or in one of the other beds. I chose to. It's fine."

Sarah settles herself on a stool at the little island and pulls the plate and coffee cup close to her. "Thank you for making something to eat."

"No problem." Dan swipes his phone open again and looks at the second video from the motion thing last night. This time he turns off the volume since he likely won't need it. Again, all thirty seconds seems to be trees blowing in the wind. For the third video, he starts it and then uses his thumb to move the progress bar along, turning it into a sort of fast motion replay. Nothing.

Sarah leans toward him. "What are you watching, anything interesting?"

"No, just watching the camera from last night."

Sarah's hand freezes midway to her mouth,

coffee cup in hand. "The camera went off last night?"

Shit. Dan frowns. "Just a few times. It's nothing. Just trees blowing in the wind."

"OK." Sarah takes a sip of the coffee and sets the cup down. "Did you sleep through the alerts last night?"

Dan sighs. "I sort of wish you hadn't asked me that. I don't want to lie to you but I also don't want you to freak out for no reason."

"I don't like where this is going."

"I turned off the motion sensor alerts."

Sarah licks her lips. "What?"

"Look, they're all trees moving in the wind." He turns his phone toward her. "It went off like a dozen times last night to basically show me the wind. I didn't want to be bothered by it all night. I wanted a little sleep." He looks at her and frowns. He doesn't need to know her half as well as he does to read the anger written there. "If I turn it back on will you stop giving me that hate glare?" He doesn't want to spend the morning arguing with Sarah. Yesterday was awful. He knew he was feeling things for Sarah that weren't reciprocated but shutting her out was not the answer. That only made her angry and he found he'd rather keep her from feeling that way. It was not Sarah's fault that he had feelings for her. It wasn't her burden to bear and he wasn't eager to hurt her again.

"It would be a start," Sarah says.

Dan keeps his phone on the table between them where Sarah can see it while he clicks the little gear again and flips the switch to turn on motion alerts. "Done," he says. "Sorry."

"Want me to download the app instead?"

He considers this for a beat. Then he imagines Sarah's heightened panic every time her phone vibrates with an alert, her anxiety spiking even as she waits for the video to load. "No. I got it," he says.

He picks up his sandwich. "Let's move past this. Talk about something else."

Sarah grimaces and reaches for her sandwich. "Where did these come from?" she asks. "I didn't see them in the box you brought."

"No, they were frozen. There's a freezer in the garage, Brent told me about it. I found them there. We can take out some meat for dinner if you want. I saw ground beef but I'm sure there are other options there too."

"We have more soup and stuff, we'll be fine."

Dan's phone vibrates with a notification from the app. "Trees moving?" he says. Sarah looks out the porch door and sees the trees swaying. She looks down at the phone screen to watch the same actions playing out on the basically live feed video Dan is showing. "Yeah, just trees."

"You'd think the app companies could come up with something that would only alert for something larger than a tree branch moving," Sarah complains. "We just want to know about animals and people. Is that too much to ask?"

Dan chuckles. "I'm not a software guy, I have no idea."

He closes the app and sets his phone back down with the screen facing up toward the ceiling.

"So what are you studying?" Sarah asks. "I feel like you told me once but I forget."

"Business," Dan says. "I've always wanted to own a sporting goods store. I figure a business degree is the best way to make sure I'm prepared for that."

"Sporting goods?" She takes a bite of her sandwich. "I guess that makes your decision to work in hardware and sporting goods at the store a good move."

He laughs. "True. Now how did you, a biology student, end up in hardware?"

"Oh see, that's easy to explain. Sporting goods runs on commission and gets me better money when I make sales."

The phone vibrates again, twice in rapid succession. The first banner shows a phone call incoming. Sarah can't see the details. The second banner is for the motion app. Dan sees that the call is from an unknown number, again, so he chooses to open the motion app.

"Trees again," he mumbles. The video is playing on a few-second delay but Dan sees an option to jump to live. He clicks it and his blood runs cold.

There is a person in the shadows of the tree line.

He stands up, dropping his phone down on the counter. "Fuck," he yells. He crosses the kitchen in two large strides and pulls the largest knife from the block on the counter.

Sarah stands up, toppling the stool to the ground with a loud bang. She grabs his phone and stares at the image, trying to see more detail. The person is just at the edge of the yard, wearing a black hoodie with the hood pulled up. She can't make out any details of their body size or shape. She's surprised at her lack of panic, staring at this image that should rightfully panic her.

She looks up from the phone to see Dan, hand on the doorknob, ready to charge out the backdoor. "Wait, don't be an idiot. I'll call 9-1-1."

"Fuck that," Dan says. "I'm seeing who this asshole is."

CHAPTER 28

Sarah follows Dan out the door and onto the large patio, his phone still clenched in her hand. "Stop," she yells. "Don't be a hero. Come inside."

Her eyes dart to the spot in the trees where the person should be. The shadows from the rising sun make it hard for Sarah to see anyone, but they have to be there. She picks up the phone, intending to dial for help.

The phone rings. The call is from an unknown number but, again, the area code is local. Sarah swipes to answer the call, bringing it to her ear without saying anything.

On the patio, Dan is pacing along the tree line near where they saw the person in the black hoodie. He's holding the knife tightly in his fist, ready to wield it to defend them if needed. His muscles are tight, he's ready for this fight. "C'mon, fucker," Dan bellows. "I know you're out here."

Sarah's breathing gets ragged and her heartbeat spikes. Dan's voice just echoed through the phone. "Oh my god," she whispers, dropping the phone to the ground. "We have to go inside," she yells. "Now."

She pulls her phone out of her back pocket and dials 9-1-1.

Dan turns his head to look at Sarah. Sarah catches sight of the dark figure darting between two trees and heading in their direction. "Behind you," she hollers.

Dan's head snaps in that direction in time to see the stranger as a blur of black coming at him. He holds out his left arm even while preparing his right arm to come down with the knife. He plants his feet, bracing himself for the impact of the person charging at him.

The blur of black lashes out with a blade of their own, biting deep into Dan's left arm. He slashes back with his right, aiming high. He feels the satisfying push back of skin underneath the blade. There's a grunt of noise from the attacker. Dan takes a step closer to them, holding up the blade again. The blade is covered in red and Dan's arm is burning but he ignores both of these things.

Behind him, he hears Sarah screaming into the phone. "You have to come now. Use my location, can't you do that? We're at an Airbnb in the woods. Hurry, they have a knife and there's blood on the patio now. You are taking too long."

"Sarah, go inside," Dan yells.

He takes another step closer to the attacker, using his arm to block an attack. Again, he feels the bite of the blade in his arm. This time when he lunges at the attacker, he feels the fabric of their clothing against his fist and knows he has buried the entire blade into this person. It is possible he will feel the guilt of this later, but at this moment he feels nothing but relief.

The attacker stumbles backward, pulling the knife from their side as they slide back into the tree line. Dan takes a step, intending to follow, but the pain in his arm stops him from doing that. Instead, he sits on the patio and pulls his arm to him. Sarah drops to the ground beside him. "They ran off into the trees," she says. "We need an ambulance. Now."

"Gimme the phone," Dan says, holding out his right hand. Sarah hands it over and Dan calmly gives the address to the operator on the other end of the phone. "They're gone right now," Dan says. "But they cut me twice, I think." There's a pause while he listens to the follow-up questions. "No, I don't think I'm going to pass out. I hope not. Hurry up."

Sarah leans down and coaxes Dan to move the arm a little away from his body. Her heart is beating so fast she's afraid she's going to collapse but she has to focus on things she can control right now. Right now Dan is bleeding and Sarah needs to see how bad it is. She can see there are two specific spots where the material of his sweatshirt is darkening dangerously. The slashes in the sweatshirt material are long. She assumes that means the ones in his skin are as well. When she touches the bottom of the sleeve in an attempt to move it up and give her access to the arm, Dan sucks in a ragged breath. She stops.

She pulls her own sweatshirt off and holds it to his arm, pushing down hard to apply pressure to the arm. She uses her stronger hand, her right, to put pressure on his elbow to act as a sort of tourniquet. Thanks to biology classes, she has a mild idea of what she's doing, but she has to focus on doing this without thinking about the smell of blood filling her nose again or the site of this blood. It's an arm, she tells herself, Dan will be fine.

"Sarah," he says. She looks up into his face. "Here," he's holding out her phone. "They're almost here."

As if his voice coaxed them, the sirens draw close enough for Sarah to hear them. "You have to let them in the front door," Dan says. "Remember what Brent said about the doorbell, it won't help to have his parents talking to them through the door. You have to go open it."

"I can't leave you here. What if that guy comes back?" Sarah asks.

"Sarah," Dan leans over and plants a quick kiss on her forehead, right at her hairline. "Go open the door. Let the heroes in. Please."

Sarah pushes herself up on shaky legs and walks through the house. As she goes, she flips every light switch and leaves them all on in her wake. The back porch door is still wide open, giving her a path back to Dan if something goes wrong. She wrenches open the front door and stands there as a police car, a fire truck, and an ambulance park in the driveway. She stands in the doorway directing them through the house and letting the reality of this experience slowly trickle in.

Then, once she's lost count of how many uniformed professionals have stomped their way past her, she collapses down to the ground in the doorway and just sits there propping the door open. Her eyes are unfocused and she is shaking. Someone kneels in front of her. "Honey, what's your name?" he asks.

She blinks and tries to focus on his face. She can't make out the details but he is in a uniform. "Sarah," she answers, her voice too quiet.

"Sarah, can you tell me what happened?"

"There was a person in the woods. Dan

went outside and they fought. He got cut twice. I think he cut them too. I'm not sure."

"OK, how did he know the person was outside? Did you see them?"

"Yes, on the camera." Her eyes focus even more and she nods, remembering the details. "The camera app is on Dan's phone. You can watch the video. It should've caught the whole thing."

"Good, that's helpful. Can you tell me where his phone might be?"

Sarah tries to remember. She had the phone, she remembers that. She had it in her hand. It rang. The caller was here because it was Dan's voice she heard on the other end. What did she do with the phone? "I think I dropped it outside on the patio." She puts her hands down, intending to stand up.

The officer puts a gentle hand on her shoulder. "It's alright, honey, I'll go look for it. You stay right here."

Sarah knows this is probably a kindness. Not only is she likely in shock, but there is bound to be a lot of blood on that patio. The officer is trying to keep her from seeing anything.

Beyond the driveway, Sarah sees a group of paramedics emerging from the side of the house with a stretcher between them. She stands and heads that way. Dan is lying on the stretcher, wincing. "Hey," she says, reaching for his leg to brush it. "How are you doing?"

"I'm good," he says. "But I need stitches.

They're taking me to the hospital."

She looks at the paramedic in charge of pushing the stretcher. "Can I ride along?" she asks.

"Absolutely. Let us get him loaded and then you can hop up front and ride in the passenger seat. Make sure you give your statement to the police before you go. That makes their job easier."

"Right." Sarah stands there, feeling helpless, and watches them load Dan into the back of the ambulance. It takes longer than she expects it to while they hook him up to IV fluids, cut back his shirt, and clean the wound. She watches them push gauze onto the wounds and tape them down. Really, it feels like a lot of the initial care is done right there in the ambulance. If he didn't need stitches, this might be it.

Then a police officer walks past Sarah into the ambulance and stands beside Dan with a clipboard. He answers the questions calmly. Sarah is so proud of him. He fought with someone today. She takes a shaky breath. What if he hadn't been there? What if they'd slept in? What if he hadn't thought about getting a knife before he went outside? What if they hadn't been monitoring that app?

More importantly, was this the killer from campus? How did he find them?

The police officer from before is back. He places a hand on Sarah's arm, which makes her jump. "Sorry, honey, I didn't mean to scare you. Is this the phone you were talking about?" He holds up Dan's phone in a plastic evidence bag. The screen protector is shattered but the case has protected most of it. Sarah nods. "Excellent. I'm going to bring this with us and follow you to the hospital. Are you riding with EMS?" Sarah nods again. "Alright, I'll see you there."

CHAPTER 29

Dan is wheeled into a small room near the emergency room. Sarah is allowed to join them after Dan has been moved from the stretcher to a similar bed that belongs to the hospital instead of the EMS team. It's not a private room but one separated from anything else deemed an emergency by curtains on all sides that happened to be pulled closed. Sarah settles into the little blue chair beside the bed and sighs. "How long do you think we'll have to wait for a doctor to come stitch you up?" she asks.

"That depends on how serious they think my injury is in relation to all the other people here. I'd say the fact that I'm not in one of the waiting room chairs is a positive sign."

Sarah nods and then lets the room fall into an uncomfortable silence. She needs to tell him that she wants to take off on her own and go somewhere. She can't shake the feeling that she's not safe and telling anyone else, including Dan, where she's going feels dangerous. She also knows Dan is likely to balk at this suggestion. He's likely to tell her she's a fool and he's not letting her go. Unless, that is, he's worried too and has already come to the same conclusion. "We need to talk," she says quietly.

Dan sighs heavily. "That's never a good opening line."

"I'm worried about your safety and mine. We were just attacked by someone with a knife because we were in the woods somewhere we thought was safe. Clearly, we were wrong about that. I need us to both go somewhere truly safe and tell no one where we are going."

"Where's my phone?" Dan asks as if he wasn't listening to her at all.

"What? The police have it. Did you even hear me?"

"I heard you. I need to talk to Brent. I need to ask him outright if he told anyone where we were. I want to hear if he's lying when I ask him. How do I get my phone?"

"Do you know his phone number because you can use my phone if you do." Sarah slides her phone out of her pocket and hands it to him.

He snags it and punches some numbers, bringing the phone up to his ear. "Hey, Brent, it's Dan. My phone is with the police so I had to call you on this one. This is Sarah's phone. Call me back when you get this."

He pushes a button and hands the phone back to Sarah. "Thanks. We should answer if he calls. If it rings, show me the phone and I'll tell you if that's his number."

"Yeah, fine." She puts the phone on her lap, the screen side up. "So, about what I said …"

Dan lets a deep breath fill his cheeks and then breathes it out through pursed lips. "Right, yeah. I can get on board with that. Do you have any ideas where we can go?"

"No. No we. Not together, anyway. I think we should both go somewhere secret and not tell each other where we are going."

"Sarah —"

"Dan, I'm serious. Either you were being targeted, which feels likely because you're the one in the fucking hospital, or I was. Either way, we are a danger to each other, obviously. Running off together almost got us killed."

"Sarah, it wasn't that serious. I just need stitches."

"This time. What happens if this person attacks you in your sleep? What happens if they attack when you're in the shower, having sex, or haven't grabbed a knife from the kitchen counter?"

"You think I'd be safer alone? That's stupid. There's safety in numbers."

The curtain swings open and someone in light blue scrubs with her dark hair pulled back in a ponytail smiles at them awkwardly. "Hey there, I'm Natasha. I hear we might need some stitches in here."

"Yes," Dan says. "That's what they tell me."

"I'm going to go," Sarah says, standing up.

"Wait —" Dan says.

"Yes, wait," another voice calls. Sarah turns to look at the newest arrival, a police officer in full uniform. "I have to get some statements from the both of you. If you don't mind."

Sarah flops back into the chair. "Fine." She waits quietly while the officer walks Dan through his statement even as the doctor is stitching his arm. She notices the officer seems clipped and almost frustrated. At one point he even rolls his eyes at Dan. Sarah notes the name on the badge, Fernandez, in case anyone asks later. The little curtained room feels entirely too small but Sarah doesn't dare leave. Dan tells the officer about the motion app, the phone call, and the reason they were at the cabin being that they were "concerned" after the recent string of killings in Flagstaff.

The officer scoffs at the phone call

mentioned. "Spam calls are highly common. No need to be hysterical here."

"Yeah, wouldn't want me getting slashed in the arm by a knife to cause hysterics," Dan says.

The officer chooses to ignore the comment and turns his attention to Sarah. "I have the preliminary statement you gave at the scene," he tells her, his voice somehow more gentle. Sarah wonders if he thinks she's fragile and needs his coddling. She's instantly annoyed and forces herself to sit up straight and put on a steely gaze. "Do you have anything you'd like to add, perhaps about this phone call Mr. Simmons is referencing?"

Sarah's shock at his tone deepens. He seems to be implying with his inflection that he doesn't believe there was a phone call and, possibly, that he distrusts Dan's account of things. "I can corroborate everything you were just told," she says confidently. "The phone you have in your possession will also show multiple phone calls from what I believe to be that same phone number in the days leading up to the attack. During the attack, I answered the call on Dan's phone, which means that call would be longer than the rest. During that phone call, I heard Dan's voice through the phone although we were standing in the backyard at the time. This points to the idea that the attacker is the one who was calling the phone. I also believe you'll want to speak to Officer Marino from the Flagstaff Police

Department, campus division, about possible connections between the case Dan just mentioned and this attack."

"Excellent. I will be sure to speak with this officer and I will follow up on this phone call thing, which is a little concerning. Thank you for bringing it to my attention."

Sarah bristles. "I didn't bring it to your attention, Dan did. Don't dismiss what he's telling you. I don't know what your problem is, but I need you to get it under control."

"Sarah, relax," Dan says. "I'm sure he didn't mean it that way."

"I can handle this," Fernandez says, the annoyance back in his tone. "I'm sorry if I offended you, Ms. Rodriguez." He rolls the Rs in her name a little too much. Sarah wants to groan, is this guy seriously giving her more credit because she happens to have a Hispanic last name? Good grief, he'd probably be disgusted if he knew that her stereotypical sperm donor never even met her and her crackhead mother decided to give her his last name in hopes that would make him give a shit.

She shakes her head. "Whatever. What else do you need from us?"

He looks down at the papers in his hand. "I think that's about all. I need you both to sign off on the statements you gave and leave me forwarding numbers in case I have further questions."

"You have my phone," Dan reminds him.

"Right." Again the condescending tone is back. Sarah wants to smack this guy but sits on her hands instead. "We are dusting it for fingerprints —"

"You'll find mine and Dan's," Sarah interjects.

"— and pulling the call log," Fernandez finished.

"Which you could pull with his permission in about ten seconds and return the phone to his possession." Sarah picks her phone up off her lap. "You know what, I think I'll call Marino. I think he'll be able to help with this."

"Give me a second to call the officer who recovered the device from the scene and see if they're done with it," Fernandez says. "I'll be right back."

He steps outside the little curtain. Sarah notes that he walks far enough away to not be overheard even while staying in her line of sight. "Legally he can't keep it," Sarah tells Dan. "You didn't forfeit it, there's no evidence on it that they can't collect and return the device to you, and they don't have a warrant. It wasn't a weapon. He'll get it back."

"Thanks."

"Alright, honey, I'm all done here," the doctor says. Sarah jumps, having forgotten the doctor was still stitching Dan's arm. "We have six stitches here on the small one and another nine on this larger one," she tells him. "I'll print the care instructions for you and have someone bring them back in before you're discharged." She pats him on the shoulder. "You did good." Then she smiles at Sarah. "Also, you're right about the phone but I didn't say that." She winks and leaves, careful to not pull the curtain shut so Sarah can still keep an eye on Fernandez.

Eventually, he returns and his attention is immediately on Sarah. "The officer will be here within fifteen minutes to return Mr. Simmons' property to him. Her name is Officer Nguyen and you can call me if you haven't seen her within the hour." He holds out a card for Sarah.

Sarah tips her head toward Dan. "Considering we're discussing his property, I'm sure you mean to give that card to him."

"Of course." Fernandez holds the card out to Dan, who takes it with his unbandaged arm.

"You two have a nice evening. I'll be in touch if I have any further questions."

Sarah waits until she can no longer hear his heavy footsteps falling on the tile before standing up herself. "Alright, I need to go."

"Sarah, wait," Dan says. "Please don't disappear."

"I'm not sure I can promise that," she says. "But let me get home and shower. I'll text you."

Dan tries to reach for her arm but Sarah easily shakes him off and then disappears around a corner. She uses an app to call for a rideshare and stands outside in the cool air, trying to use the sharp sting of the wind to keep herself from crying or falling apart.

CHAPTER 30

Sarah confirms her address with the rideshare driver and settles into the backseat. He tells her this ride might be a bit pricey because of the distance. Sarah figures she has no other option and agrees to it. She stares out the window, watching the trees go by, and wonders what she's supposed to do now. Going into the woods was a disaster. Who knew they were there? Dan's roommate Brent knew. Alicia and their boss at the mall both knew they were going but didn't know the address. Sarah didn't tell anyone else.

So where does she go now? She can't think of anyone she'd ask for help or any place she would go.

Her phone rings in her hand. The number is local but not saved on her phone. She wavers on whether to answer it and, in the end, decides it's worth a shot. If it's the killer, maybe she'll at least be able to have a number saved on her call log for the police. She'll keep them on the phone as long as she can.

"Hello."

"Hey, this is Brent. I'm looking for Dan. He called me from this number."

"Right. Sorry, I left. He should be getting his phone back soon. Call him on that."

"What the hell happened? I saw the police lights and stuff but I didn't know if I was allowed to watch all the other videos. Are they evidence or something?"

"Call Dan," Sarah says. "I don't really want to rehash the whole thing."

"Yeah, alright. Fair enough. Bye, I guess."

"Bye." Sarah hangs up. She swipes open the maps on her phone and checks her location. They're not far from home now. She watches the rest of the drive in silence, making sure every turn is correct.

"Thanks, have a nice day," she tells the driver. She checks her entire apartment for anything unusual, drops her cell phone on the charger, and double checks that every door and window in the apartment in locked.

After a hot shower and a cup of coffee, Sarah starts to feel a bit more like her old self. She flops down on her couch and reaches for her cell phone. She scrolls through phone numbers, wanting to talk about something other than this chaotic murder case with someone.

She settles on Brenda, a girl she went on a few dates with a while back who decided they made better friends. There's never been hard feelings between them, since Brenda found the love of her life shortly after dating Sarah. They are always able to chat. It's nice, relaxing, and exactly what Sarah feels like she needs right now.

She hits dial.

Brenda answers after three rings. "Hey girl, what's new? I haven't heard from you in ages."

"I've been alright, just needed a friendly voice. Tell me what's up in your life,"Sarah says. "How's Georgia?"

"She's good. We're good. I just got offered a promotion at work. They want to offer me an extra fifty cents an hour to make the schedule for everyone in the deli department. I'd be the scheduling manager or some such nonsense. I'm trying to decide if it's worth it, you know? I'd be the one everyone shits on if they don't like their hours."

"True, but you're good at listening and you're good with time management. You'd be good at scheduling."

"You sound like Georgia, that's exactly what she said." Brenda makes a clicking noise with her tongue. "I'll probably take it. Fifty cents an hour adds up."

"That's awesome. Good for you." Sarah flops back on the couch, getting comfortable. "You're still taking a full schedule though, right?"

"Yup, fifteen credit hours this semester. I'm trying to get this shit done. I need that degree. I don't want to be working at a deli all my life, you know? The more credit hours I take in a semester, the faster I have to stop paying for this nonsense."

"You are speaking my language," Sarah agrees.

"I know you didn't call me to ask how many credits I was taking," Brenda says. "What's really up, girl?"

Sarah sighs into the phone. "I don't really want to talk about it."

"But you will."

"If you make me."

"Girl, I know you work at the station desk. Is this about those boys that got killed?"

Sarah throws her head back, staring up at her ceiling. "I met the most recent victim," she admits. "Only once, but still. He was a total douche. I hated him pretty much on sight."

"Shit, do they think you're a suspect?"

"What? No, no, nothing like that. I just feel guilty." Sarah's knees start moving up and down in rapid succession and she warms up to the worst parts of her story. "I found the second body."

"Holy shit, no joke?"

"No joke. I'd met him a few times at the station and stuff but I didn't really know him. He had a class with me though."

"Wow, small world," Brenda says.

"Right. Then he didn't show up to class one day. I was skipping out a little early because the lecture was boring me to sleep. So I'm walking in the hallway and I just see him there on the ground." Sarah's voice catches. "Sorry, I don't want to say more than that." She blinks a few times to control her tears.

Brenda whistles. "You have been going through it. Tell me you have a support friend or something," she says. "Tell me you ain't doing this alone, waiting to call me until all this shit gets to be too much."

"I think that's the worst part," Sarah says. "I have this friend at the mall job, right? He's a nice guy and he's been supportive through all of this. Forcing me to take breaks and things, making sure it doesn't get to be too much for me."

"I like this dude already."

"So he takes me up to this secluded cabin this weekend, forces me to take time off and says we'll relax and recharge out where it's safer."

"Smart," Brenda says.

"That's what I thought." Sarah takes a deep breath before launching into this part of the story. "Someone showed up at the cabin and attacked

Dan. He got two slices from a knife on his arm and needed like fifteen stitches to close them. The police came and took statements, but they almost seem to be treating this like a random attack. I don't think it was. I think the killer tried to get to us."

There's silence from the other end of the phone. Sarah's knees pick up speed and she sits upright on the couch, suddenly nervous. "Brenda, are you there? Did you hear me?"

"Shit, I heard you. I'm just processing. This is a lot. Are you ok? Don't answer that. Where are you right now?"

"I'm at home, but don't come here. I think I'm going to go to the station. I want to talk to Marino, he's in charge of the case. I have the day off but I still think it needs to be done."

Brenda blows out a breath into the phone. "That's a good plan. A good plan always makes me feel better. Keep going, what else are you going to do today? Walk me through it."

Sarah thinks about it. "I'm going to get some lunch on campus, somewhere public. Then I'm going to the station to talk to Marino. Then I'm coming home, locking all my doors, and working on homework for a few hours. I'll call both of my bosses after that and talk about when it would be all right for me to come back. I'm going to watch something stupid on TV and go to bed early."

"This is a good plan. How do you feel?"

"A little better," Sarah admits. "More in

control."

"OK, perfect. Hey, one more thing you have to do today," Brenda says. "Call me after you get home. I want to hear from you at least once a day for a bit. I don't care what time of the day or night, you hear me? You need people right now and I'm one of your people."

"Thanks, Brenda."

"No problem, girl. Go get some lunch. Talk later."

As Sarah walks herself through the steps of her day, she focuses on the tasks she gave herself. She finds it easier to get through the simple things when she repeats the tasks in her head like a checklist. She stays in populated areas, taking main streets and walking down sidewalks crowded with students. All the while repeating to herself lunch, Marino, homework, movie, sleep.

At the police station, Alicia comes around the desk and hugs Sarah right in the lobby. "Why are you here? I didn't expect to see you today."

"There was an incident," Sarah says, blinking rapidly to keep her eyes from betraying her and dropping tears at the station. "Dan was attacked."

"Oh no. Where is he? Is he alright?"

"He's fine. He had stitches but he's fine. I need to talk to Marino, is he here?"

"Come back here and sit down, I'll call him." Alicia puts her arm lightly on Sarah's back and ushers her through the employee door. Sarah drops into a folding chair a little ways back from the desk and Alicia picks up a phone and dials an extension. "I have Sarah here at the front desk to make a statement for you." Pause. "Yeah, I'll tell her." Alicia hangs up and turns to Sarah. "He'll be a few minutes."

"That's fine. Have there been any changes in the case?" Sarah asks.

"The husband I told you about had an alibi, rumor has it. So he's out as a suspect. I don't know much else." Alicia settles into the cushioned chair at the desk, wincing a little as she sits.

"You OK?" Sarah asks.

"Cramps, I'll be fine." Alicia rolls her eyes. "It sucks having a uterus sometimes."

Sarah doesn't know what to say to that, although it's a sentiment she has agreed with many times in the past. Instead, she steers the conversation back around to the case they were discussing. "Did Andy have any family? Anyone who came in to give statements or anything? Has anyone reached out to Greg?"

Alicia rolls her eyes. "I'm hearing some seriously bad shit about this Andy guy. Not sure he had anyone who might have loved the way he was."

"Everyone has someone," Sarah says, shocked at the vehemence in Alicia's tone.

"I don't know about this one is all I'm saying."

"Sarah, sorry to keep you waiting." Officer

Marino steps into the lobby. Alicia spins in her chair, facing the front of the lobby again. "Why don't you come back here with me, we can chat."

Sarah follows him back to the interview room, the same room she settled in to give her statement when she found Keith's body. She drops into a chair and Marino takes his time settling into the chair across from her. He sets a yellow notebook and a pen in front of him. "What can I help you with?"

"First, I want to say that I gave your name to an officer named Fernandez. Have you heard from him?"

"I just spoke to him this morning, actually, so I have some of the details from that case he's opened. Sarah, I'm sorry you're going through this. Do you have any idea why this might have happened to you?"

"What?" Sarah sputters. Sure, she had already had this same conversation with herself and then with Dan but to hear a respected officer ask, it hurt. Is he implying she has something to do with this?

"I just don't often get the same person in here twice to give statements about two unrelated crimes."

He also can't often get murder cases, but Sarah decides not to mention that. Instead, she jumps on the last two words he said, seeing her opening. "I don't think they're unrelated," she says. "I think they might be the same. I remember when I met Andy at the coffee shop he complained that he kept getting spam calls. I gave him a call-blocking app that I use as a recommendation. Dan's phone was getting spam calls this weekend. Did Fernandez tell you about the one I answered during the attack?"

"He did."

"Well, I think that's a connection." Sarah's hand flies to her mouth. "Oh my God, I found Keith because his phone was ringing. I followed the ringing to his body."

Marino nods. "I can look into this a little but phone calls like this might be just a coincidence," he tells her gently. "I don't want you getting ahead of yourself. You and Dan are alive and you're doing alright, all things considered. I want you to stay safe and keep a level head."

"I'm trying," Sarah says honestly. "It's been a little difficult. I spoke to a friend this morning who made me feel a bit more normal. This is all really scary."

"Would you feel more comfortable if we could get you some kind of protection?" Marino asks. "Are you afraid the attacker might try again?"

"Do you have any idea who the attacker might be? Any leads at all?"

"I can't talk about that, Sarah. I'm sorry. Fernandez seems to be trying to establish whether you folks were targeted or whether the idea of the house being empty was the target. According to the owners, the Airbnb was not officially rented this weekend, which is why they let you stay there. That means on the websites it would've shown as empty. That could be why it was targeted. You two may have just been in the wrong place at the wrong time."

Sarah wants to believe that with her entire soul but that does not explain the phone calls. She knows Marino and has worked with him for a while now. She has faith he will look into this if he says he will. She decides to let it go on faith, for now, and not bring it up again. "I think it might not hurt to have patrol cars or something check on my house from time to time if I'm going to stay in town. I also want you to let me know if you find anything that tells you I'm not safe here. If this wasn't random, we deserve a chance to be safe."

"Of course." Marino clicks the pen closed then seems to reconsider how this looks and offers Sarah an awkward smile that might be apologetic. "Is there anything else?"

"Not at this time. I'll be in touch if anything changes."

"Thank you, Sarah." Marino stands up and waits for Sarah to do the same, then he gestures to the door. "When are you back at work? No rush, of course, we just miss you around here."

Sarah considers what she'd imagined doing, running off somewhere. She has nowhere else to go. She'd been on her own for years. There are no parents, grandparents, aunts, uncles, cousins, or roommates waiting off in the wing with spare bedrooms or whole ass houses in the woods. There's no one coming to save her. She will just have to toughen up and handle this herself. "I'll be back tomorrow. No safer place than a police station, right?"

Marino chuckles. "See you tomorrow."

CHAPTER 31

The next evening, Sarah's phone buzzes with an incoming text where it sits facedown on the desk beside her at the police station. She checks the cameras, looking for anything unusual before she lets herself pay attention to the phone. When nothing seems out of place, she grabs the phone and flips it to read the banner. An alert indicating a text message from Brenda is showing halfway down her screen. She clicks.

How's it being back at work? You having regrets?

She smiles at the screen and types out a response. *Actually, no. It feels normal. I'm sitting here trying to stay awake, drinking too much coffee, and studying for a test I don't give a shit about.*

Perfect. I'm fighting my insomnia so you call if you need me, alright?

Will do.

She sets her phone down again and closes the textbook she was trying to focus on. This math course she needs as part of her degree is a total waste of time. It's entirely too similar to the other course she needed, which she took last semester, meaning she already knows most of this stuff. According to the syllabus they'll get to new material about three weeks before the class is over. She should've tested out of it but didn't take the time to find out if that was an option for this particular class. Plus, testing out of it often involves earning the credit for that particular course but not the actual credit hours required for a degree meaning she'd have to take something else. So stupid.

Instead, Sarah pops an earbud in her ear and uses her phone to navigate to an audiobook. She chooses something with a pastel-colored cover that looks like there's no way for it to include blood or murder. Then she settles back in the chair, arms crossed over her chest, and turns the audiobook up to 1.5 times the normal speed.

Two hours later, she's made a huge dent in the adorable romcom story which, in Sarah's opinion, would only be improved if the two female best friends had tried dating each other instead of merely agreeing to help each other find the perfect candidates. She pops the headphone back into its little hard plastic case and decides that's the route she's hoping the story inevitably takes.

Then she starts a pot of coffee. Alicia warned her that Greg was also back today and Sarah wants to make his transition as easy as possible.

As if called by the coffee, Greg's car pulls into the lot. He navigates it to his favorite spot, parks, and hustles up the walkway to the door. Sarah hits the button to allow him access and stands up. "Hey," she greets. "How are you?"

"This is so fucked up," Greg says. "But I'm hanging in there. Thanks for asking. How are you?"

Sarah can't help looking at him differently right now. Her mind is filled with the ideas that Dan put there. Ideas that Greg might be obsessed with her, might be dangerous. She's never seen him that way before and knows she's being ridiculous. They're friends. They've been friends for a long time. She owes him more than that.

Greg removes a bag from his shoulder with a wince. Draping the bag on his arm, he gingerly touches his side. "That coffee smells heavenly," he says.

Sarah's eyes stay focused on the place Greg

is touching. Her mind is racing and her heart is beating out of control. "What happened to you?" she asks.

Greg steps through the doorway into the employee area and Sarah takes a step back away from him, still staring at the place where he is holding. When Dan gave his statement to Fernandez he said he hit the attacker with the knife at least once, probably twice. They should have a cut. Sarah remembers Dan handling the knife with his right hand. The attacker would be injured on their left side. Greg is currently holding his left side.

"What?" Greg says. He looks down at his hand, almost as if he hadn't noticed he put it there. He shrugs. "Oh, I pulled a muscle in my side or something moving furniture around my apartment. I think I was going a little stir-crazy during this time off or whatever. I rearranged my living room like three times." He crosses to the coffee pot and picks up the carafe. "Don't move couches by yourself, that's my advice. Want some coffee?"

Sarah shakes her head, barely, and clears her throat. "Did you hear about the attack at the cabin? I'm not sure what Alicia told you."

"I heard about it." He pours a cup of coffee and replaces the carafe. When he turns to her, his jaw is set and his eyes are angry. "I can't believe that asshole put you at risk like that. What the fuck was he thinking?"

This sudden anger does not bode well for Sarah's concern about Greg's intentions. She takes another step back, her bottom hitting the countertop behind her. "He was thinking we were in danger here."

"So he took you out into the woods where there are fewer people around and response times are slower? What the hell kind of sense does that make? How do we know he isn't the killer? How do we know he didn't bring in someone else to attack you and make it look like it wasn't him?"

Sarah rolls her eyes. "I wasn't attacked. He was."

"Whatever, I'm sure I'm overreacting. I'm glad you're both OK. I just think it was a stupid idea. I wish you'd asked me, I would've told you not to go."

"You're not my babysitter." Sarah bends her knees without taking her eyes off Greg. She grabs her bag and stands back up. "I was sorry to hear about Andy."

Greg's anger dissipates and his shoulders sag. "Yeah, that sucked. Honestly, you were right about him. I was afraid to say that before and I probably shouldn't say it now but he was an asshole. I think I thought I could fix him if I stayed friends with him. He didn't deserve this, that's not what I'm saying, I just hate that I'll never get to see him be a better man than he was."

Driving to the cabin with Dan, Sarah had rejected the idea of Greg being the killer for a few reasons, she recalls. One of those was that he was friends with Andy and, therefore, wouldn't have killed him. At this moment, listening to him talk about how he wanted to change Andy and got frustrated when he couldn't, she's questioning that.

"Hey, I'm going to go," she says. "Nothing noteworthy happened and we're not waiting on anything so it should be a normal morning for your first day back. Take care of you."

She walks out of the room quickly, unable to find a way to do it that doesn't require her to put her back to Greg. She doesn't slow down until she's in the car with the doors locked. Then she checks the parking lot and finds nothing unusual. The door to the police station closed behind her. Greg didn't follow her. No one else is around.

She's safe. For now.

CHAPTER 32

Sarah checks the lock on the front door no less than eight times after she gets home that morning. It's Saturday morning, which means she has no classes she needs to rush off to and nowhere else to be. In fact, since she is easing herself back into things, she doesn't even have the mall job to worry about today. This is time she should be using for laundry, homework, cleaning her apartment, and much-needed sleep. Instead, she's pacing her living room and watching the front door like it might burst open at any minute.

Could Greg be the killer?

That's the question that has Sarah in a panic spiral. There's the fact that he did seem to like her and that he was always doing nice things to impress her, like bringing her a perfectly made coffee or trying to hold the door open for her. Then there's the fact that he was friends with Andy until Sarah pointed out how bad this guy was at which point he talked about trying to "change him". It is conceivable that he might have done something drastic if he learned Andy couldn't be changed. He knows where she lives. He knows her phone number. He was nursing an injury on his body that could be a cut from Dan fighting back.

Fuck, she needs to calm down.

Sarah grabs her phone and stares at it. What she'd really like to do is call Dan. Dan is reliable and smart. He's helpful. But she cannot drag him further into this. He got sliced with a knife and got stitches in his arm because he helped her before. She can't let that happen again.

Instead, she dials Brenda. "Hey girl, what's new?"

"Nothing," Sarah says. "OK, that's a lie. I'm panicking. Got a second to talk?"

"Hang on, let me take care of one thing real quick." The phone goes into the deep silence which usually means the other end has hit mute. Sarah waits. Finally, Brenda returns. "Alright, all good. Lay it on me."

"I think a guy I work with might be the killer and I need you to talk me down from this ledge."

"OK, whoa. That's a big accusation. You got any facts?"

"He has some kind of injury on his body about where the cut Dan would've made when he fought with the killer is," Sarah begins.

"Girl, I sure as hell hope you have more than that. Did you see this cut?"

"No. He was just holding his side like it hurt. He said he pulled a muscle."

"OK, OK. Keep going. Give me more."

Sarah sighs. "He knew the third victim. When I met Andy, that's the victim, he was introduced as a friend of Greg's."

"Greg would be your suspect?"

"Right. So he was a friend of Greg's but I didn't like him at all. I told Greg this. Then today he was all about how he thought Andy was different and he thought he could change Andy but he was wrong. Brenda, did he kill this guy because I told him he was an asshole?"

"No. This is a new way for you to try and blame yourself for this Andy guy dying. Go back to the first victim, did Greg know him?"

"I don't think so. I mean, he might have but I don't know. He didn't say he did one way or the other. But I didn't know he knew Andy until a few days before the murder."

"Look, Sarah. This whole thing is

unprecedented and scary. I hate that it's been near you in so many ways. I hate that you are so broken by this. But I can't have you blaming yourself. I can't have you looking at everyone in the world like they might be a murderer. This Greg guy, he ever make you feel scared before you decided he might be killing people in his spare time?"

Sarah thinks. Greg has made her uncomfortable before, mostly because he was obviously flirting when she wasn't looking for that from him. He's frustrated her, showing up late or early for a shift and messing with her routine. He's done stupid things like holding the door open for her that were probably intended to make her feel grateful and only made her feel like smacking him for being out of touch. But he's never made her scared, not before this morning. She sighs. "I don't know anymore."

"Girl, I love you but you can't think this guy killed someone just because of one coincidence. By all means, be cautious around him. If anything else breaks, you tell someone. But please don't go calling the police or confronting this guy on this suspicion."

"See, this is what I needed. I needed you to calm me down. Thanks, Brenda. I owe you for all this. You've been the best lately."

"I try. Are you better now?"

"Yes," Sarah says, mostly honestly. "I'm better. Get back to work. Talk later."

They hang up and Sarah sets the phone

down on the table in her living room. She doesn't feel completely better, but she's aware that her attempts to explain why are not working. This morning with Greg she got a bad feeling. Listening to him talk about Andy like that, something was off. The anger he got when they talked about Dan wasn't right either. There's something under the surface of that boy that she doesn't like, something she's never seen before.

On the table, Sarah's phone vibrates. Goosebumps break out over her arms even as she reaches for it. She doesn't even realize how much she expects to see that unknown caller banner until it's something else. Mariana's name and the cute photo of her beautiful smile fill the screen. Sarah answers with something sounding like skepticism in her voice. "Hello?"

"Oh, thank God. I was so worried. What the fuck happened? You were attacked?"

"What?" Sarah tries to follow the thread of Mariana's rapid speech. "How did you hear about that?"

"So you were. Oh my God. Are you freaking out? What can I do?"

"I'm fine. Honestly, I'm fine. How did you even hear about it?"

"I have a study group on Friday nights with this girl who knows Alicia from the police station with you. It's sort of like big news all over campus. Everybody is talking about how someone got attacked. People think it's the same person who killed all those other guys. Then the girl tells me your name and I totally panicked. I mean, I fucking know someone who was attacked."

Sarah cannot believe she ever found this girl attractive. How did she miss the focus on gossip? It's like this girl's entire personality is who she knows and how she's connected to them. She rolls her eyes. Then something else Mariana said clicks in her head. "Did you say Friday night?"

"Yeah, that's when the study group is."

"So you heard about this last night and called me in a panic this morning?"

"Well, yeah. I didn't want to wake you up."

Sarah pulls the phone away and checks the number. Is she being pranked? Is this real? She puts the phone back to her ear. "You must not have been that worried if you thought I was sleeping peacefully." She shakes her head. "It doesn't matter. What matters is that I am fine. I wasn't injured in the attack and I'm fine."

"That makes sense since the killer seems only to be killing men. Who were you with? Is he ok? I mean all serial killers have a type, right? Were you with someone who was like a closet dirtbag with a history of being an asshole?"

"What?" This time the word is not said out of confusion but a sort of warning. Sarah heard her. She also cannot believe someone would have the guts to say this sort of thing to her right now. How can anyone be so insensitive?

"I mean that's what everyone is saying.

Everyone is saying the guys who died were all total assholes. I'm just thinking maybe that guy you were with was the target."

"Mariana, you're way out of line right now."

"What? Why? I'm just saying what I heard. Everyone is saying it."

Sarah shakes her head again. "You know what, you keep worrying about whoever the fuck this everyone is. I don't need you to call me again. Have a good life." She hangs up the phone and slams it satisfyingly on the couch beside her.

"What is wrong with people?" she asks the empty room. She's not perfect, she's always known that. But she's suddenly really glad that whatever flaws she has don't seem to lump her in with this "everyone" Mariana is getting her information from. She never wants to be that tone-deaf in her life. Blaming the victims of an actual murderer for not being perfect people before they were slaughtered is a crazy low she doesn't ever want to stoop to. What makes the killer someone who is allowed to run around and play God, deciding who's worthy of death and who isn't?

But Mariana did voice one thing she was worried about herself, Dan. What if Dan was the real target of this maniac? Suddenly Sarah feels incredibly selfish for not checking on her friend since the hospital. Pushing him away feels like a good answer but what if she's wrong?

She flops back on the couch. "Fuck," she

groans. She just wants life to go back to how it was before. Classes, work, homework. No killer, no death, no knowledge of what blood smells like. Just getting shit done. The police station didn't have a pending murder case that was all anyone could talk about. The mall job wasn't filled with gossip. It was just Dan, making her laugh and helping her pass the time.

She whines into the empty room. "Fuck," she repeats. That will never be her life again, will it?

CHAPTER 33

Sarah turns on the TV in her apartment and pulls her homework out of her bag, spreading it out on the little table in front of the couch. She jumps whenever there are noises outside and keeps finding her brain spiraling back to the conversation with Greg, the attack, or the smell of blood. When she tries to pull her brain along to better topics, it cycles back to thoughts of what her life was like before. Everything starts to feel dark and lonely.

She picks up her cell phone and, practically

without thinking, dials Dan's number. It rings in her hand only twice, which isn't long enough for her to notice what she's done and change her mind. Then his voice fills her ear. "Sarah?"

"Yeah, hi. Sorry. I'm sure it's tacky to call you out of nowhere like this. I'm sorry, I can let you go. You're probably busy."

"No, I'm good. I've been worried about you. How are you?"

Sarah doesn't want to talk about how she is. She doesn't want to talk about any of this over the phone. She also doesn't particularly want to be alone right now. "Hey, are you home? Can I, maybe, swing by?"

"Yeah, that's fine. I'll text you the address."

"Perfect. Thanks." Sarah hangs up the phone and stands up, leaving all her stuff scattered across the small table. Part of her need to see Dan right now is that he was as entangled in all of this as she was. He was there at the cabin. He got the phone calls. He'll understand what she's feeling. He won't downplay any of it.

Also, she can admit this only to herself, she just really wants to see him. She's spent her day remembering what it was like hanging out with him before and she hates that she ruined that friendship. She needs that friendship right now.

Lastly, she's terrified that Dan might be targeted by this maniac again. She wants him to be safe. She needs him to be safe. For that, he needs to understand everything she knows.

So she grabs her keys, locks her front door, and heads to her car. It takes her seven minutes to drive to Dan's.

She finds a parking spot and knocks on the door for the apartment number he gave her. It swings open and Dan is there, looking tired and weary, but happy to see her. "Hey, come on in."

The apartment is clean and smells like vanilla. Sarah immediately likes it. The furniture looks comfortable and inviting. She spots a TV and a video game console but also a bookshelf full of spines that look interesting. This is not a stereotypical apartment for a couple of college roommates. They've done a decent job keeping it maintained. Sarah is impressed.

She walks through the living room, Dan right behind her, and makes her way to a little table in what seems to be serving as a dining room. She pulls a wooden chair out and sits. Dan sits across from her. "So, what's up?" he asks. "You sounded like you wanted to talk about something serious."

"How are you?" Sarah asks instead of answering. "I mean, how's the arm? I don't want you to think I don't care. I was just worried about you getting hurt again."

Dan shrugs, which makes Sarah think he isn't exactly forgiving her for that, just moving past it. "I'm a little sore but I'll be alright." He rests his arm on the table but doesn't lean on it. "Now, talk. I have a feeling that's what you came here for."

"Right. I went back to work yesterday at the police station."

"OK."

"I saw Greg and I remembered what you said about him possibly being a suspect."

"Which you shot down," Dan reminds her.

"I know, but then it was in my head when he showed up for his shift. So I was paying attention." She locks eyes with him. "He had an injury on his left side that he was favoring. He kept wincing when he moved the wrong way."

Dan sits up a little straighter. "Holy shit."

Sarah can tell by the expression on his face that he's as blindsided by this as she was. He's taking her seriously. She leans into him. "Exactly. So I asked him what he did to hurt himself. He gave me some bullshit story about moving his couch around and pulling a muscle. Then one of us mentioned Andy, it might have been me, and he was so weird about it."

"Weird how?"

Sarah purses her lips, trying to remember. "Like he was mad at him. That's how it seemed. Like he was mad at Andy for not being a good guy for all those years he knew him. He said something about how he always thought he'd be able to change him."

"Fuck," Dan says. "I didn't want to be right, you know that. But this makes sense. He was friends with Andy and thought Andy could be fixed or whatever. Then when you meet Andy and tell him what an asshole he is, Greg knows it's him or you. So he makes an easy decision."

Sarah runs her hand down her face. "Please don't tell me this is all about me. This can't be all about me."

"No, obviously not. I mean you didn't kill Andy." He reaches for her hand, rubbing the back of it lightly with his thumb. "I'm sorry I made it sound like that. I'm just saying in his fucked up way of thinking, it might have made sense."

Sarah sighs. "Here's the part I can't get around. The other two guys. Explain them."

Dan sits back in the chair and takes on a serious expression. Sarah lets him think, just watching him. Finally he leans forward again, this time putting the weight on his good arm. "I don't know enough about the first guy. Hell, I don't think I even remember his name. But the second guy —"

"Keith," Sarah supplies.

"Right. Keith knew you from class or whatever. Maybe Greg thought something was going on there. Did you ever tell Greg about having that class with Keith or about meeting him?"

"I don't think so. I might have mentioned it, but I don't remember."

"I think he worked at the mall though," Dan says. "Someone at work told me the kid who was murdered worked at the chicken place in the food court."

"So maybe I'd talked to him a few times there, too. That's possible. But none of this seems like a good reason to kill anyone."

"Sarah, nothing is ever going to be a good reason to kill anyone when you think about it like you or I would. I think we have to stop assuming this killer has logical reasons for anything."

"Fine," Sarah relents. "But Brenda, my friend, says that I can't take any of this to Marino. She says it's not proof it's just a bad feeling."

Dan nods. "So let's get some proof."

This time it's Sarah who slumps back in the chair, her back making an audible smack on the wood. "I hate that idea but what are you thinking?" she asks.

"We're either going to be right about his obsession with you or we aren't, right?"

"I guess."

"Then we need to find out if his obsession makes him dangerous to other people who catch your attention, right?"

Sarah nods. "He did mention being angry with you for taking me into that dangerous situation as if I can't take care of myself and you did all the fucking thinking for me."

"Perfect. I think I have a plan. Call Greg. Invite him to dinner tonight. If he accepts, we're on the right track."

Sarah frowns. "When do I get to know steps two through whatever?" she asks.

"When we know step one is even happening. Call Greg."

"Calling him would be way not my style. I'll text." She picks up her phone and does just that. *Hey, sorry about the awkward shift change at work today. I was exhausted. Dinner to make up for it?* "Done," she says, setting her phone down.

"How long does he usually take to respond?" Dan asks.

"We don't text all that often. Although I suppose the longer he ignores me the less likely it is that your obsession angle is —" She's interrupted by the vibration signaling an incoming text. She grabs the phone. "It's him." She locks eyes with Dan over the table. "He's in. Better tell me step two."

CHAPTER 34

Sarah's leg bounces nervously under the table. She was the first to arrive at the restaurant. That wasn't precisely part of the plan but more of a direct result of her nervousness. This little operation of theirs had spiraled into something that sounded serious faster than she was comfortable with. She almost hopes Greg doesn't show up for dinner after all. She really, really wants to be wrong about what he's been doing with his free time.

She uses her phone to check the time and

then shoots a text message to Dan. *Are we still sure about this?*

The response is immediate, as he promised he would be. *Absolutely sure. Everything getting set at this end. You just focus on the conversation.*

Got it. She answers.

"I'm not late am I?" Greg's voice breaks through her concentration.

She sets her phone face down on the table and stands up. "Not at all, I was just early. Thanks for coming." Now that she stood up there's an awkward moment where she has to decide what she did that for. Does she hug him? No, that feels like a really bad idea. Instead, she sticks her hand out. Greg gives it a strange look but ends up shaking it. They both sit.

"Are you getting food, appetizers, or dessert?" Greg asks, picking up the menu and opening it.

"I was thinking dessert and coffee. I'm dying for a cheesecake," Sarah says.

The waiter makes his way over and they both order a dessert and a coffee. Then Sarah braces herself and dives into the act she rehearsed at Dan's apartment and again in her car on the way here. "Can we talk?" she asks, hopefully sounding distraught. "I just need a little advice."

"Shoot," Greg says.

"So when we went to the cabin, me and Dan, he was a little aggressive." She watches Greg's face for signs of anger or any reaction. "He made me feel sort of uncomfortable." Dan had told her it was important to sell this part. If they were right about Greg, this would be something he wouldn't be able to stand for. She checks his face for signs of anger. He looks confused, his eyebrows uneven as one arches up toward his hairline. "He was just being sort of an ass, even before the attack. I don't know, it just got sort of overshadowed by what happened and I'm not sure if I should bring it up to him or what I should do about it."

"I don't know what to tell you," Greg says. His voice is short and he rolls his eyes to punctuate it.

Sarah is a little taken aback. She expected him to rush to her aide or offer to help. Instead, he seems upset at her. "Sorry. I just thought I could maybe get some advice."

"I didn't know you wanted to whine," he snaps. "I thought you wanted a date."

Sarah pulls back a little from the table. The urge to get up and leave is strong. This is not the kind of thing she would normally stand for. Who the hell does this guy think he is? Instead, she takes a deep breath and forces herself to remember the plan. She was supposed to make him angry. Sure, they originally thought it would be a good idea to make him angry with Dan but angry is angry.

"Sorry," Greg offers. He shakes his head and his expression softens. "Seriously, I'm sorry.

I'm being a dick. What do you want me to say?"

If Sarah were being herself right now, instead of the version of herself they need for the plan, she'd tell him to stop placating her. It's obvious by the way he put the mental workload of the conversation on her. What do you want me to say is such a bullshit move. He doesn't want to have this conversation. Fake Sarah offers him a smile. "I don't know. Nothing, I guess. In the end, there were bigger problems with the weekend."

The waiter arrives with their desserts and coffee, setting them down on the table with the lack of flourish that comes from a small order which likely means a small tip. He's gone before Sarah has to worry about the mood dying.

"Almost sounds like you're saying he deserved what he got," Greg says quietly.

Sarah, who had been looking down at her cheesecake, snaps her head up. "What? Fuck no." She realizes that was real Sarah talking and tries again, a little calmer. "I mean no one deserves that."

"Of course." Greg grabs his fork and digs into his slice of apple pie.

Did Sarah imagine that little eye roll just then or did he actually do it? Does he think some people deserve injury or death? If they're right about who he is, that would be true.

Sarah feels suddenly nervous about what they're doing. She wipes her palms on her jeans then picks up her fork and takes a bite of her cheesecake. The creamy texture might have been a bad idea. Although she normally loves it right now it feels like it's sticking in her throat behind her nervousness. She takes a large sip of her coffee in an attempt to work it down. "How are your classes going?" Sarah asks in an obvious attempt to change the subject.

She's sure he notices the change. He offers her a grateful smile. "They're good. I just had to ask for a week of bereavement but everyone was willing to work with me on it. I probably need to put some effort into it today and get caught up as much as I can."

"I took some time off as well," Sarah says. "Everyone was pretty cool about it. We're not exactly dealing with a common situation right now."

"That's true. Do you think that's why they're being agreeable about it?"

Sarah shrugs. It's strange but with the threat of a killer possibly having dessert with her like it's a normal evening, she's finding it hard to give a shit what her professors think. "I'll get all caught up when this is all over," she says.

Greg nods. "Exactly what I was thinking."

OK, she's for sure not imagining what sounded like a threatening tone in that phrase. She's not sure what it's supposed to mean, but it's making her feel like she has bugs crawling all over her. She tries to ignore the feeling, but it's not easy to shake. She focuses on the cheesecake, knowing it would be suspicious if she didn't at least attempt to eat most of it. Again, she washes it down with large sips of coffee.

In practice, it seemed like it was going to be easy to find a way to make this next part happen but, in reality, an easy bridge just isn't presenting itself. She'll have to go for direct. "Did you have to drive here to meet me or do you live close?" A lot of people like walking in this town but they're not exactly close to the part of town most students live in. It's silly to think he might have walked here. She's hoping he thinks she's exactly that, silly, instead of suspicious.

Again, one eyebrow tips up in confusion. "I drove. I live over by central campus."

"Oh yeah? My apartment is near there. Which ones are you in?" She has to find a way to bring up Dan's apartment. How do you just work that into casual conversation?

"Still Lakes," Greg answers.

"Oh, I know that one. It's across from Wood Crest where Dan lives. Funny to think if you were home tonight you two would just be hanging out in apartments across the street from each other if you weren't here with me instead." She feels her shoulders relax. She worked it in. It wasn't perfect. Actually, it was pretty sloppy, but it got the job done.

Greg takes the last bite of his dessert and stands quickly. "Hey, I'm sorry to be rude. I have to get started on that homework we talked about."

Sarah has to bite the inside of her cheek to keep from smiling. It worked. He's practically running out of here. She swallows. "Right, of course."

"Great. It was nice chatting with you. Call me. We'll do it again."

Then he's gone. Sarah fishes her phone out of her pocket and texts Dan. *I think it worked. He dashed out of here as fast as he could move when I mentioned you were across from his apartments and alone. I gave him the name of your complex.*

She sends that and then waves to the waiter, hoping he'll know to bring the check. She imagines Dan at home in his apartment, as planned, waiting to see if the next step goes down or not. Either Greg is the person Sarah thought he was at the start of all this and Dan will go to sleep tonight laughing about how they wasted their time or Greg is the killer she fears and Sarah just pointed him right at Dan. *Be careful.* She sends.

CHAPTER 35

Sarah walks quickly across the parking lot and jumps into her car. She forces herself to pause and take a look around the lot, watching for Greg's vehicle. Nothing. She pulls out onto the main road and heads for Dan's apartment. The choice of restaurant tonight was part of the plan. Sarah wanted to be close to the apartment complex in case Dan needed her and she needed to get back there quickly. Dan wanted her to have a longer drive so she could keep her eyes out for anyone following her. He told her to look for headlights that changed lanes when she did, sped up when she did, or slowed down when she did. He told her to "be annoying" when she was driving. Drivers around here will go around you if you are being too cautious or slowing down for no reason. Two-lane roads were made for that, after all. They'd settled on a place that was sort of in the middle, one she could drive to in under ten minutes.

Sarah follows Dan's directions, slowing as if she's checking street names at intersections and then speeding up on straight paths. She changes lanes, slows to check a street, and then speeds up again. Then she changes back into the original lane.

Behind her, someone honks their horn, pulling her attention to the rearview mirror. "Sorry," she mumbles. She hates driving like this but it's good to know it's having the desired effect. Then she spots it, at least two cars back, someone else changes lanes with her. Her blood runs cold. "No way," she whispers. Part of her thought this was never going to work. Part of her convinced herself she was safe.

Her car alerts her to an incoming text. She clicks the screen. "In a text message, Dan Simmons said: Just got a call from an unknown number. No one there when I answered," the digitized voice reads.

Sarah tightens her grip on the steering wheel and watches the rearview mirror as she slows down for a coming street. The car directly behind her honks and changes lanes, speeding off. The car she was watching doesn't. There's now only one car between them.

Dan's apartment complex is coming up on her left now. She slows down, turns on her blinker, and turns into the lot. The car directly behind her continues straight down the busy street, accelerating too fast for the situation to show their irritation with her driving.

More interestingly, the car she was watching follows her. Sarah squints in the rearview mirror and side mirrors alternately, trying to see the driver. In the dark all she can tell is that they are relatively tall, thanks to the shadow seeming to come close to the roof inside the car. It could be anyone back there. Hell, it could be Dan if she didn't know better. She doesn't recognize the car, all she can tell is that it's a darker-colored sedan of some sort. Greg drives a car that would fit that description, but she can't see the details of the car. At least none that she would recognize. Plus, no matter how slow she goes on this street, the car stays a few lengths behind her.

When she turns down a little path that will take her to Dan's unit, the car continues straight. "Maybe I was wrong," Sarah mumbles. She pulls her car into the first available spot and turns it off, waiting to see if anyone else pulls into this parking lot. No one does. She knows there are other lots, but she can't see them from where she is sitting. She counts to ten and then exits the car, rushing up toward Dan's landing. As they agreed upon, his front door is unlocked. She turns the knob and quietly identifies herself. "Nothing yet," Dan answers. "Get in here."

Sarah pushes the door shut but doesn't latch it, leaving a small sliver of light from the outer porch light in. "Are you sure you want it open like this," she whispers.

"It looks like I confronted you at the door. It plays into the angry guy routine you sold him."

Sarah crosses toward the couch she can barely see in the glow of the television, the only light source in the apartment right now. Dan is on the couch, sitting up straight and rigid. The television is turned down so far it may as well be muted. She drops onto the cushion beside him. "Now what?" she asks.

"Now we wait."

"Right." Sarah sighs. "What are we waiting for, exactly?"

"Did he get mad when you mentioned me?"

Sarah nods. "A little. Honestly, he seemed more mad at me than you though. He didn't want to talk about you and how you made me feel. He accused me of whining."

Despite the tense situation, Dan lets a little chuckle escape. It's a quiet thing, made only of exhales. Sarah merely smiles. "You must have hated that," Dan says.

"Right?"

Dan squeezes her leg, just above her knee. "You did good. Were you followed, do you think?"

"Maybe," Sarah says. "There was a darker sedan type car that was changing lanes when I was and things. I couldn't tell whose car it was or when it started following me. But when I pulled into this lot it kept going."

Dan's phone rings. He flips the phone toward Sarah so she can see the number he has programmed into his phone as "death" is calling. He answers it and clicks the speakerphone button. "Hello," he says, his full-volume voice echoing in the apartment and making Sarah jump.

The silence on the other end of the phone feels heavy. "You got something to say, fucker?" Dan prompts.

Again, silence.

Dan hangs up the phone and tosses it on the floor. He stands up. "Enough playing around, asshole. If you're here, quit with the tricks and get your ass in here."

"Dan," Sarah whispers. "Maybe don't anger the murderous attacker."

"Fuck that," Dan says. "Let's do this."

Then the television and the outdoor light click off at the same time, plunging the entire apartment into pitch blackness. Sarah blinks rapidly but the absolute darkness doesn't change.

This wasn't part of the plan.

PAGE 308

CHAPTER 36

"I didn't think about the power being cut," Sarah whispers. She reaches out for the place where Dan was standing a few seconds ago. Her hand closes around his arm, the soft feel of his long-sleeve shirt comforting her despite her racing heart.

"All the cameras are battery operated. We're good." His voice is quiet again, barely a whisper on the breeze. That information was for her, not for anyone else. "At least we know he's here."

Sarah traces her hand down his arm until it meets with his hand. He squeezes her fingers. With her free hand, she pulls her phone out of her pocket. The screen lights up, providing a small circle of visibility. Sarah thumbs out the numbers, nine one and one. She shows Dan and he nods. She doesn't hit send. Not yet. Stick to the plan. Be sure.

On the floor, Dan's phone rings. "Are you kidding me, you fucking coward?" he yells. But even as he is yelling, he is bending down to grab the phone. "Do I answer it?" he whispers.

"Yes," Sarah says.

He does, again turning on the speakerphone. "Hey, fucker. I'm right here. I'm unarmed this time. Let's fucking do this." There's a loud click from the phone and Dan shrugs. "I guess he hung up this time," he says. He keeps the phone in his hand. Sarah watches him thumb open the camera app.

They stand, fingers clenched tightly between them, waiting for something to happen. Sarah's entire body hums with adrenaline. All her muscles feel tightly coiled, waiting to be used. She isn't sure whether they'll have to run, brace themselves, or fight. She's not sure she's ready for any of those options, but she trusts Dan to have set up everything they talked about. She trusts Dan to keep her as safe as he possibly can.

The window beside the front door slides open. Sarah tightens her grip on Dan's fingers.

"Why the window? The fucking door was open," his voice comes out as barely a breath. Both Sarah and Dan tighten their grips on their phones, Dan pointing his toward the window.

When it opens and a figure starts to slide through, darker than the darkness by a shade, Dan clicks the shutter and a flash erupts from his phone. The entire living room lights up with the flash, including someone in all-black clothing halfway through the front window.

Sarah thumbs the green button to send her phone call.

"Smile, motherfucker, you're on camera," Dan says. The flash fires again, lighting up the living room and the progress the attacker has made. They hear feet hit the floor.

A laugh, low and dangerous, comes from the area of the window. Dan fires off another shutter just to give them light. Sure enough, the attacker is now fully in the room. "Are you planning to beat me with film, asshole?" the attacker asks.

Sarah's grip tightens even further on Dan's fingers. She's sure she's turning the fingertips white at this point. She yanks on his arm, trying to get his attention. "That's not Greg," she says in a desperate voice above a whisper. "I know who it is but it's not Greg."

CHAPTER 37

"What?" Dan keeps his eyes on the attacker, trying not to be distracted by Sarah's revelation.

"That's not Greg," Sarah repeats.

Again, the attacker laughs. "You thought I was Greg? Greg." The laugh gets higher in pitch. "No. No way Greg cares enough about women to take action like this to rid the world of the scum plaguing us."

"Us?" Dan says, confusion clouding his voice. He swipes up on his phone, flipping on the flashlight app.

The attacker is now fully illuminated. They have not moved from their spot in front of the window, but now they do. As Sarah and Dan look on, the attacker takes two slow steps in their direction. Then, they reach up and grab the bottom of the ski mask obscuring their face and fling it back.

Sarah, who had recognized the voice, doesn't startle. Dan does.

"Yes. Us," Alicia says. "Women everywhere who are fucking tired of assholes like you thinking you run this world. We've had enough. It was time for someone to stand up for us. Craig was a chauvinist. I met him at a bar once, talking a big game about how he can screw anything with developed breasts. He was sleeping with a married woman, Sarah, just like I told you. The worst part was that he wasn't doing it because he loved her. He wanted to prove he can even wreck a relationship with this penis. That's what he told his buddies at the bar. He was my first victim and, honestly, he was a good place to start."

"Fuck," Dan mumbles. "You're fucking crazy."

Alicia shifts and brings a gun level with her elbow. Sarah yanks on Dan's arm again. This time she doesn't have to say anything, he gets the warning. Until this moment the killer had always used a knife. Always. When they planned for this, they didn't plan for bullets. You can't wait for a confession while running from bullets. Sarah glances down at her phone, still lit up with the call she connected. How is she supposed to alert them to the gun without saying it out loud? She randomly presses buttons with her thumb, hoping that this action that was not the plan will send some kind of message that things have gone off the rails. They can't let Alicia sit here and monologue all the deaths. This isn't a movie. Sarah is truly in danger now and it's time to throw the plan out the window.

"Keith was different. I would never have found him if it wasn't for the police investigation into Craig's death," Alicia says. "He mentioned knowing Craig in high school so I looked him up. That's how I found out he had three girls accuse him of sexual assault while they were still in high school. He was out of state so we didn't recognize the name but he made the news in his hometown. Asshole got away with all three, barely served any time. Do you know why?"

She takes another half-step toward them and Sarah flinches. "Because he had a promising future in sports. So he got a slap on the wrist for ruining the future of three girls, giving them PTSD, and more all because he could play some fucking sport. He's not even playing the sport in college, can you believe that? He got community service and some fucking slap on the wrist for nothing."

"That's wrong," Dan says. He drops Sarah's

hand and holds it up in a giving-up gesture. "It is. We hear you. But I'm not like that."

"Andy tried to say he wasn't like that, too. He was what gave me the phone call idea, you know. We went on one date, one. I told him I wasn't going to have sex with him on the first date. He asked me out again and I said no. He called me incessantly. He cyber-stalked me. He showed up at my fucking apartment. He tried to rape me. So I showed up at his apartment and displayed all the evidence for him. Then I killed him the second he found it. That one was karma."

She takes a step closer. Sarah feels tears falling down her face. She isn't sure what to do. Alicia is only about six feet away from them now. Too close. Way too close. "Now there's you, Danny boy."

"I'm not like that," Dan repeats. "Nothing in my past like that, I swear."

"No, you just think a killer on campus is a good excuse to get laid up in the woods. You saw death as an opportunity to work your way into the vagina of a girl who otherwise kept you at arm's length. You're scum."

Dan shakes his head, sputtering things that might have been words if he was a bit more focused. "We didn't sleep together," Sarah says.

Dan's head turns a little in her direction. "That's what you're focused on? She just admitted to killing a bunch of people and you want to straighten her out about our sex life?"

"You didn't? Smart girl," Alicia says.

"Fuck, I didn't even try. That wasn't what that trip was about," Dan says. He throws his hands up, making the flashlight beam jump. "This is ridiculous. We're standing here at gunpoint right now. This isn't the time to have a conversation about our relationship."

"We don't have a relationship," Sarah says automatically. "I don't do those."

"But he might convince you otherwise," Alicia says. "That's the problem. Boys like him come along and make everything worse. They turn someone who could have a real future into a sniveling mess." She shakes her head. "I have things to settle with you."

Finally, blissfully, the front door opens with a bang, and Officer Marino fills the doorway. "Hands up," he calls.

CHAPTER 38

Sarah keeps her eyes on Alicia, nerves keeping her from finding the ability to look away. She watches the gun barrel waver a little, pointing up toward the ceiling. She hears Marino repeat the command to put up hands. She's aware of her body complying as if he was talking to her, her hands rising to either side of her head.

Alicia puts her hands up as well, but the gun doesn't fall. "Put the gun down," Marino barks. Alicia lowers the barrel as if she is going to comply then there's a loud bang and a flash. It takes a fraction of a second for Sarah to realize that means the gun was fired.

There's a second bang, this one from a different direction. Alicia falls to the ground in a heap and officers swarm her. Sarah blinks her eyes, slowly clearing away the fear and the fog she'd been focused on. Dan is directly in front of her, his mouth is moving as if he's talking but all Sarah can hear is the ringing in her ears. "What?" she says. "I can't hear you."

Dan steps closer and puts his mouth directly next to her ear. "You're bleeding. Did that bullet hit you?"

Sarah turns her head and looks at her shoulder. She sees a spot of blood on her shirt and what looks like a large tear. Then the pain hits.

"Oh my God," Sarah shouts. "She fucking shot me."

Marino looks up from where he is crouched on the floor. "I saw that. I didn't expect her to shoot. I'm sorry, Sarah. We'll get a medic in here."

"What the hell took you so long?" Dan says, taking a step closer to Marino. "You said when Sarah dialed 9-1-1 you'd be here. She could've shot us multiple times while you were waiting for that full confession. Which, by the way, should be perfectly captured on the laptop sitting on the fucking table. You're welcome."

"We had eyes on the apartment," Marino says. "We made a mistake. We assumed it was a knife she was wielding. It's always been a knife."

The officers on the ground who had been swarming Alicia drag her up to her feet. She moans. "She's alive?" Sarah asks.

"Yes," someone answers.

"Wait, so this whole thing was about women you thought were mistreated?" Sarah says. "Seriously?"

"Fuck you," Alicia says. Her voice is quiet but full of venom.

Sarah shakes her head. "Fucking stupid."

"I was standing up for women everywhere. Women who are tired of being tread on and treated like shit."

The officer on Alicia's right tugs her arm. "That's enough," he says.

"No, it's ok," Sarah says. "I want her to hear this." Sarah walks even closer until she can speak quietly to Alicia. "The fact that you think women need to be saved is part of the problem. We don't need a savior, Alicia. We are strong enough to fucking save ourselves. People like you who think we are too weak to stand up are the problem."

"You should've just kept dating women, Sarah. Then this wouldn't have had to come to your door. I never would've had to help you handle a toxic woman."

Sarah shakes her head. "I don't need you to help me handle anyone. I don't need you. Women can do anything."

A slow smile breaks across Alicia's face. It's creepy, the smile Sarah has seen so many times breaking out on the face splattered with blood. Sarah wonders if the blood is the spatter from the shot in her shoulder or the shot in Alicia's side. "Women can do anything," Alicia agrees. "Even be serial killers."

Then she laughs. But the laugh is cut short by a cough that sprays blood onto the floor.

"Alright, that's enough. We have to get you both checked out," the officer says. He applies pressure to Alicia's arm, dragging her out the front door of Dan's apartment. Sarah lets Dan lead her to the couch and drops heavily onto the cushion.

CHAPTER 39

The police officers remaining in the room step to the sides, leaving the center space open for the EMTs that come through the door. They drop large black bags nearby and come close enough for Sarah to hear them even when they speak quietly. There are two of them, one woman and one man. The man approaches Dan while the woman approaches Sarah. "Where does it hurt, honey?" she asks.

"Just where I got shot," Sarah answers. "In my shoulder."

"Nowhere else?" The woman offers a kind smile. "No headache, nausea, or vision problems?"

"No. None of that. I was having trouble hearing when it first happened, but that seems to be better now. Maybe it was the sound of the gun?" Sarah feels bile or something climb up her throat at the thought of the gun going off.

"Alright, let's see what we're dealing with." The paramedic's hands are gloved which keeps Sarah from feeling how cold they probably are. She peels back the jacket from Sarah's shoulder, making Sarah wince. Then she stuffs a wad of gauze directly on the shoulder and presses hard.

Sarah turns her attention to Dan and his paramedic partner. "Honestly, I'm fine," Dan insists. From the tone of his voice, Sarah assumes it's not the first time he's tried to convince the professional of this. "I wasn't hit at all. I'm good. Worry about her."

"I'd feel better if you'd let me get some vitals really quick. I want to rule out shock. Something like what happened here can have lingering effects."

Dan rolls his eyes. "I'm. Fine," he repeats, his voice taking on a sterner tone. "Deal with her."

"Alright, man, if you say so." The paramedic throws up his arms and then turns his attention to his partner. "What do we have here?"

"GS to the upper left arm, through and through. Heartbeat a little elevated. Breathing normal."

"Stretcher is outside on the porch, can she walk to it?"

Sarah puts her right hand up between them. "She is capable of speech, strangely enough," she says sarcastically. "Yes, I can walk. Do I need stitches?"

"Yes, you also need to be checked out by a doctor. We're going to take you to the hospital," the lady explains.

"Can he come?" Sarah says, tipping her head toward Dan.

"Of course," the woman says.

Dan's voice overlaps with hers. "No, I'm good," he says.

"Can we have a second?" Sarah asks, looking pointedly at Dan. "We'll be fast, I promise."

The male EMT frowns but, thankfully, it's the woman who answers. "Make it quick. I can only buy you a minute. We need to get you to the hospital."

"Got it." Sarah pulls her leg up on the couch so she's facing Dan. "You ever have those moments in life when you realize you've royally fucked things up?" she asks.

"Like getting shot teaches you to be more careful who you poke with a stick?"

"Like avoiding someone and realizing that has sucked all the joy from your day," Sarah says. "Like realizing you were not at all worried about yourself," she looks down at her shoulder wound, "even when you should have been. Like realizing you did all this because you were so worried about someone you didn't realize was important to you." Sarah takes a deep breath. "I can't believe I knew this girl the entire time and I never suspected anything. She was harboring all this hatred and anger. She didn't care who she threw it at. I can't do that. I don't want to be that person. I can't treat you like shit and push you away just because I've been hurt before. I didn't mean to do that to you. I'm sorry. I think, maybe, I was wrong about the whole relationship thing."

Dan shakes his head, the gesture is almost sad. "Sarah, you can't say that."

"What? Why?"

Now he turns his eyes fully on her and the depth of that sadness takes her breath away. "You can't choose me in trauma, Sarah. We've been through the fucking wringer here. It's like that movie from the 90s with the lady who has to drive a bus. She didn't want Keanu, she just wanted the hero she went through trauma with."

Sarah would love to tell him to get more recent movie recommendations but she actually likes this one so she refrains. "I don't think that's …"

"You didn't feel this way at the cabin before the first incident. Remember? I asked. You didn't feel this way until I got stabbed and now you got shot." He sighs. "Sarah, you know how I feel but that's not about a trauma response. It's not fair to put us together like this." He reaches over and squeezes Sarah's hand but lets go before she can squeeze back. "I don't want to be your Keanu, at least not from that movie."

He leans over and plants a soft kiss on Sarah's lips. It's equal parts sweet and sad. It sets Sarah's heart beating faster than it should but also breaks it.

"Alright, honey, that's the best I can do. We need to go." The female EMT lays a hand on Dan's arm. "She's gonna be alright," she says.

"I already knew that," Dan says, keeping his eyes on Sarah. "She's stronger than the world." He sighs and smiles at her. "Take care, Sarah. Try to schedule a little relaxation and fun into that chaotic schedule when this is all over. You deserve it."

"Honey, is your pain worse?" the EMT asks, reaching down to guide Sarah up off the couch.

"Not the pain from the gunshot," Sarah says. "This one is more of an emotional roller coaster."

"Oh, honey, we don't have anything in the truck for that." The girl puts a comforting arm around Sarah's shoulder and Sarah lets her tears fall as she's guided to the stretcher.

CHAPTER 40

Two weeks later, Sarah finds herself standing outside the campus police station for a mandatory informative meeting. Marino had called her personally and explained that he needed her here. He apologized, again, for taking up any of her time. She shrugged it off and told him she was looking forward to seeing them all. She had a few things she probably needed to say to Greg, at least.

She pulls open the heavy door and walks into the lobby. Marino is standing behind the desk in the spot she'd spent so many hours working after dark. She waves and he returns the gesture. "Come on back," he says. "Everyone else is already here."

"Everyone else" turns out to be Greg and a tall guy Sarah vaguely recognizes as the other desk clerk, Ted. They're sitting around the table in the very same room where her questioning took place all those weeks ago when her part of this whole nightmare started. Sarah takes a chair on the other side of the room from where she sat last time. She remembers what her therapist told her, you have to visualize positive memories and let go of the negative thoughts. You came through it and those thoughts don't control you.

"Thank you all for coming," Marino begins. "In light of what happened, we have made the decision to stop using students for the front desk after hours. Obviously, none of this is a reflection of any of you. You were all outstanding employees and we appreciate everything you have done. I'll personally write you all letters of recommendation and I hope you'll use me as a reference when you need one." He pulls a packet of papers from a nearby table and holds it in front of him. "I was able to negotiate a decent severance package for all of you, with three months of standard pay." He clears his throat. "I'm truly sorry I wasn't able to do more."

"None of this is on you," Ted says.

Marino grimaces. "I should've seen the

signs." He shakes his head, perhaps realizing he shouldn't be talking about this. "Never mind. I'm sorry about the program being cut. Do you guys have any questions?"

Sarah joins the rest of the room in shaking their heads. Then Marino passes out physical checks to each of them. Sarah smiles down at the amount, which should pay off the rest of the hospital bill she has waiting for her at her apartment.

"Alright, that's all," Marino says. "Thank you for coming in."

Sarah stands up and follows the boys out of the room they came in. Marino brings up the rear, pulling the employee door shut behind them. Sarah finds it interesting that there's so much symbolism there, with the door she used to work behind being closed behind her. She's been telling her therapist that she didn't think she could return to work at the station but it feels strange to have that decision made for her. She'll have to learn to deal with that, she supposes.

Sarah turns and spots Greg at the door. "Greg, hang on a second," Sarah calls. He stops and she jogs across the lobby to catch up with him. Together they take a few steps across the sidewalk until they're out of the way of nearby buildings. "I just wanted to apologize for that night. I'm learning I need to be honest with people so I want to say that I honestly suspected you might be involved, which I realize is hard to hear and I'm sorry about that. I'm glad I was wrong. I was baiting you at that dinner to see what you would do. It was wrong of me and it was immature. I'm very sorry."

Greg frowns. "That's what that was about?" He shakes his head. "It's probably my fault she followed you, you know?"

"How do you figure?"

"I told Alicia we were going to have dinner. It was an offhand comment, but she must have taken note. I guess we both have things to be sorry for."

Sarah shrugs. A week ago this would have consumed her thoughts for hours. She was stressed about all the unanswered questions surrounding the case: how did Alicia find them, why did Sarah get shot when Dan would've fit the profile of Alicia's victims better, what was happening with Alicia now? This step toward one of those answers would've sent Sarah down the path of looking into all of the answers again, hyper-focusing on all the details of the case as she knew them and trying to find something she might have missed.

That's exactly what her brain had been doing when she finally decided she was going to need therapy. It was the middle of the night in her apartment but as bright as day because Sarah could no longer tolerate the dark, when she opened her laptop and found herself a therapist she could connect to virtually through her camera app. She's already had three scheduled meetings, which is a lot for a week. Sarah assumes that's a testament to how seriously they're taking her PTSD. She's already learning to let things go. She doesn't need to have all the answers.

She offers Greg a small smile. "Right, I wanted to apologize and I've done that."

"Absolutely." Greg offers her his hand. "I've done the same."

Sarah shakes it. "So, we're good?"

"I think we're just fine. It's been a pleasure knowing you, Sarah."

She gets the brush off he's hinting at. They won't be working together anymore and this seems to be Greg's way of telling her they won't be anything else, either. She clarifies that, no longer wishing to live in a world where things are implied instead of stated outright. "Are you closed to the idea of our friendship continuing?" Sarah asks.

For his part, Greg appears to look like he's considering what she's saying. Sarah braces herself for him to give her some kind of placating half-truth where he claims they should keep in touch. Instead, she watches as he almost flinches from something he's remembered. She wonders what that memory must be. "You know what, Sarah, I think we've run our course," he says. "I wish you the best of luck in life but you need to learn how to relax and have fun. You're too uptight."

Sarah appreciates that he doesn't say, "no offense" which is a classic move by people who know they're about to be harsh to try and put the blame on you because you were offended when they clearly told you not to be. She hates that. Her mother did that. She nods. "Noted. Good luck in life, Greg."

"Thanks. Bye, Sarah."

She watches him walk away across the parking lot she's seen him cross in the other direction so many times. Watches him get into his car. Waves when he seems to look in her direction. Then she pulls out her cell phone and deletes his number from the directory. She doesn't want to be tempted to call him in a moment of weakness. There are not a lot of numbers in Sarah's phone. A direct result, she supposes, of always keeping people at a distance from her personal life and thoughts. Perhaps that's why her D contacts and her G contacts are visible on the same page. Maybe that's why Dan's name jumps out at her while she's staring at her phone screen. Maybe it's because she's spent hours thinking about him every day for the last two weeks. She could tell he needed time so she hasn't reached out. But that doesn't mean she hasn't been thinking about him, wondering how he's dealing with all of this. She hopes he's finding happiness.

She closes her phone and slides it in her pocket. She'll find out today. It's her first shift back at the mall since the attack.

Sarah takes herself to class, practicing her breathing exercises to calm herself down only once when she feels like there is too much chaotic energy in the room as people are funneling in. She finds the bright lights of the classrooms calming, for the most part, and the return to her notes and techniques are comforting.

Back in the classes, she finds she's a little further behind than she thought. She takes the time to talk to the professor of the first class after his lecture. She explains some of what she's gone through and apologizes for missing so much. This, of course, had all been covered in her email to him but she wanted to talk to him face-to-face. Some professors take you more seriously in person.

He offers her placating words and a promise to give her as much of an extension as he's capable of. But, he cautions, she will still need to do the work if she isn't dropping the class. He can give her more time but he cannot excuse her. "Not even for something like this," he adds.

Sarah thanks him but wonders, briefly, what the hell would someone be excused for if not two brushes with a serial killer.

After her second class of the day, Sarah grabs herself a salad and a coffee to go. She takes her time eating it at a table, checking her watch to make sure she has enough time. Her new schedule is much less taxing than her old one, which is probably a good thing. Her classes, of course, are still the same. But the decision to drop down to one job, which someone made for her, helped her to change her hours with the remaining job. She can pick up weekends and let herself get some sleep because she won't be working overnight.

The money was her biggest concern, especially with medical bills and therapy bills, but if she uses some of the savings she's been accumulating she should be fine. Plus, the plan is to pick up a second job in the summer when she's not taking classes and build that savings account back up.

Really, this time has allowed Sarah to adjust her priorities. Before her plan was to work as hard as she could right now and worry about the rest when she had a job. She wanted to graduate, get a job, and not be like her mother. Follow her dreams.

Now that it was all almost taken away from her, she has a new perspective.

She wants to enjoy the life she's given, while still reaching for new things. She does want that degree and she does want the job. But at what cost? Sleep is important. Books are important. Movies are important. Friends are important. Sarah is painfully aware, now, of how close she came to having it all taken away from her before she'd allowed herself time to accumulate any of the things she always thought she'd have more time for. She had experience but she had nothing else.

It turns out there are worse things than

ending up like her mother, although she's still not in a rush to be like that either. She doesn't want to be like Alicia, prejudging everyone by the worst mistakes she can dig up about them. She doesn't want to be a no-one, leaving the world before she even thinks it starts.

She wants to be Sarah, whatever that turns out to be. It starts with admitting her truths and giving herself time and space to enjoy life.

So, she sits at a table and eats her lunch before she ducks into the bathroom to wash her face, put on her polo shirt, and drive to work.

She lets herself feel the nostalgia of parking in the same lot and walking up to the machine where she swipes her badge to start her shift. The security officer pokes his head out of the doorway beside the clock. "Sarah, right?" he greets.

"Yeah." She's worked here for over a year and although she recognizes this guy who looks like he might only be about four years older than her, she has no idea what his name is. "I'm sorry, I don't actually know your name," she admits.

"Mike." He offers her his hand, which she shakes. "I'm on the security team and I'm closing tonight. We've had a few extra cameras installed while you were out. I wanted you to know that I'll be watching as much as I can tonight. If you need anything, you just holler for me or wave your arms. I'll come running."

Sarah's knee-jerk reaction, which she has to fight down, is to tell him to relax. She's tempted to ask if he gave this same speech to every male employee or if this is only a bullshit assumption that women can't take care of themselves and need him to save them. Honestly, if she had to guess this guy is probably ten to twenty pounds lighter than her. So unless he's packing some kind of weapon in that mall security outfit of his, what the hell help can he offer?

But she swallows all of that down. He's being kind. He's heard about the terrible shit she's been through and this is the best he can do to make her feel safe in their shared environment. She hopes he did give this same speech to Dan, actually. That thought makes her smile. "Thank you for that," she says. "Maybe I'll meet you right here after closing tonight and we can walk out to our cars together so neither one of us has to walk alone in the dark,"

"I was about to suggest the same thing," Mike says. "See you at closing. There's a group of us planning on doing that."

"Perfect," Sarah says. She's a bit surprised to find that she means it. It was the mention of the group that did it. That tells Sarah her second instinct was right, he did tell others. Other people are scared of what happened here, too. They're changing things, just like she is.

She smiles at people as she passes, waving at a few who know her name. When she gets to her department and deposits her bag underneath the desk, she looks around for Dan. Instead, she finds another assistant manager, usually on the day shift, near the treadmills. She waves him over. "Where's Dan?" she asks.

"Oh, you didn't hear?" he shrugs. "I thought you guys were friends. He quit. We're looking for another assistant manager to take his shifts. You should apply."

Sarah tries to pretend like he didn't just fill her veins with ice water. She offers a strained smile. "Yeah, maybe. Thanks." The news makes her sad. In the last few weeks, she's figured out one really important thing above all the other things she's figured out. You have to allow yourself to enjoy the things in life that bring you joy.

Dan brought her joy. He was the best part of her day.

Now, it appears, it's too late for her to spend time cultivating that.

CHAPTER 41

Sarah lets herself get lost in the details of her shift at work. She enjoys working with customers and helping them with the problems that seem small and manageable after the things she's dealt with. She doesn't think much about Dan again, and how different this shift would be if she could enjoy it with him, until her lunch break. The lunch break, a misnomer borrowed from a traditional 9-5 shift that would more accurately be called a dinner break in this strange shift she's found herself in, is normally the time when she and Dan would take off down to the food court to share something quickly. The break is usually only twenty minutes, which is not long enough to leave the premises to get something real. It's barely long enough to stand in line and wait for something fast. It's never been the primary source of food for the night, but a quick something in her stomach. Actually, if Sarah is being honest in her introspection, that's how most of her food consumption has been for her entire life.

"I'm taking a lunch break," she tells the new manager. He nods his understanding and Sarah starts a timer on her watch for twenty minutes before letting herself out into the food court.

She takes her time looking around instead of heading immediately to the same storefront where she knows they are the fastest at bringing out your order. She decides to try something from the sandwich shop she's never actually been to. She takes her time ordering, choosing a bread she's never had and any veggies that sound good. She even asks the employee to recommend the best drink, which nets her a lavender lemonade that looks beautiful with the dual colors layered in the clear plastic cup.

Then she settles herself down at a table and takes her time eating the sandwich. There's a part of her that wants to rush, to eat like this is a race. That's the part of her that knows there's a time limit and thinks there's some kind of prize for beating that time. That's the irrational part of her that hasn't learned to enjoy life yet. She doesn't want to be that person.

Instead, she takes her time, not letting herself get up from the table until there is only two minutes left on her timer. Then and only then she gets up, throws the trash away, and walks to the store. She's three steps into the doorway before the timer goes off. Perfect.

Back at the counter, the phone is ringing. The manager on duty is helping someone so Sarah jogs to the phone and grabs it before the customer can hang up. "Hardware, this is Sarah, how can I help you?" she greets.

The line is silent in her ear. Sarah feels a cold sweat break out on her upper lip. She tries to repeat the greeting, but can't find her voice. Her eyes widen and she stands there listening to the silence and thinking lots of dangerous thoughts that will lead to her not being able to be productive for the rest of the night.

"Who is that?" the manager asks, tipping his head toward the phone. "You good?"

Sarah holds the receiver out to him. She tries to find words, but nothing will come. He takes the phone, putting it to his ear. "This is Brad," he says into the phone. He pulls the phone away from his ear, looks at it, looks down at the screen to watch the numbers that indicate the length of the call click up, and then puts the plastic handset back to his ear. "Hello?" he says. He shrugs, pushes the hang-up button, and then puts the handset down in the cradle. "No one there," he says, "Did they ask for a manager?"

"Uh, I didn't ..." Sarah chokes on the words. Then she shakes her head. "No, they didn't say anything."

"Weird." Brad shrugs. "Anyway, thanks for getting the phone. Was your lunch over?"

Sarah closes her eyes and takes a deep breath. It was not Alicia. That would be impossible. Alicia is in police custody. This was just a customer who didn't know how to use a cell phone or who still accidentally had their phone on mute. She opens her eyes and nods. "Yeah, it was over."

"Perfect." If Brad notices Sarah's discomfort at the phone call, he ignores it. "I'm going to go take my lunch now. I'll be in the food court if you need me."

"I won't need you," she says.

The phone rings again just as Brad is leaving the area. Sarah looks down at the phone and takes a calming breath before answering. She plasters a fake smile on her face. "Hardware, how can I help you?"

Again, nothing.

Sarah slams the receiver down and takes a step back. She shakes her head. She will not let herself get sidetracked by this stupid string of phone calls. She is going to focus on her job and get through the night. No problem.

She busies herself straightening and front facing containers near the register. She helps a few more customers who wander in, including one that promises to bring in a lot of sales later when they come to pick up a few kits for a school shop class once they have the purchase order in hand.

By the time Brad comes back from lunch, nodding once in Sarah's direction, her plan has succeeded in making her forget about the phone calls.

That is until it rings again. It's strange how quickly Sarah's blood runs cold at the sound. She stands where she is, ten steps from the phone, just staring at it. Brad rushes to the receiver and grabs it. She hears his voice but doesn't focus on the words. Then she registers that he's looking at her, his mouth moving.

She shakes her head and forces herself to focus. "Sorry, what?"

"It's for you." He holds the receiver out toward her. "Someone named Marino?"

"Oh, right." She crosses the space, feeling herself relax a little after the scare of the phone. This is typical. This is normal. Well, as normal as her former boss and a police officer calling her at her place of work can possibly be. "He's the supervisor from my other job," she says. "My old job," she clarifies.

"Yeah, cool."

Sarah takes the phone and brings it to her

ear. "Hey, Marino?"

"Yeah, sorry to call you at work. You weren't answering your cell phone and I wanted to get you some information before you saw it on the news."

"The news?" Sarah parrots.

"Yeah. Look, I'm just going to say this. Alicia died in custody. We aren't sure what happened, we're still investigating and I probably shouldn't even tell you. But the news got word of it so it will probably show up on the channels. I wanted you to hear it from someone you trust."

"Alicia died?" Sarah can't think of anything else to say.

"Yeah. Hey, are you alright? You seem a little distracted."

Sarah rolls her eyes. "I'm at work." She blows a breath out. "Hey, did you try to call this number a few times earlier tonight? Maybe like with the phone on mute or something?"

"What? No. Why would I do that?" Marino asks.

"I don't know. Someone did. There were calls that had no one on the other end. It was weird because —"

"Hey, no," Marino interrupts. "No, it's not the same. I can tell you that. Alicia had no access to a phone inside and, even if she did, she honestly passed hours ago and I've been ordering the investigation and doing some paperwork before I called you."

"Hours?"

"Yes. Hours. I promise."

"Ok. Thank you."

"No problem," Marino says. "Hey, Sarah, can you please stay away from reporters for me?"

"Absolutely," Sarah agrees. Honestly, that is an easy promise to make. Sarah has no desire to end up as the face of the tragedy that has fallen on her little town and changed her entire life. "No media."

"Thanks, Sarah. Good luck. Call me if you need anything. I'll let you get back to work."

"Hey, thanks. Bye." Sarah hangs up the phone and turns around to find Brad still standing there, awkwardly watching her. "Hey, sorry about that. I know it was technically a personal call."

"No problem. Seriously, I don't care. Everything alright?"

"Yeah. I think it will be, actually. Someone really bad tried to hurt me and they can't get to me anymore."

Brad sets his lips in a hard line and nods like he understands. Sarah wonders how much of the story he already knows from the news. He'll probably be able to put the final pieces into the puzzle tonight after his shift. He'll catch it on the news and be able to tell all his friends that he works with the girl that they're talking about, the one who was attacked. Well, one of the ones who was attacked. "Shit, can I make one more personal call?" Sarah asks. "There's just one more person I should probably tell about this."

"Yeah, totally. I'll cover the register."

Sarah grabs her cell phone from the clear bag and shakes it as she walks to the little private office in the back. "Thank you, I'll be quick."

She hits the button to dial Dan's number, hoping she'll feel better when she hears his voice. She feels a pang of sadness when his answering machine picks up with a soft beep. "Hey, it's Sarah. I know we haven't talked in a bit but I wanted to call and give you some information. Um, Marino called me to tell me that Alicia died in custody. Man, that feels heavy to say out loud." A little huff of a laugh escapes her. "Oh my God, I'm such a bad person. I'm glad she's dead. Isn't that awful? Anyway, I miss you at work. It's not the same being here without you. I really, really hope you didn't quit because of me. I hope it's not about wrecking your future just because I messed up. That's what I did, I see it now. I hate that you're avoiding me. I hate that I made you feel like you had to avoid me." She sighs. "I'm rambling. I should go. But I wanted to tell you about Marino's phone call and, also, hear your voice, if I'm honest. The answering machine version of your voice made me smile." She sighs again, this one louder and more drawn out. "Seriously, I need to go. But I did mess up. I'm sorry for how I handled this. I thought getting too close to someone would ruin my chances at a future and, instead, it turns out you were the best part of my day. I miss you." Sarah hears footsteps outside the door, likely a customer in the department who needs help. She has to wrap this up before Brad gets frustrated and reports her. "Bye, Dan." She hangs up the phone, slides it into her back pocket, and opens the door with a sad smile on her face.

CHAPTER 42

When Sarah clocks off of her shift for the night she joins a handful of other closing employees, including the security guard, at the time clock. Together, they walk out the big doors and into the employee lot. By the rules of the store, they've all parked in the back half of the lot, past the space that is painted with a bright blue line signifying they are allowed to park out there. Sarah pulls her jacket closer, huddling against the wind that is biting at her exposed skin. There isn't much talking in this group, although two girls Sarah has seen before at the jewelry counter keep up a light banter. Mostly, everyone keeps their eyes up, scanning the lot and looking for the best route to their cars. Slowly, people begin to drop off, headed down the path that takes them to their vehicle.

Sarah pulls her keys out of her pocket and hits the button to unlock it, turning on the inside light. This allows her to see there are no unusual shadows that would indicate someone is sitting inside waiting for her. Of course, that's ridiculous. If someone were inside the car waiting for her they'd likely be lying below the window level. That thought does nothing for her nerves.

She gives a small wave toward the people still walking with her. "Goodnight," she says. The word sort of dies on the wind and no one acknowledges it. This walking to the car group is about safety, not really about camaraderie. Alicia's actions have changed the safe feeling of this little sleepy town and everyone is adjusting. Including Sarah, who spends an extra minute looking in the windows and checking the floorboards of the car before she gets in. Spotting nothing, she jumps in the driver's seat and immediately shuts and locks the doors. Only then does she set down her items, turn on the car, and fire up the heat.

All the way home Sarah checks her rearview mirror for possible tails. She uses the same techniques she employed on her drive home from the restaurant before the attack, which brings back memories she has to try and detach from their emotions. She changes lanes, slows down at random spots, and generally tries to be annoying to other drivers. Although at nine-thirty at night in a quiet town, there aren't many people on the road to be annoyed with her. As near as she can tell, she's not followed.

At her apartment complex, Sarah follows a routine that has been new to her since the attack. Instead of driving straight to her spot, she takes the loop that brings her close to her front porch. She slows down and looks at her door. It still appears solidly closed and exactly the way she left it. The parking lot curves out away from the units and Sarah follows it but turns to look at her visible apartment window. Nothing looks unusual or out of place there either, although she isn't sure what would look different if something was amiss. Right now, normal is acceptable.

Finally, she steers her car into the spot and turns it off. She sits there for a beat, listening for anything out of the ordinary. Her heartbeat is racing and her cell phone is clutched in her hand like it might save her life. Which, in the case of an emergency call, it might.

When nothing else changes or seems out of place, Sarah finally opens the car door. The night air is cold and Sarah pulls her jacket tight before slamming the car door and walking quickly toward her apartment. She hates that this is her new routine now. Nothing will ever be the same again now that this is her reality. She can no longer just walk to the car, drive home, and go inside. This has become a drawn-out routine courtesy of PTSD and one person's vendetta against humanity. It's irritating. She lets the anger warm her.

Her eyes land on the bottom of the staircase that would lead up to her landing. Someone is standing there, moving their feet to keep warm, right at the foot of the stairs. Sarah stops in the parking lot to watch. She tries to remember if her lower neighbor smokes or something that would cause them to be outside. She can't remember who lives below her or what their name is to call it.

The shifting stops as the person notices Sarah. They take a step forward into the light from the neighbor's porch and put up their hands. "Shit, sorry," Dan says. "This was a bad idea. I didn't even think about what this would be like to come home to after everything we've been through. I should've called."

Sarah relaxes her shoulders. "It's fine. But it's freezing out here. Come inside."

"Yeah, that would be great."

She leads the way up the stairs and unlocks her door. She tries to appear normal, but can't stop herself from checking each of the three windows and then walking through the bedroom and all the way into the bathroom to make sure nothing is out of place. Dan stays in the doorway the entire time. When Sarah comes back into the living room from checking the shower she notices his hand is still on the doorknob and he has his cell phone in his hand, ready to call for help if they need it. "Everything good?" he asks.

That question could mean a lot of things in this context. A person could be asking if you're ok since you just took time to look through your entire apartment like you were worried someone was inside and that seems like the action of a person who might not be ok. They could be simply greeting you, wondering if life has been good since they haven't seen you. Or, and this is the context in which Sarah instinctively knows Dan means it, they could be just as damaged as you by the things you've been through and genuinely wondering if their anxiety can go down a notch based on your walkthrough. "We're good," Sarah says. "Everything is the way I left it."

"Perfect." Dan pushes the door shut and flips the lock. Sarah turns on the light and sets down the things she's been carrying. She opens her fridge. "Want a drink? I'm having one of those sparkling water things but I also have ginger ale, beer, and yellow sports drink stuff."

"I'll take a ginger ale. I haven't had one of those in years," Dan says. "So, you're probably wondering why I just randomly showed up here."

Sarah closes the fridge and brings the drinks into the living room. She hands the soda to Dan, opens her can, and drops onto the couch. She tries to appear perfectly relaxed and comfortable. In reality, her pulse is racing just because he's here. But he made himself pretty clear the last time they spoke. It's no longer acceptable for her to go to him, touch his arm, hug him, or be near him. That is too hard, for both of them. So she sits on the couch, holding onto her can like the lifeline that it is, letting the cold keep her in reality instead of in a fantasy where things are different.

"I got your message," Dan says. He is still holding his cell phone, which he now holds up as a way of showing her what message he's referring to. "Did you mean what you said?"

Sarah can't remember what she said in that message. She knows she rambled a little. She shrugs. "Honestly, I said a lot of things, didn't I?" She meets his gaze and holds it even when it makes her heart speed up, even when she feels that tug of longing, and it makes her so sad for what might have been. "I didn't lie about any of it, though."

Dan's smile is lopsided and it matches the tilt of his eyebrows, Sarah notices. "I'm the best part of your day?" he asks. His voice isn't teasing, like she would have expected. It's almost pleading instead.

Sarah gets the feeling that this answer matters to him. That alone makes her hope, just a little. "Without question," she says. "I'm sorry I didn't see that before there was trauma. This isn't a trauma response, Dan. I don't want you because you're safe. I don't want you because you kept me safe. I just want you because you make me a better person and my day is better when you are in it. That's all."

Dan nods but he doesn't take any steps to close the space between them. Sarah can feel it like a figurative elephant in the room, just looming there begging one of them to cross it. Sarah holds the can tighter, unwilling to let herself be the person who closes it. She promises herself that if he takes even one step, she will know that is a sign that he wants to be closer to her. "You always said no relationships, nothing serious."

"I was wrong."

"Why? I know what changed but why change that?"

"Because life is too short," Sarah answers. "Because I almost didn't make it out of this year and into what I thought was my real life starting. Because I always said real-life stuff, like relationships, were for after you had finished the preparations. Real life started with a job. I was wrong." Sarah takes a sip of the seltzer. "I was wrong," she repeats. "This has all been my real life all along and I want to enjoy it."

Sarah watches Dan process this. He nods his head a few times, takes a sip of his soda, slips his cell phone into his back pocket, and then reaches to set his can down on the TV stand at his side all without ever moving his feet. Sarah starts to doubt her idea that he might ever take a step closer. Maybe he came here to tell her that he already said what he needed to say. She's too broken for him.

He takes a step toward her. His eyes are on her the entire time and his step is slow as if he's afraid he's going to spook her. She smiles and he takes another step.

Sarah leaps from the couch and closes the rest of the gap, pulling him into a hug. She pulls back and looks into those beautiful eyes up close where they're even more amazing. She takes a breath, enjoying the scent that is so comfortingly Dan. "So what are you thinking?" she asks.

Dan sighs. "I'm thinking I've missed you too." He puts his thumb under her chin and tilts her face up toward him. "Can I kiss you?" he asks, his voice a whisper against her skin.

Sarah nods and, again, closes the gap. The kiss is gentle, yet somehow more passionate than anything Sarah has ever felt before. When he pulls back, she sighs against him. "That was lovely," she admits.

"So here's what I'm thinking," Dan says, his arms still around her waist. "I think I need you in my life. If friendship is all you can do, I won't be happy about it but I think I can handle it. If you need just for fun dating, I can —"

"Dan," Sarah interrupts. "What if I want an exclusive relationship?"

Dan snaps his mouth closed and looks down at her in shock, his eyes wide. Sarah laughs.

"Miss nothing serious wants to jump right to exclusive?"

"Only if you do."

"Sarah, I can't think of anything more I want than that."

This time, the kiss is a lot more passionate.

THANK YOU

If you enjoyed this story, we'd love a review! In fact, if you are on social media talking about this book, we'd love for you to tag us or let us know.

Tabatha is a wife, mother, and book addict from Arizona. She welcomes emails and social media posts from other readers. Get all her details and find her other available titles at <u>tabathashipleybooks.com</u>